"IF ONLY YOU COULD SEE YOURSELF...."

Nikolai's voice was tormented. "You look so beautiful when you dance, Tiffany; so elegant, perfect. Your face is angelic...."

His emotions seemed completely out of control, and Tiffany was stunned at the depth of his feelings.

"Why must you be as you are?" he choked. "It is torture for me to endure your beauty, your sensitivity, when I cannot let myself so much as touch you. I can only watch you. My useless longing will come to nothing...."

Tiffany wanted to run into his embrace, to beg him to reveal the terrible secret that forced him to deny his deepest passions. But she couldn't. Nikolai would tell nothing—not even to save their love.

AND NOW...

SUPERROMANCES

Worldwide Library is proud to present a
sensational new series of modern love stories—
SUPERROMANCES

Written by masters of the genre, these longer,
sensuous and dramatic novels are truly in keeping
with today's changing life-styles. Full of intriguing
conflicts, the heartaches and delights of true love,
SUPERROMANCES are absorbing stories—
satisfying and sophisticated reading that lovers
of romance fiction have long been waiting for.

SUPERROMANCES
Contemporary love stories for the woman of today!

LISA LENORE
DANCE OF DESIRE

A SUPERROMANCE FROM
WORLDWIDE
TORONTO • LONDON • NEW YORK • SYDNEY

To Craig Broude, my one true love.

———————◆━◆━◆———————

Published, May 1982

First printing March 1982

ISBN 0-373-70018-0

Printed in U.S.A.

PROLOGUE

Five Years Ago

IF TIFFANY HAD KNOWN who the mystery visitor was, she might have panicked and ruined her performance. But she did not know. Madame Vorshak, Tiffany's ballet instructor, was in the habit of bringing unannounced guests to her students' classes. As far as Tiffany knew, the gray-bearded, distinguished-looking man who now stood beside Madame Vorshak was just another of her numerous friends from professional ballet, not special in any way.

Soon Tiffany was too swept up in the beauty and passion of her dance to pay any attention to the observer. She was dancing the Swan Queen's solo from act 2 of *Swan Lake*, and as always happened when she performed such an enchanting piece, the dance transformed her. The lyrical rousing melody of the Tschaikovsky score filled the old ballet studio—only now it no longer came from the battered tape recorder. Now, in Tiffany's mind, the music poured forth from a full gleaming orchestra of tuxedoed musicians. The studio with its long wall of mirrors suddenly disappeared, and in its place Tiffany found herself dancing on the stage of her dreams, leaping and pirouetting at the edge of the beautiful glistening Swan Lake, with the bright stars twinkling above in the midnight sky. The lush aroma of the green forest was fragrant in her nostrils, and a cool breeze wafted over her.

She was no longer eighteen-year-old Tiffany Farrow; she was Odette, Queen of the Swans, and this was her golden moment. The music surged around her, uplifting her spirit. Tiffany did not just dance— she soared; she floated; she and the music became one. A single pirouette turned into a double of amazing speed and grace. Incredible leaps, twirls, *pliés* and *glissades* were performed as if by magic. Her body moved with a life of its own, inspired by the wondrous forces that always overtook her at moments like this. . .moments crystal clear with the beauty of her lightning swift, flawlessly executed movements. Leaps took on amazing elevation; *balancés* and *arabesques* seemed suspended in gravity-defying grace.

Tiffany soared with rapture as her body met every demanding challenge of the dance, calling upon skills she had perfected during the past eight years of vigorous intense training. The rapture went on and on. . . .

Then the last, clear, ringing notes of Tschaikovsky's score sounded in the brilliant night sky and faded...and the night faded with them, as did the magical Swan Lake. Tiffany returned to the mirrored ballet studio. Her lovely white swan feathers vanished with her dream world, revealing instead her worn ballet tights and frayed woolen leg warmers.

There was a moment of disorientation. Tiffany always felt it when coming out of the almost trance-like state her dancing put her in. Then she heard a noise and realized that her fellow students were applauding her. She smiled and bowed shyly before scurrying back to the *barre* to get ready for the next class's practice exercises.

Tiffany took her towel and began wiping her face. When she glanced up, she saw Madame Vorshak motioning her forward urgently. Tiffany went to her.

"Yes, madame?"

"Tiffany," said the elegant old woman, "your *rond de jambe*—it is atrocious. Atrocious!"

"Yes, madame," Tiffany said softly. She was not distressed. She knew Madame Vorshak was never satisfied and would have found something to criticize even in a performance by Margot Fonteyn. The woman's chronic look of irritation did not bother Tiffany, either, for she had long ago learned it disguised a truly warm loving personality.

"And that final *bourrée*, Tiffany! It was—it was...." She paused. "Well, we shall leave the critique for later. For now, I wish you to meet a friend. Julian, may I present Tiffany Farrow."

The distinguished-looking man was staring at Tiffany with great interest. He bowed graciously just as madame said, "Tiffany, this is Julian Temple."

Tiffany was stunned. Julian Temple, dance master of the National Ballet Theater? He was the man responsible for selecting the dancers and overseeing the productions of the most prestigious ballet company in the United States, and now he was looking at her in a strangely foxlike way and saying, "I've been hearing quite a good deal about you."

Tiffany glanced at Madame Vorshak, who was attempting to look impassive. She had known for a long time that she was madame's pride and joy, the star pupil of her renowned New York Ballet Academy, but she had never imagined madame would speak to anyone of Julian Temple's stature about her—or bring him into class to watch her perform!

"Nothing I've heard, however, equals what I've just seen. Young lady, you're a very promising dancer."

"Thank you," Tiffany said in a quiet small voice. Now that she knew who this stranger was, she most definitely did feel nervous and embarrassed. She glanced at the other students. Led by an assistant, they were supposed to be intent upon their exercises, but they kept stealing sidelong glances at Tiffany as she stood with madame and the mystery visitor. Meanwhile the rehearsal pianist continued to plunk out a basic two-four practice rhythm. "I'm pleased you liked my dancing, Mr. Temple," Tiffany said.

Julian Temple smiled in a tight nonjoyous way. "Wednesday," he said.

"I beg your pardon?"

"Wednesday, the day after tomorrow. That's the day you'll report to me at NBT. We'll sign the contracts, and you'll go right into rehearsal. We're preparing for *Coppélia*, and there happens to be an opening in the corps. We'll start you in the corps, of course, but with talent like yours we won't keep you there long. I expect you'll be demisoloing within six months, and we should have you soloing before the year is through."

It was a dream come true. Tiffany could do nothing but stare at him, wide-eyed. She swallowed. "But...don't you want me to audition for you?"

"You just have."

Tiffany was amazed. Only in her most secret fantasies had she ever imagined she would one day dance with the NBT. She knew she was good enough—her natural modesty did not prevent her from being coldly objective about her talent. And she knew she had that mysterious spark in her soul that separated the merely excellent dancers from the world-class ones. But still she had never really believed it would happen to her—and certainly not in so abrupt a manner.

"Mr. Temple is a very busy man, Tiffany," said madame. "A simple thank-you will suffice. Then you may change and rush home to tell your mother. I'm sure this is a moment you'll wish to share with her." She added, somewhat bitterly, "Despite her unfortunate attitude toward dance.'' Then turning to Julian Temple, she said, ''Her mother is Victoria Farrow.'' Temple's eyebrows raised in surprised interest.

''Well, madame,'' he said, ''perhaps this explains such extraordinary talent.''

''I—I—madame, is this for real?'' Tiffany blurted out.

Julian Temple smiled again, and now Tiffany saw why his smile seemed so strange. His eyes were not friendly at all. They were pure business. This was a man who knew what he wanted and did not fool around about getting it. ''I assure you, Miss Farrow, I am not careless about extending invitations to join my company, and I do not do so as a practical joke. I expect to see you in my office on Wednesday morning at eight o'clock sharp.''

This was the culmination of everything Tiffany had hoped and worked for, everything she had struggled eight years for, since the age of ten—sacrificing her social life, torturing her body, devoting herself single-mindedly to this one pursuit, which was the love of her life. And now it was happening. She had been selected by NBT. She was about to become a member of that most rare of species: the professional ballet dancer.

Not trusting herself to words, she made a *révérence*—a low courtly ballet bow. Then impulsively she kissed Madame Vorshak on the cheek and hurried away to the dressing room.

Moments later the other students burst into the girls' dressing room, boys and girls alike, to share her joy and congratulate her enthusiastically. There was much kissing and embracing and patting on the back, and Tiffany admitted, with moist eyes, that it was the happiest day of her life.

THE NEXT MORNING Tiffany phoned Julian Temple at his office and told him in a quaking barely audible voice that she could not accept his invitation, though she thanked him very much for offering it. All she would say when pressed for a reason was that she was giving up ballet forever. For "personal" reasons.

Two days later she accepted a low-level position as researcher with Grayson Productions. Now that she was no longer devoting her life to ballet, there was no reason not to take a full-time job.

She never returned to Madame Vorshak's class. And it seemed certain that no one would ever see her dance—in class or in public—ever again.

CHAPTER ONE

The Present

WHEN TIFFANY'S JET touched down at Kennedy International, she wanted nothing more than to return to her apartment for a long leisurely bath, then to sleep for a hundred years. She was on her way back from filming a three-month-long Egyptian archaeological dig. The documentary, for which she had been assistant producer, had gone exceptionally well, and Tiffany was convinced it would boost her career greatly. But for now she did not want to think of her career, or ancient tombs, or the blasting Sahara. All she wanted was to unwind and relax.

She was surprised when a uniformed chauffeur approached her at the baggage check and said, "Miss Farrow? Mr. Grayson has sent a car for you. I'm to take you to his office right away."

"Now?" Tiffany said, amazed. "I just got back. I haven't even had time to change."

"Those are his orders, miss."

Steve Dunhill, standing beside Tiffany, said to the

chauffeur, "What about me and my crew? Are you taking us back, too?"

"I'm sorry, sir. Mr. Grayson's orders were to pick up Miss Farrow only." He looked uncomfortable. "I imagine Mr. Grayson wants to give you time to collect your baggage and relax before reporting back."

Steve Dunhill laughed good-naturedly. "Sure. Who am I, after all? Just one of his top staff producers, with twelve years' experience behind me. Now if I happened to be a beautiful young assistant producer, maybe I'd rate a car then, too." He touched Tiffany's elbow. "You go ahead, Tiff. I'll take care of the baggage."

"Steve," she said apologetically, "I don't know what this is all about."

"Don't worry about it," he replied, smiling, taking it in stride. "I'll cuss Rolf out next time I see him. And he *still* won't send a car for me when I come back from my shoots!"

The Grayson Productions building was in downtown Manhattan. Tiffany wondered, as the sleek silver limousine sped her through the streets, what Rolf wanted her for. Surely it was not to criticize her work? Steve Dunhill had given her more latitude on this shoot than she had ever had before, and as far as Tiffany was concerned, her work had been extremely good. She'd been acting almost like the principal producer, rather than the assistant. If Rolf was unhappy with the end result, Tiffany would take as much heat for it as Steve.

She hoped he wasn't displeased. In the five years she had been with Grayson Productions, Tiffany had moved up from lowly researcher to her present position—and she loved her work. It filled the gaping hole left by ballet. She did not want to lose it.

Tiffany glanced in the courtesy mirror attached to the rear-seat mahogany cabinet. She wished she had had time to change. She was still wearing her tailored khaki safari suit, her hair curling down to her shoulders in luxuriant waves. Tiffany's hair was a dark shining brown that contrasted nicely with her emerald green eyes. Her skin was very fair, perhaps a shade too fair, for this made her generous mouth and shapely lips far too noticeable. Sometimes she wished her lips did not look quite so sensuous. It disturbed her that everywhere she went men would turn to stare at her. It was almost as if they felt that her stunning looks gave them an invitation to stare.

When Tiffany entered Rolf Grayson's luxurious inner office, Rolf was pacing in front of his enormous, polished, teak desk, dictating in commanding tones into a machine. He glanced over at her and grinned in his usual dynamic irresistibly powerful way.

"Welcome back!" he exclaimed, coming to her across the plush Oriental-style carpet. He put his arms around her and embraced her. And though Tiffany made an effort to submit to the embrace without responding, as usual she found she could not quite do so. It was impossible for her to be unresponsive in the presence of such a bold handsome charismatic man.

"I'm sorry I had to hustle you over here so quickly, darling," Rolf said, "before you even had a chance to unpack. But you may not have to unpack. I've got another assignment for you—a big one— and I'm sending you out again just as soon as you're ready."

"Rolf," she protested laughingly, "I can't take another assignment yet. I'll need at least three or four months to edit the Egyptian shoot and supervise the narration."

"The Egyptian piece can wait. It's not all that topical. Besides, Steve can oversee the editing. This new assignment is *very* topical, and you're the only producer I've got with the background to handle it properly."

"Producer?" Tiffany said, startled.

"Congratulations, darling. You've just been promoted. That Egyptian shoot was excellent. I've been watching your dailies as they've come in, and I know. Did you think it was an accident Steve gave you so much leeway in supervising the crew and directing the filming?" He shook his head, smiling at her. "I told him to. I wanted to see how you could handle yourself in the role of producer. I had to, because this new assignment is going to tax your skills to the limit."

"Oh, Rolf, I don't know what to say." She was pleased and almost flabbergasted.

"You can start by saying thank-you. But I

wouldn't advise it. Wait until you hear what the shoot involves. I'll tell you frankly, Tiffany, you're not going to like it. And your first inclination might be to turn it down flat.''

Tiffany was bewildered. She could hardly imagine disliking anything so much she would turn down her first chance at being a full-fledged producer.

Rolf splashed some Cointreau into two crystal glasses and handed one to Tiffany as he motioned her toward the sofa. It was Tiffany's favorite liqueur, and she sipped at the sweetish orange ambrosia gratefully. Rolf never forgot such things as what her favorite drink was, or her favorite flowers. Despite his brusque, super-charged, sometimes ruthless manner, he could really be quite a considerate man— when he wanted to be.

Tiffany watched him as he stood silhouetted against the giant wall of windows that overlooked the magnificent Manhattan skyline. He was an extremely handsome man, with a long aristocratic face, a square jaw and a very tall trim body bursting with energy. His jet black hair was tinged with sophisticated gray at the temples, as befitted a man on the verge of turning forty. His attire was strictly Ivy League, from his exquisitely tailored, charcoal pin-striped suit to the gold pocket watch on a gold chain attached to his vest.

''This assignment I'm about to give you, Tiffany— it can make you or break you. And as I say, you're not going to like it. I'll give you exactly fifteen minutes to raise Cain about it and tell me how you absolutely refuse to do it. Then we'll cut the protests short, and you'll go do the assignment like I want you to. Right?''

Tiffany could not help smiling at his overbearing attitude. Rolf was a man you just had to hate—yet she liked him, though not in the way he liked her. "Liked" was not the word, Tiffany reflected. She knew how strongly Rolf Grayson felt about her. They had been seeing each other for two years and had only recently stopped. They had stopped because Rolf had proposed to her—and she had turned him down. Though she did care for him a great deal, she didn't love him, and to Tiffany marriage without love was out of the question.

Shortly thereafter she told Rolf she would have to stop seeing him socially. It was either that or resign her position and not see him at all, because Rolf was not the kind of man you could accept on a casual halfway basis. It would be impossible to continue working for him, she told him, if he kept trying to force his affections on her and force her into a relationship she did not want.

She was very fond of his foibles, his charming mannerisms and his basic integrity. Though he could be a ruthless hard-driving businessman, he never lied, and he never pretended to be anything other than what he was. Single-handedly he had used his skills to found Grayson Productions, to build it into one of the most prestigious media conglomerates in

America, to make himself a millionaire many times over. In addition to the documentary production company, which was his pride and joy, he also owned several nonnetwork television stations, three radio stations and a string of newspapers. He was on the boards of several arts foundations, and his power and prestige in the cultural arts were immense.

"Rolf," Tiffany said, smiling, "this new assignment can't be as bad as you're making out. The way you're talking, I feel as if I should ask for a blindfold and a last cigarette before hearing about it."

"You don't smoke, and a blindfold is out of the question. You'll need your eyes wide open to tell your crew where to set up and what to shoot. Which is why I'm sending *you* on this assignment, instead of someone with more experience."

The suspense was finally getting to her. "Well, what is it?"

"I want you to cover the Volgaya Ballet Company at the International Dance Competition in Zurich. Next to the Bolshoy and the Kirov, the Volgaya is the best ballet troupe in Russia. Some say it's even better than the Bolshoy. I want you to fly to Moscow with your crew to start filming background material on its new lead dancer, a man named Sharmonov. He's the focal point of the shoot. You'll follow the Volgaya as it tours across Europe, ending up in Zurich."

Tiffany stared at him, her brow furrowing. For a moment she did not speak. She had not really thought he would do this to her—give her an assignment she would truly feel tormented by. "No, Rolf," she said. "I won't do it."

"Tiffany," he said forcefully, "I know how you feel about ballet, how you refuse to have anything to do with it. But don't you think it's time you came to grips with this mysterious hang-up you have about it? And it *is* a mystery! You never explained to anyone why you walked out on your chance to join the NBT five years ago after having devoted your life to dance, or why you're so painfully sensitive about my even bringing up the subject. But the fact is, you've got the background knowledge essential for this piece, and you're the only person I've got on staff who's qualified to handle it."

"You can save your fifteen minutes, Rolf. I won't argue. I'll just tell you that the answer is no." She set her glass of Cointreau on the coffee table. "I'm sorry, but I won't cover ballet for you. I've told you that before."

He held her stare for a moment, apparently feeling very mixed emotions. Finally he walked over to his desk and leaned back against it. "I'm sorry, Tiffany, but I'll have to insist. It's either use you for this assignment, or bring in a free-lancer with a specialized background. If I have to bring in a free-lancer, you know what that'll mean to your career." He paused. Some of the hardness in his eyes softened a bit. His voice softened, too. "You're the one who told me to treat you as I would anyone else on my staff. You said you didn't want our personal rela-

tionship to interfere with our business relationship.
Well, if you still feel that way, you're going to have
to make a choice. You either take this assignment
or...." He searched for a less blunt way of saying it.
"You know how I deal with employees who tell me
no."

"Yes," she said, looking away. She knew. Rolf
hated the word *no*. If she did not mean so much to
him, she never would have survived turning down his
proposal. She had once seen him fire an associate of
ten years' standing for refusing to do something very
minor Rolf had asked of him. Rolf had had to buy
out the man's contract, which cost him a large sum of
money. But in the end Rolf had had his way—the
man was out of the building and on the street.

"Tiffany," Rolf said, "I don't *have* to treat you
so...equally, like any other employee. Just say the
word and our relationship will stop being so damn
businesslike."

Tiffany said nothing. She felt perplexed and defiant. She was about to tell him exactly what he could
do with his ballet-tour assignment, but she stopped
herself. The fact was, she loved being a filmmaker.
Next to ballet it was the most important thing in her
life.

But ballet was still such a sensitive painful subject
to her! It tortured her to watch others dance and to
think about what might have been had she continued
her ballet career. That was why she couldn't bear going to performances. It was too much to bear! Yet

even though she avoided performances, she still practiced rigorously several times a week. She did this secretly, though, alone, at an old ballet studio, late in the evening. Her love for ballet was still the major force in her life, whether she wanted it to be or not.

Grayson strode over and sat beside her on the sofa. He looked at her sympathetically. "Tiffany," he said gently, "take the assignment. This is your first shot at being a full producer. Don't turn it down."

Tiffany still did not respond. But nor did she get up and walk out on him. Grayson knew her well enough to take this as a good sign. "Look," he said, "just let me tell you a little about the assignment. You don't have to make up your mind now. Just listen; you can decide later."

Tiffany still said nothing. She picked up her Cointreau from the coffee table, though, and leaned back in her seat. Rolf Grayson was not a particularly sensitive man, but he was definitely sharp-eyed and perceptive. He interpreted this, too, as a positive sign, and he quickly crossed to his desk and pulled out a folder. Leafing through it, he began speaking.

"Nikolai Sharmonov is the main focus of this shoot. He's a young maverick who's just burst on the scene out of relative obscurity, and he's taking the ballet world by storm. He was Zhukov's protégé and disciple." Rolf looked up. "You're familiar with Zhukov, the Volgaya's former *danseur noble*?"

"Yes," said Tiffany. "But. . . former?"

"They booted him out for political reasons—only

last week. That's why you haven't heard. Well, Nikolai Sharmonov was always in his shadow, dancing as a soloist, doing a few principal leads. Now that Zhukov is out, Sharmonov has been promoted to lead status, and from all accounts the man is absolutely brilliant. A legend is growing around him. Those who've seen him dance are comparing him to Nijinsky. This Zurich competition will be his first chance to shine internationally as *premier danseur*. A documentary on him will be an extremely marketable item. Everyone in ballet is already asking just who this young hotshot is. We'll give them the chance to see for themselves—to see him in action.''

''Will there be a language problem?'' Tiffany asked.

''Sharmonov speaks English, as a lot of Muscovites do. But even so the Russians are assigning us an interpreter, a man named Vronsky. To tell the truth, I think he's more of a government 'watchdog' than anything else—to make sure Sharmonov doesn't step out of line. Sharmonov's got a reputation as a young hothead—a temperamental rebel.''

That sounded intriguing. Tiffany found herself wondering what this Nikolai Sharmonov was really like. As Grayson told her more about him, she became more intrigued. Finally Grayson handed the folder to her and said, ''Your visa will be approved by the Soviets almost instantly. They're cutting through all the red tape that usually interferes with projects in the iron-curtain countries. For some reason they really want to see this documentary get made." He looked a bit curious. "They're even helping us get around the rules about using local crews instead of our own and developing the film in-country. That's unusual." He wondered about this for a moment, then shrugged.

He offered his hand to Tiffany and helped her to her feet. "You better go rest up, so you can get an early start on your basic research. I'll give you more information on the shoot over the next few days." He was too wise a man to ask her again if she would take the assignment. He simply acted as if there had never been any question about it.

"Welcome back, kid," he said, winking at her in his fiercely charming way as he escorted her to the door. "Start thinking about caviar and vodka. Because before you know it, I'll be wishing you bon voyage—in Russian."

CHAPTER TWO

ROLF WAS RIGHT. For some reason the Soviet government seemed very eager to have an American documentary done on the Volgaya's tour and its new star, Nikolai Sharmonov. Tiffany received approval for her visa application within a week. Within three weeks she was aboard a narrow-bodied Aeroflot Ilyushin jet, winging over the crystal blue Baltic Sea on the way to Moscow.

The fact that she was about to be exposed to professional ballet again after years of avoiding it should have dampened Tiffany's spirits. It was impossible to not be excited, though, as she gazed out from her window seat at the sights below. After crossing the Atlantic nonstop from New York, they had flown over northern Europe, then over the Baltic Sea. Now the Baltic had been passed, and they were crossing the western zone of the great Russian plain.

In the eastern reaches of Russia, half a world away, were the dominating mountain ranges, the Verkhoyansk and the Chersky. But here in western Russia, now below her, Tiffany could see lush forests and green grasslands. Beneath them was the mighty Volga River, flowing along verdant banks toward Moscow.

"Look," said Mary Blakely excitedly, "is that it?" She was seated next to Tiffany. She pointed toward an area far ahead of the aircraft that seemed to be a break in the forested Russian plain. "Is that Moscow?" She craned her head close to the window, but neither of them could tell yet from this distance.

"It's coming up soon," Tiffany said. "It has to be. Look there." She nodded toward the window on the far side of the plane. Through it they could see, off in the distance, another great river that had just become visible.

"The Oka," said Mary, all agog. "You're right. Moscow has to be coming up soon. It's situated between these two rivers." She leaned even closer toward the window, nearly crushing Tiffany in her eagerness to see out of it.

"Hey!" said Tiffany, laughing.

"Sorry." Mary sat back in her seat.

Tiffany liked Mary. That was the reason she had chosen her to be assistant director on this shoot. That and the fact Mary had a deep fascination and interest in Russia—which could come in quite handy. She was always talking about it. She was enchanted by the incredibly savage, yet culturally rich heritage of the land and the romantic figures it had produced: geniuses like Tschaikovsky and

Dostoevski, conquerors like Peter the Great and
Ivan the Terrible. Mary was a very efficient curly-
haired girl who wore glasses and had an impish
look. And her excitement about Russia was con-
tagious.

Russia, thought Tiffany, as she gazed out the
window, land of the Mongol invaders and the legendary cossacks; the largest nation ever to exist
on earth, with a full one-sixth of all the land area
on the planet. Tiffany was amazed at its sheer enor-
mity. There were eleven time zones from east to
west, in a nation that spanned almost half the
globe. Its museums were said to contain more art
treasures than those of almost all of Europe com-
bined.

Tiffany glanced at the other members of her crew,
who were sitting nearby: the cameraman and his
assistant, the sound man and his boom operator, the
best-boy grip. They, too, like almost every other
passenger on the Ilyushin jet, were looking out
of the windows expectantly for the first signs
of the great city of Moscow, the most populous city
in Russia, the ninth most populous in the entire
world.

In addition to being producer, Tiffany was also
director on this shoot. And Mary was the UPM—
unit production manager—as well as assistant director. This was the way Tiffany wanted it. A seven-
person crew was just barely manageable; a larger
crew would have been impossible.

"There!" declared Michael French, her cameraman. "Isn't that it off in the distance?"

Everyone looked toward the east. A tributary of the Oka branched off and began winding northward. "That's the Moskva River," Mary said. And yes, there on its banks were the beginnings of the enormous city of Moscow.

The first things Tiffany noticed were the countless ribbons of moving steel glinting in the afternoon sunlight. These were the railroad trains, she realized, streaming into and out of the city. Moscow was the focal point of all the great rail lines in Russia, which radiated from it like spokes on a wheel. Rail transportation was nonstop to accommodate the almost eight million people of this urban center.

Soon the city itself came into view. It consisted of concentric rings formed by the major boulevards. Ring after ring became visible as the jet flew in toward the center of town. Their destination was Sheremetyevo International Airport, on the city's farthest edge. After they had passed the innermost rings, they saw at the very hub of the circle a sight that made everyone who had never seen it before gasp. The Kremlin.

Tiffany had heard about it, of course, but had never imagined it could be such an awesome sight. It was enormous, absolutely monumental. In Russian *kremlin* means "citadel," and this structure they were now approaching was a citadel to end all citadels. Its three sides formed a roughly triangular shape, with twenty mighty towers, each with formidable crenellated battlements. It looked medieval, a castle of sorts, only more heavily fortified and impregnable than any castle that had ever existed.

"Look at those walls," Tiffany whispered, looking down. They were blood red and seemed to shoot straight up to the heavens.

"They're sixty-five feet high," Mary said.

"They're so—so massive!"

"Twenty feet thick in some places. Can you imagine that? Those walls are *thicker* than most fortress walls are *high*."

The jet was passing alongside the Kremlin now, though not directly over it. By looking down and to the side, Tiffany could see inside the Kremlin walls. Again she was awestruck. It was a city within a city—but what a city! A city composed almost entirely of extravagantly beautiful palaces, churches and cathedrals. These buildings were brilliantly multicolored, and even from the air Tiffany could see they were works of incredible architectural splendor.

"That's Uspensky Cathedral," said Mary, pointing to a building topped by five golden domes, each blazing brightly as it caught the sunlight. "It was built in the 1470s for the crowning of the czars. Over there is the Grand Palace. That's where the czars used to live. Now it's the home of the Supreme Soviet, the Russian parliament."

"What's that?" Tiffany asked, pointing. "It looks like an enormous bell."

"It is a bell—the Czar Bell."

"Why isn't it hung in a bell tower?"

"Look at it. Can you imagine building a bell tower big enough to hold it? That's the biggest bell in the whole world—which is why we can see it from this height. It's twenty feet high—and you know how much it weighs? Two hundred tons!"

Michael French, in the seat across the aisle, whistled softly.

"You better believe it," Mary said to him.

"Everything is so big here," Tiffany said. "The world's biggest this, the world's tallest that. How can there be so much of it in one place?"

"That's one of the things that makes Russia so fascinating," Mary replied, "the sheer awesome size of everything. And the beauty! You just wait until we get on the ground and have a chance to look around." She gazed down at one of the buildings below, which was almost out of sight now that the jet had passed the Kremlin's farthest wall and was quickly leaving the fortress city behind. "You see that palace? Granovitaya Palace is what it's called. If you think it looks beautiful from up here, wait until you can see the inside. The floor is made of agate jasper tiles, given to Ivan the Terrible by the Shah of Persia. They're supposed to be so brightly polished they're like agate mirrors. The walls are covered with murals by the Russian artist Feodosy—

they're supposed to be the equal of the frescoes on the Sistine Chapel's ceiling.''

Tiffany had to admit she was anxious to see these splendors for herself. Mary's enthusiasm had definitely whetted her appetite. For now, though, there were other things to think about. For one thing she noticed that Michael was looking very disturbed. Tiffany guessed what was troubling him. She knew she was right when Michael said, ''I wish I had my camera.''

''I'm glad your camera is safely locked up in the baggage compartment,'' she replied. ''All we need is for you to try to film the Kremlin from above. We'd be minus a cameraman. You'd be in jail, while we'd be filming the Volgaya with your assistant.''

''What did they need such a massive place for anyway?'' he asked.

Mary began telling him about the constant invasions throughout Russian history, but Tiffany looked back out the window at the winding Volga River and turned her thoughts to something else. She was thinking about the man she had come all this way to film: Nikolai Sharmonov.

She wondered what he was like. Before she had left New York, one of the last things Rolf had said to her, in somewhat of a warning tone, was, ''You sure you can handle this fellow alone? I don't know if you picked this up from your research, but he's a descendant of Taras Sharmonov, one of the fiercest cossack chieftains who ever lived. And some say he's a throwback. He's not known for his . . . cooperativeness, shall we say. Maybe you should take Langerhorn along as your AD."

"I told you, Rolf," she said, "I want Mary Blakely as my assistant director. She's a good AD, and besides, she knows all about Russia." She added, smiling, "And I can take care of myself. I don't need Langerhorn."

Langerhorn was a seasoned veteran, and Tiffany knew that if she agreed to take him, this would no longer be her shoot—except in name only. Langerhorn had enough experience and status that he would take charge—whether Tiffany wanted him to or not. The fact that Rolf suggested him meant he was not overly confident Tiffany could handle this Nikolai Sharmonov by herself. But why not, she wondered. Was there some reason to believe he might give her trouble?

Tiffany did not have time to give the question any more thought. The seat-belt light was on, and the jet was beginning its descent into Sheremetyevo Airport. Soon there were a hundred other more immediate problems to worry about: getting her crew and equipment safely through customs, getting settled in the rooms reserved for them at the Metropole Hotel, calling to check in with the American embassy's cultural-affairs office. A problem came up in getting Michael's fresh undeveloped film through customs, and Tiffany spent the entire afternoon trying—and failing—to solve the problem.

It was not until the next day that Tiffany went with her crew to the Volgaya Ballet, had her first encounter with Nikolai Sharmonov and realized that Rolf's worries had been entirely justified. There was going to be trouble on this shoot, she realized, trouble that could utterly ruin the shoot—and with it, her career.

CHAPTER THREE

TIFFANY SAT in the front row of the empty sumptuous Volgaya Theater, watching Nikolai Sharmonov on the stage before her. He was dancing the role of Albrecht from the ballet *Giselle*.

Tiffany could not take her eyes off him. He was absolutely brilliant. No wonder the Volgaya had chosen him as their new lead dancer. His *grands jetés* were breathtakingly high; his *fouettés* and *tours en l'air* were done with incredible speed and control. All of his movements were performed with such precision and grace, he seemed not to be earthbound at all, but rather a soaring elegant bird in flight that touched down on the ground only at whim. His technique was so bold and innovative, it was like a slap in the face to those who watched him if they were accustomed to the more traditional *danseurs*.

Tiffany grimaced with frustration. Oh, if only Michael were here with his camera! She wanted so badly to get this rehearsal on film. Michael was back at the customs office, though, trying to free his undeveloped film. He would be there shortly. Comrade Vronsky, the "interpreter" Tiffany had been assigned by the government, had gone along with him, promising to solve the problem with the greatest dispatch.

Well, Tiffany sighed to herself, if she missed this performance, there would be others to film later.

"Look at that," said Mary in a reverent whisper as Sharmonov began whirling like a dervish before them, moving so fast his body seemed to blur. He glided out of that movement into a perfect *arabesque penché*, weight on his forward leg, his other leg raised gloriously high behind him. "Isn't he just the most delicious creature?"

Tiffany had to admit his glowering intense looks were really quite striking. The man was not so much handsome as he was extremely virile-looking—and potently sensual. He had a wild mane of golden hair, bright as a sunburst. It whipped about as he bounded across the stage, despite the rolled red bandanna he wore as a sweatband. And like his dancing, his looks, too, were an arrogant challenge to one's beliefs about what dancers were supposed to be. Everyone knew male dancers were supposed to be slight and somewhat fragile-looking. It was a popular image! Yet here was Nikolai Sharmonov, more than six feet tall, with a powerful chest that rippled with his movements and very broad shoulders and muscular arms that made him look more like the cossack descendant he was than a classic ballet dancer. His waist was slim, his stomach seemingly hard as granite, and his legs and calves were pure sinewy muscle. The black cutaway shirt and woolen tights he wore did nothing to disguise the raw power and animal strength radiating from him.

Looking at him, Tiffany could not help thinking of the great sculptures of Michelangelo, those marble icons of ultimate male beauty. His face, though, was far too voluptuous—and too arrogant—for a Michelangelo sculpture. He had heavy eyelids with long golden lashes. His cheekbones were very prominent in his lean face, and his thin lips, though sensuous-looking, seemed more suited to snarling than smiling. The image he projected was one of insolence and haughty disdain.

As Sharmonov's solo came to an end, his partner appeared onstage, and he lifted her high into the air effortlessly. As the two dancers began their *pas de deux*—dance for two—Tiffany looked at the ballerina and for an instant saw herself. She felt a sudden deep heartache and a pang of remorse. She quickly fought down the feeling, though, wishing once again that Grayson had not insisted she take this assignment.

The *pas de deux* was wonderful, and Tiffany was entranced. She kept stealing quick glances toward the theater entrance, wishing Michael would hurry up and arrive. Finally the doors opened and he appeared, carrying his camera and accompanied by his assistant and his sound man. His expression was apologetic as he hurried forward to set up his equipment. Behind him was Comrade Vronsky.

Michael quickly placed the camera on its tripod, had his assistant check the lighting, then put his eye to the eyepiece and prepared to begin filming. It was then that a major obstacle became glaringly evident.

Nikolai Sharmonov, seeing the camera set up to film him, turned to Tiffany and glowered directly into her eyes. Then he pivoted on his heel so that he was facing the back of the stage, instead of the front. He continued his *pas de deux*, redirecting his partner so that she, too, was facing the back of the stage. Michael was left with nothing to film but their backs.

Tiffany was astonished. And she was not the only one, either. The director of the Volgaya Ballet, Ivan Gargarin, looked horrified at this sudden new interpretation of the traditional choreography. *"Stoi! Nazad!"* he shouted, calling the dancers to a halt. Someone shut off the record player. Gargarin stormed over to Sharmonov and began gesticulating angrily, berating him in Russian.

Tiffany could not understand the language, and Vronsky declined to interpret this particular outburst. The message was clear enough, though. The director was demanding that Sharmonov perform the material as it was written and not impose his own interpretation on it—especially not such an absurd interpretation.

Sharmonov turned to Tiffany again and glared at her with deep hostility. Tiffany was startled. What had she done to make him feel so antagonistic toward her? She didn't even know the man! Mary turned and looked at her curiously. Nikolai Sharmonov continued listening to the shouting agitated director, while keeping his eyes on Tiffany. Then, when the director had finished his tantrum and paused for an answer, Sharmonov said to him, *"Nyet."* He refused to allow himself to be filmed facing the camera.

The director became even more infuriated and began ranting again. Sharmonov turned and walked off the stage without a backward glance. This was incredible—Tiffany had never seen anything like it.

After a few moments the rehearsal resumed, but without Sharmonov's participation. The other members of the dance troupe—the corps de ballet— came onstage and danced wonderfully. Tiffany had Michael film the rest of the rehearsal as she sat and watched. But her arms were crossed over her chest, and she was fuming. From the way Sharmonov had glared at her, it was almost as if he had some personal grudge against her. She didn't know what the problem was, but she did know that if it continued, if the *premier danseur* refused to let himself be filmed, it would ruin her assignment—and prove to Grayson she really couldn't handle a major shoot on her own.

Tiffany felt anger much more than bewilderment. Here she had finally forced herself to accept the assignment, to face the torment of being exposed to ballet again, and now it might all be for naught. If she couldn't get the film she needed, Grayson would assume it was due to some deficiency on her part. He'd send in Langerhorn to take over, keeping her on only as an assistant because of her knowledge of ballet. The situation was infuriating.

"Is no problem," said Vronsky, leaning forward from the seat behind her. "Is only temporary misunderstanding. I assure you, will be worked out very quickly."

"Why doesn't he want to be filmed?" Tiffany asked, turning her seat.

Vronsky was a jowly beefy-faced man, with dark bushy eyebrows and a sturdy, somewhat squat body. From the way he shrugged Tiffany could tell she would not be able to get any useful information from him. "Is only small problem," Vronsky said. "Please not to worry. Gargarin will straighten situation out very quickly."

"I hope he does," Tiffany said, turning back to the front to watch the continuing rehearsal.

But Gargarin did not straighten out the problem very quickly. That evening Tiffany set up interviews with the key soloists and principal dancers of the Volgaya. Everyone came but Sharmonov; he sent the excuse that he was ill.

The next evening Tiffany threw a small party in the Metropole Hotel's banquet room for the members of the Volgaya. The purpose was to get to know the members of the troupe on a more personal basis. She believed that the warmth and idiosyncrasies and foibles of people came out best when one got to know them as people, not just as subjects for a film. It was this sort of human touch—the kind of contact one got from informal interviews, impromptu fooling around on the stage, and so on—that could make or break a documentary. Everyone in the Volgaya came to Tiffany's party except Sharmonov, and everyone seemed anxious to cooperate with the filming—except Sharmonov.

He had sent word that he was ill. Again. But he was well enough the very next morning to do a vigorous *pas de quatre* during the morning's rehearsal without showing any signs of having been the slightest bit sick.

As Tiffany had Michael set up his camera and the rest of the crew take their positions to prepare for the filming, she wondered whether there would be a repeat of that first day's situation. She prayed there would not be. And to her vast relief, when it came time for Sharmonov to move into the foreground while the corps de ballet performed in the background, he danced as he was supposed to, without turning his back to the camera, without storming off the stage.

His dancing was brilliant. He leaped, he twirled, he moved with elegant grace and lightning speed. The dancers were in costume now, and Sharmonov wore a royal cape and glittering bejeweled tunic, looking extremely dashing in his role as Albrecht.

The filming was going extremely well, and Tiffany was pleased. Just to shoot Sharmonov dancing during rehearsals and performances would not be enough to "make" her documentary, of course. She would also have to interview him in informal settings, and she hoped to film him while he was experimenting onstage or working out by himself in an innovative manner—personal touches of that nature. With luck this, too, would come in time, now that she could see he was willing to cooperate at least to this extent.

"His solo is coming up soon," Mary said quietly in Tiffany's ear.

Tiffany nodded and watched the stage. She was looking forward to this. His performance in this particular solo contributed largely to the legend growing around him. Originally it had been Zhukov's *pièce de résistance*, and Zhukov had become renowned by performing it better than any other dancer ever had; it was what he had built his reputation upon. Now word had gone out that Sharmonov, Zhukov's protégé, did this solo better than even Zhukov himself and indeed put Zhukov's rendition to shame. It was supposedly one of the thrills of a ballet-lover's lifetime to watch him execute it. And Tiffany was about to get it on film. She leaned forward in her seat, eager with anticipation.

The corps danced off the stage; the starring ballerina moved to the sidelines. The stagelights dimmed, and a single bright spotlight picked up Sharmonov's leaping figure. Then, as the music built to a crescendo, Sharmonov launched into his solo. To Tiffany's great frustration and surprise, he glared at her contemptuously for an instant, then turned away from the camera and began to dance facing the back of the stage.

The director went wild. Ballet directors the world over have the reputation of being a harried, nervous, emotionally excitable lot, and Gargarin fit the image to perfection. He jerked his hands up to his wiry salt-and-pepper hair and made as if to pull it out. He began howling at Sharmonov in Russian, undoubtedly cursing. The music ceased. The stagelights came back up.

Sharmonov listened to Gargarin with glowering displeasure, saying nothing in his own defense. As the director's tone gradually changed from browbeating anger to half-anger, half-pleading and cajolery, Sharmonov's head turned. His striking cobalt-blue eyes alighted on Tiffany, and once again—without any apparent reason—they were filled with hostility. Tiffany felt so stunned by this look she wanted to scream at him in helpless frustration, "You don't even know me! How can you hate me?"

Suddenly, as if reading her mind, Sharmonov left the director in midharangue and leaped down from the stage. He grabbed a towel from around a fellow dancer's neck and strode up to Tiffany, wiping his face as he came.

The camera followed him. Michael French was no fool; he knew that this was potentially great material. But when Sharmonov came near, he took his towel and snapped it down over the lens of Michael's camera.

"Hey!" Michael yelled, pulling his head back from the camera's eyepiece.

Nikolai Sharmonov offered no apology as he held the towel tightly over the camera, blocking the lens, while he stood in front of Tiffany, towering over her, glaring down at her. When he spoke, his voice was deep and low and manly. It was also heavily accented, though his command of English was excellent. "My director threatens to remove me from my role in this ballet. I wish to thank you for that."

"Me?" she said, astounded. "If he feels you're incapable of dancing the part as it was written, how can you blame me?"

"How would *you* know how it was written?" he said scornfully.

Tiffany held his stare, quietly breathing fire. Then she said very slowly and deliberately, "Vernoy de St. Georges did not write *Giselle* to be performed facing stage rear. Jules Perrot did not choreograph it to be danced that way. When Lucien Petipa first danced it in its premier performance in Paris, in 1841, he did not dance it that way."

Sharmonov raised an eyebrow, clearly impressed. Tiffany was obviously not some shallow unknowledgeable "outsider," as he had assumed. His change in expression lasted only a fraction of an instant, though, before he once again became sardonic and disdainful. "Perhaps you are correct. Perhaps my director *does* now believe I am incapable of dancing the part as it was written. But he did not think this thing until you came into the theater with your camera and propaganda crew.''

Tiffany eyed him with growing anger. "We're not a propaganda crew. We're here to film a documentary. Your own government has given us permission to film the Volgaya. You must know that."

His aggressive tone was unrelenting. "Because it is my government does not mean it is not propaganda."

This was a very bold and dangerous thing for him to say, and an audible gasp arose from the others in the theater. Tiffany had forgotten all about them, however, for Nikolai's presence was so overpowering she had unthinkingly focused all her attention on him to the exclusion of everybody else. Now she looked around her, aware suddenly that all eyes in the large auditorium were riveted on the two of them.

The other dancers, the director, her own crew—everyone was watching them. And most threatening of all, jowly beefy-faced Vronsky was watching them, too. Beneath his bushy eyebrows his eyes were narrowed ominously. From the briefing Rolf Grayson had given her, Tiffany knew that Vronsky was not primarily an interpreter. His main role was that of government security agent with the KGB. He was present to make sure nothing was filmed—or said—that might reflect badly on the government.

Tiffany looked at Sharmonov. He seemed not to care at all that he was putting himself in danger. His jaw continued to jut forward aggressively, and his striking blue eyes were filled with seething hostility. "Hothead" wasn't a strong enough word for him, Tiffany reflected, remembering what Rolf had called him. The man seemed to have no sense of fear or self-preservation. Well, she thought, he could get himself into dangerous political trouble on his own time. She certainly had no intention of being a party to such temperamental self-destructiveness. She decided to change the subject quickly. "Why are you avoiding me?" she asked.

"I?" said Sharmonov. "You deceive yourself that you are important enough for me to wish to avoid."

"I've been in Moscow three days now. I've done a preliminary interview with every key dancer in the Volgaya—except you."

"I took ill the day you requested the interview. I sent word; surely you received it."

"Yes, I received it. I received it the very evening you were busy performing a vigorous rehearsal in the studio, which I didn't find out about until afterward."

"A miraculous recovery," he said, shrugging.

"And then last night I hosted a small party so I could get to know you and the others informally, so we might become a bit more relaxed and friendly with one another. Everyone came—except you."

"My most sincere apologies. I took ill."

"Again?"

"The very same sickness. Fortunately I recovered in time for today's rehearsal."

His expression was taunting, mocking, arrogantly domineering. Tiffany was furious. She stared back at him defiantly. How dare he treat her so disdainfully? Why, she did not even know the man! And she had done nothing whatever to provoke him. She knew she should end this argument right away. She wasn't doing her chances for a reconciliation any good by continuing it. But Tiffany had always had a stubborn streak of willfulness that seldom bowed to reason when her ire got up.

"Why are you so hostile to me?" she demanded.

He laughed a snorting contemptuous laugh. "Perhaps it is your very charming personality."

"You don't even know me! You don't have any idea how charming or uncharming my personality is!"

"This is true. Then there must be another reason for any antagonism you detect, mustn't there?" He was about to repeat his earlier words about Tiffany's "propaganda" crew; she could see it clearly in his eyes. Their gazes locked. She pleaded with him not to say it—wordlessly, letting him see her wish in her expression.

He was a perceptive man; he saw her message. He glanced at Vronsky, understanding that Tiffany did not want to be a party to any reprisals he might suffer as a result of his outspokenness. He did not say the words. Instead he waved his hand sharply through the air, dismissing the subject with disdain, as if it were beneath him.

"I do not have time for this," he snarled. "Here's what I came down here to tell you. I wish to make an offer. You desire to watch me dance, yes, facing the front of the stage?"

"Yes. That's just what I want."

"Fine. I will do that. And in return you will agree to take your camera away, out of the theater. I do not wish to be filmed by you."

"I can't do that, and you know it. My whole purpose in coming all the way to Moscow is to film you and the others." She paused. "If you don't want to get publicity for yourself for some reason, at least you might think of the others. I'm sure many of them would like to be in this film."

"Fine. Then you film them; to that I have no objection." He turned on his heel and leaped back onto the stage, where he took up his position in the center. The director looked at him questioningly, hopefully, wondering if at last they might return to their purpose for being there. Sharmonov nodded curtly at him. The director gestured to a man across the stage, who started the record player, and music filled the air.

Sharmonov went into his preparatory position, down on one knee, his arms held close to his chest, his powerful shoulder muscles bulging. He glanced at Tiffany to see what she would do.

Tiffany reached over and jerked the towel off the front of Michael's camera, baring the lens once more.

This was what Sharmonov had been waiting for. To the director's shouts and frustrated ranting and raving, Sharmonov stood up and stormed off the stage. Vronsky, sitting next to Tiffany, looked coldly menacing. He left his seat and walked backstage in the direction in which Sharmonov had disappeared.

The director ordered the record changed. New music came on, bouncier and more lyrical. The corps de ballet paraded into a new position at his instructions and began rehearsing their dance. As they bounded and swirled across the stage, the director hurried down the side steps and approached Tiffany. He looked harried. He collapsed dejectedly into the seat next to her.

"I don't understand," Tiffany said. "Why is he so against me? Is he like this to *everyone*?"

The director shook his head. He was an older man, with graying hair and bags under his eyes that made him look like a sad dog. "You wish to speak to Nikolai, yes? You have interviewed the others, and now you wish to interview him, too? I believe I can arrange it."

"I don't see how. He certainly doesn't seem very eager to talk to me—or to listen to you."

The director sighed with helpless frustration at the truth of this observation. "I tell you, Miss Farrow, I am most unhappy at this situation, most unhappy. Nikolai is very good dancer—best dancer, maybe, that I have ever seen in all my years with the Volgaya. I would like very much to keep him as my Albrecht and feature him in other lead roles. But if he continues behaving in this crazy way...." He shook his head, a hangdog expression still on his face. "The government—it does not tolerate mavericks."

"That's why Zhukov was let go from his position, too, wasn't it? Because he was a maverick in a political way."

The director looked shocked and nervous. He quickly glanced to the left and right. "We do not talk of such things," he said stiffly, in a hushed voice. He seemed on the verge of getting up and leaving.

"Wait," Tiffany said, putting her hand on his arm. "I'm sorry. I just...well, let me ask this. Why did they allow Nikolai Sharmonov to be promoted to *premier danseur*, knowing he was such a rebel?"

"He was not such a rebel earlier. A little bit, yes. But that is expected of temperamental geniuses. Never, though, has he behaved like *this*, as we see today. Only since you have come."

"Me? What does he have against me?"

Gargarin threw up his hands, unable to answer.

"Oh, great. It makes me feel wonderful to know that I might somehow be responsible for one of the world's great dancers being banished from ballet. And the thing of it is, I didn't even *do* anything. I don't have any idea why he's acting this way toward me."

"You will find out, yes? *Please* find out. Please find out and do something to change the situation. I will try to arrange a dinner meeting between you and

him for tonight. I will prevail upon Nikolai to go.
Maybe he will go. I think he will go. Vronsky is with
him now, telling him what—how do you Americans
say—what 'hot water' he is in." He stood up and
started backing away. He said to her plaintively, "If
I can arrange for him to go, then please work out the
problems between you two? Convince him to cooperate?"

"I'd love to!" she called after him as he retreated
quickly back onto the stage. "After all, it's not *me*
who's—" But he was on the stage now, instructing
his dancers, deliberately turning his back to her.

CHAPTER FOUR

ARRANGEMENTS WERE MADE for the meeting to take place in the main restaurant of the Rossia Hotel. At eight o'clock Nikolai Sharmonov arrived at Tiffany's hotel room to escort her. Right from the start she could see that if this evening's dinner date was an attempt to make peace between them, it would fail.

"Good evening, Nikolai," she said, answering the door, trying to establish a casual rapport.

He bowed slightly, his expression stony, his eyes insolent.

"Would you like to come in for a moment while I get my wrap?"

"Da," he said. No "Thank you." No "Yes, please." He swept past her into the room, his entire attitude belligerent. As Tiffany got her white fur wrap, Nikolai walked about the hotel room possessively, his hands on his hips. He acted as if he owned the place, as if he were some feudal lord scornfully inspecting the premises of one of his serfs. He went to the large veranda windows and gazed at the patio and the rooftop garden beyond. He went into Tiffany's bedroom and inspected her perfumes before

her dressing-room mirror. He even went to her closed closet doors as if he were about to yank them open and inspect her wardrobe.

"Are you quite ready?" Tiffany said to him icily.

He looked at her. *"Da,"* he said. He did not offer to help her on with her wrap.

Seated in the back seat of the taxi as they drove down the Moskovretskaya Embankment, Tiffany turned her eyes to him. He was sitting at ease, yet with the stiff-backed elegance of a dancer who never relaxed his posture totally. His eyes were directed straight ahead.

He looked very handsome with his profile so resolute and strong, his cheeks sunken. His sunburst of golden hair was brushed into a semblance of order now, across his forehead, half covering his ears. He wore a dark blue turtleneck under a tan leather coat that was surprisingly well-cut and expensive for a society that frowned on displays of materialism. Tiffany remembered something from her research: Nikolaï was a rebel in economic matters as well as those relating to social conventions. He did not hide his scorn for Soviet antimaterialism. He had a taste for expensive clothing and other articles, and he indulged it on the black market.

Tiffany herself had dressed quite modestly, believing Nikolai would do the same and not wanting to make him feel self-conscious. She wore a pale green gown that accented her slender but quite shapely figure. Her dark hair was done up in a modified bun, with ringlets framing her cheeks. Her earrings and necklace were of gold and simply designed.

Her concern about making him feel self-conscious, she now realized, had been greatly misplaced. Looking at his supremely self-assured features as he pulled out a silver cigarette case and offered her a Troika, she could see that nothing in the world could make this arrogant man feel ill at ease.

"No, thank you," she said a little too coolly, in reaction to his own haughty aloofness.

He took a Troika for himself and lighted it with a silver lighter. The smoke from the Russian cigarette was unusually fragrant. Nikolai opened the window and settled back to watch the view.

"You're an excellent conversationalist," Tiffany said, unable to restrain herself from the sarcasm.

She was not used to being ignored so totally. Most men she met became nervous in her presence and began acting fawningly toward her. Other men, stronger men, put on a show of bravado and tried to impress her with their charm or virility. No one, though, ignored her completely, as Nikolai Sharmonov was doing now. It bothered her that he could be so unaffected by her looks. Normally Tiffany was genuinely modest and tried to minimize the effect her beauty had on people. She tried to pretend it really didn't matter. Now, though, she wanted it to matter. She wanted to penetrate that wall of cold reserve surrounding him.

"You're the one who requested this meeting,"

Nikolai said. "If you wish to hear conversation, go ahead and speak."

"I didn't ask for this meeting. Your director set it up and asked if I would please attend. For your sake, I might add."

"You wanted to interview me from the very first. Do not deny it."

"I'm not denying anything! And I don't like your tone. I want to interview you, yes, for professional reasons. But I do not force myself upon men or invite them to have dinner with me, as you seem to suppose."

"Well, I certainly didn't ask to have dinner with *you*. It was arranged for me. And if my behavior seems a bit rude to you, perhaps you should ask yourself how you would act if you were a captive being spied upon to make sure you behaved properly."

"Spied upon!" she said indignantly, ready at last to give him a piece of her mind. "If you think that I—"

"Turn around," he said. "Look out the window behind you."

Tiffany did so. She saw Vronsky seated beside the driver of the green Russian Lada sedan that was following them. "What's he doing here?" she said, surprised. "I didn't ask for an interpreter tonight."

"Whether you ask or not, you receive. He is here to report on me. So you see, this 'social' dinner date you have planned is not really so social at all."

"Well...I'm sorry, I had no idea. It's certainly

not my doing that he's following us. You realize this, don't you?"

He said nothing. The taxi reached the circular driveway of a very tall building. Nikolai relented from his stern rudeness enough to get out first and hold the door open for her. They entered an elevator in which they were taken to the twenty-first floor. When Tiffany emerged, she was amazed. There were enormous windows facing the elevator, and through them, twenty-one stories down, she beheld a view of a stunningly beautiful fairy-tale-like building, illuminated by floodlights.

"St. Basil's Cathedral," Nikolai said.

It had many giant towers with onion-shaped domes, each topped by a tall spire and a golden cross. Every tower was unique, with its own vivid coloration and its own distinctive motifs. The nearest one was orange and white, with a blue-striped dome. Its carved decorations took the form of arrowheads pointing to the heavens. On either side of it were blue-and-white towers with semicircular designs incorporating paintings of tree branches with green leaves. The onion domes on these were brown and green, with crisscross latticework in relief. There was more—there were pillars, statues, arches.... The enormous cathedral was an extremely complex work of art, from the very bottom to the top of the highest golden dome. The wealth of beautiful colors alone, floodlit as they were, was a staggering sight.

"It's beautiful," Tiffany said, conscious of the inadequacy of such a statement.

For once Nikolai did not make a cynical remark or affect a mocking expression. He seemed quietly pleased that Tiffany could appreciate a work of such grandeur. She had a vague feeling that this was somehow related to the fact that she had surprised him earlier by knowing more about ballet than he had expected.

"I'm glad you like it," he said. "I suspected that you would, that you would be able to."

"Who wouldn't?" she replied.

"There are many who would not appreciate it the way that you do."

For an instant Tiffany detected a look in his eyes that was different from anything she had seen from him so far. It was a look of acknowledgment, as if he had formed an opinion about her sensitivity, about her ability to value beauty and works of art, and was pleased to see that his opinion was right. It was as if he were allowing himself to feel an empathy toward Tiffany despite himself. For a moment there seemed to be a truce between them. He seemed to have let down his guard ever so slightly. As Tiffany let him guide her to a table, as they followed the maitre d', she hoped this new attitude would last.

The moment they were seated, however, something happened that made her realize it would not: the elevator doors opened, and Vronsky stepped out. This was unfortunate. Tiffany had hoped he would

be content to leave them alone once they had entered
the restaurant. But no, evidently he wanted to watch
them every minute. He glanced around worriedly until he caught sight of them, then he turned his eyes
away quickly, pretending he had not been looking for
them at all. When the maitre d' seated him in a corner, he made a production of busying himself with
his menu as if unaware of Tiffany and Nikolai's
presence. He acted as though he had just wandered
into this particular restaurant by "coincidence."

Nikolai glanced at the menu, then said to Tiffany,
"I suggest the *tsiplyata tabaka*—spiced chicken flat-
tened between two searing-hot stones. Shall we order
it for...three?"

She saw the mocking look in his eyes as he gazed at
her from under his lowered brow, but now there was
a hint of sympathy in his look, too. He seemed to be
saying that even though he would not cooperate with
her now that Vronsky was here, he realized it was not
her fault that the man had shown up. She and
Nikolai were antagonists once again, but at least they
were antagonists who could sympathize with each
other's predicament.

This was not good enough for Tiffany. She was
tired of being in predicaments that needed to be sym-
pathized with. Here she was on the verge of finding
out why Nikolai had been so hostile toward her these
past three days, and now Vronsky had shown up and
ruined her chances completely. Well, she wouldn't
stand for it!

She rose from the table and walked away without explanation. Crossing the dimly lighted, attractively appointed dining room, she went straight to Vronsky's table and stood looking down at him.

For a moment he pretended not to be aware of her presence. Then he looked up from his menu, an expression of surprise on his face. "Ah, Miss Farrow. *Dobraii vecher*—good evening. So you have discovered this fine Soviet restaurant, too, I see. What a coincidence, eh, seeing—"

"Comrade Vronsky."

"Yes?"

"May I ask you a question?"

"Yes. Yes, dear lady, of course."

"Are you planning to stay here for dinner tonight?"

"Why, yes. I was planning to. I do not disturb you, I hope?"

"Not at all," Tiffany said. "I was just curious. So you are eating dinner here tonight?"

"I am eating dinner here tonight. *Da.*"

"Fine." She nodded. "Good evening, Comrade Vronsky." She returned to her table. Instead of sitting down, though, she said, "Nikolai, let's go."

Nikolai raised an eyebrow in interest.

"Our good friend the interpreter is staying, but there's no need for us to."

Nikolai looked at her for a moment, then a grin broke out over his sensuous lips. It was a very charming boyish grin and was the first sign of real warmth he had ever displayed to her. It was very appealing. Tiffany began to feel that if he was capable of this, perhaps he really was not as conceited and horrible as he had seemed. Maybe it was just possible that he actually thought he had a legitimate reason for treating her as rudely as he had.

Nikolai stood up, said a few words to the maitre d' and handed him a five-ruble note. Then he led Tiffany toward the elevator. She saw Vronsky's alarmed expression as he realized he had been tricked. He could not leave to follow them now without making his true role more obvious than it already was.

As they were passing his table, Nikolai said in a seemingly friendly, actually taunting voice, "Enjoy the borscht, Vronsky. It is very good here." Then they were in the taxi and driving away from the restaurant.

Nikolai was smiling broadly now, more alive and animated than Tiffany had ever seen him. "That was very nicely done," he said. "I congratulate you."

"Thank you. But I don't want your congratulations. I want to know why you keep avoiding me and why you have such a strong hostility toward me when you don't even know me."

Nikolai narrowed his eyes as he looked at her, debating with himself over something important. Finally he said, "You have earned the right to know. I think I will tell you—maybe." He leaned forward and gave the driver a new address—on Marx Prospekt.

Tiffany recognized the place. "That's my hotel!" she protested. "You're taking me back?"

"If you wish to talk seriously, a restaurant is not the place to do it. Look out the window behind you." Tiffany turned and saw that Vronsky was once again following them. By this time she was not really surprised. "He would not stay behind," Nikolai explained, "despite losing face by making himself obvious. He has a job to do. He intends to follow us wherever we go."

"So instead of going anywhere, you're taking me back to my hotel?"

He nodded.

"And we'll talk there?" she said hopefully.

"*Nyet*. I am afraid we will not talk there."

"So you've decided against telling me after all?" She was upset and agitated. "Why must you be so mysterious about all this? If you don't like me for some reason, the very least you can do is tell me why. I don't think it's fair for you to—"

He raised a finger to her lips, silencing her. "Wait and see," he said.

When the taxi pulled up in front of the Metropole, Nikolai led her into the lobby. She got her key from the desk clerk, then turned to see what Nikolai was looking at. He was standing by the stairway but not ascending. He was watching the green Lada now pulling to a screeching halt in front of the hotel. Vronsky disembarked; his beefy face was sweating, and he was mopping it with a handkerchief.

Nikolai took Tiffany's arm and waited. Then, just as Vronsky burst in through the hotel doors, he started leading her up the carpeted stairway. He held her arm tightly, indicating that he did not want her to look back at Vronsky.

They arrived on the second floor, where Nikolai guided her to her room. Tiffany inserted her key into the door. She was upset and bewildered. First he'd said she had earned the right to know why he was acting so hostile to her, then he'd said they would not talk here at the hotel. Evidently he had decided against telling her his motives after all—at least not tonight.

"Well," she said coldly, "good night. You obviously don't trust me with your mysterious secret reasons, whatever they are."

"Not so obviously," he said.

She turned to enter her room, but he stopped her, his hand upon her arm. He held her there like that, not moving. There was the sound of labored breathing coming up the carpeted stairway. Now Nikolai turned Tiffany to face him. She looked into his eyes questioningly, not knowing what he wanted. An instant later Vronsky's squat figure burst upon the landing, huffing and puffing.

At that moment Nikolai put his arms around Tiffany and hugged her tightly, his lips descending on hers. At first she was stunned by the unexpectedness of his clasp. Her next instinct was to protest, to resist. How dare he take such liberties with her! She wanted to resist, hotly and indignantly—but her body betrayed her. Feeling his hard masculine chest and hips pressing against her, his firm lips moving voluptuously upon hers, she felt suddenly weak and powerless. It was as if all her strength had deserted her and she could do nothing but watch her body submitting to his passionate embrace, as if she were divorced from it, up on a cloud somewhere looking down.

She opened her eyes and watched his strong, sensuous, strangely harsh face as he was kissing her. It was the face she had been secretly, guiltily, seeing in her dreams for the past three nights—those heavily lidded eyes with the long golden lashes, the prominent cheekbones that gave him such a chiseled look. The image of that, along with the feel of his lips upon hers, nearly made her swoon.

Vronsky, at the edge of the landing, saw what was happening and realized he would soon be observed. He turned and retreated a few steps, just enough to be out of sight.

Tiffany by now had managed to gather her wits and strength about her again. Through a major effort of will she succeeded in pushing herself slightly away from Nikolai, though he still held her within the circle of his arms. "How dare you!" she said, keeping her voice low so Vronsky would not hear. "If you think you can treat me like a—"

Nikolai put his finger to her lips once more, silencing her. Tiffany felt like slapping his hand away.

His eyes, however, were filled with meaning. He was giving her a signal. He was telling her through the look in his eyes that she must playact at the present and do as he wanted.

"We'll go inside now, my love," he said in his deep masculine voice loud enough for Vronsky to overhear.

Tiffany hesitated. No matter what he might be trying to tell her, the fact was Nikolai Sharmonov had a reputation throughout Russia as a lady's man *extraordinaire*. She had learned that from her research. She had learned, too, that he constantly denied the reputation. But at the moment such a denial did not seem particularly convincing, especially since his hand was just beneath the small of her back, unconsciously resting on the curve of her derriere. And he was still holding her in a close embrace, his body pressing against hers.

The sensations emanating from within her were distracting her. What she really wanted to do was slap him and raise her chin defiantly, then leave him standing in the hall. But she did not do this. She understood that he seemed to be acting this way for Vronsky's sake, to create a deception that might somehow be to Nikolai's advantage.

Tiffany gazed into the depths of his clear cobalt-blue eyes and made a decision. She would trust him— for now. "All right," she said loudly enough for Vronsky to hear. She opened the door and entered her room, allowing Nikolai to follow her in. And even though she felt she was being compromised, she did not protest when he put the Do Not Disturb sign on the doorknob and shut the door firmly.

He turned to her now, his expression smoldering with sensuality, yet at the same time bewildered. From his look Tiffany could see that his kiss *had* been purely for show—to deceive Vronsky for some reason. Nevertheless the "show" had got to him. It had penetrated to his emotions in a way he had obviously not expected.

So she had not been the only one, Tiffany reflected with a tinge of satisfaction, to become involuntarily swept up in the passion of the moment.

"Just what is this all about?" she demanded.

Nikolai made a strong effort to regain his composure. The startled look caused by his unexpected feelings of tenderness quickly vanished. In its place came a steely expression. He seemed embarrassed at having let himself lose control of his emotions for an instant, and now he overreacted with a brusque coolness. He grasped her hand and took her with him across the room to the veranda windows. He flung the windows open and led Tiffany outside onto the patio. He crossed the garden to an interior stairway exit at the far end.

"Where are you taking me?" she asked, pulling back a bit.

"You wish to interview the Volgaya's *premier danseur*? You cannot do it here. We go to a place where you can do it."

Tiffany didn't argue as he took her down the secondary stairway, past the lobby, into the basement mall. If Nikolai was finally going to explain to her why he was acting the way he was, she would go where he led her.

The Metropole Hotel was a prerevolutionary building constructed at the turn of the century. Nikolai guided her through an underground basement, then up again to the street level. Tiffany passed a memorial plaque designating the hotel as an important historical monument; a battle had been fought in 1917 by revolutionary troops seeking to occupy it. Outside, out of sight of the lobby entrance, Nikolai hailed a taxi. Tiffany stood before the facade of the building, which was adorned with an enormous brightly colored enameled relief: *Dream Princess*. It seemed to Tiffany that almost everywhere you turned in Moscow you were confronted with beautiful facades, statuary and works of art. Many of the buildings were architectural marvels, encompassing a variety of periods. Surprisingly, some of the most famous Russian buildings were designed in the manner of the Italian Renaissance.

"Here," said Nikolai as the taxi arrived. He ushered Tiffany inside quickly and gave the driver an address.

Tiffany still had no idea where he was taking her or why they could not talk in her hotel room. As the cab sped through the darkened Moscow streets, she could not help thinking about how mysterious this whole affair was turning out to be. He had kissed her at the door to deceive Vronsky into thinking they were still inside the room now being...romantic. But instead they were escaping to some unknown destination.

When the taxi pulled up outside an old-style apartment complex on Sadovaya Street, she followed Nikolai inside. His attitude was still brusque, an overreaction from his earlier moments of weakness. They reached a particular apartment; Nikolai banged on the door.

"Where are we?" Tiffany asked.

The door opened.

"You wish," Nikolai answered, "to interview the Volgaya's brilliant *premier danseur*? Here is the Volgaya's brilliant *danseur*, the man you *should* be interviewing and filming." He gestured with a grand sweep of his hand to the surprised man standing in the open doorway. "The Volgaya's great dancer— Serge Zhukov!"

CHAPTER FIVE

TIFFANY DID NOT KNOW what to say. The man in the doorway was older and distinguished-looking and had a graying goatee and mustache. He had once been quite a dashing figure. Tiffany had seen him many years ago, while he had been on a tour of the United States. This was indeed the great Zhukov, the former star dancer of the Volgaya Ballet.

Tiffany and Zhukov stood looking at each other in awkward silence. Nikolai stood beside Tiffany, looking fiercely self-righteous. Zhukov turned to Nikolai, and his expression showed that he was annoyed by this situation. Then he sighed tolerantly, though, and broke the silence with a courtly invitation.

"Come in, won't you please," he said to Tiffany in quite good English. "Forgive my hotheaded young friend for not introducing us properly and for putting you in such an uncomfortable position. His manners vanish as his temper rises." He glanced at Nikolai sidelong in a reprimanding way, but Tiffany could see there was genuine warmth between the two men. Zhukov had been Nikolai's mentor. "My friend suffers from an affliction common to many creative geniuses," Zhukov said. "He is temperamental and has absolutely no common sense." He bowed to Tiffany. "My dear, I am Serge Zhukov."

"I'm pleased to meet you, Mr. Zhukov. I'm Tiffany Farrow. I'm in Moscow to film the Volgaya for a documentary, following it to the ballet competition in Zurich."

Tiffany entered the apartment, and Nikolai followed after her, his movements sharp and abrupt. The apartment was cozy but quite small, as were most dwellings in Moscow, where living space was at a premium. Almost everyone wanted to live in Moscow due to the temperate weather in the summer and the relative abundance of consumer goods and cultural activities. Citizens could live in Moscow by permission only, however, and the waiting list was four years long.

Zhukov's furniture was plump, comfortable and aged. One wall was a floor-to-ceiling bookcase filled with books and knickknacks gathered from the countries he had toured in during his years with the Volgaya. Another wall was completely covered with photographs of Zhukov costumed for some of his most famous roles: Romeo, Siegfried in *Swan Lake*, Don Basilio in *Don Quixote*. The pictures captured him in candid moments or during performances with other dancers. In just the briefest of glances Tiffany saw and recognized some of the greatest names in ballet of the past quarter-century.

"Now," Zhukov said to Nikolai, "what is this all about?"

"Very simple. This Miss Tiffany Farrow is desirous of filming the Volgaya's great *premier danseur*. I have brought her here so she may do so."

Zhukov looked at Tiffany in bafflement. "You wish to film me? I do not understand. I am no longer with the Volgaya."

"I know that," Tiffany said. She lowered her eyes. "My assignment is to film Nikolai Sharmonov—and the other dancers."

"But don't you see!" declared Nikolai hotly. "If you film me, you give added weight to those who say Sharmonov is the greatest dancer. You add to the propaganda effort to sweep Serge Zhukov under the rug, to make people accept the change without protest!"

"Nikolai! Do not speak of this!" Zhukov demanded.

"She must know what she is doing," Nikolai said. "She must be aware of the injustice she is helping to perpetrate."

"Nikolai," Zhukov said in a half angry, yet half plaintive tone, "do you wish to end up like me? You're not far from it, you know. You become more of a political liability to the Volgaya each time you open your mouth on this subject. Why don't you just *accept* it? I have. I have had my day of glory, and now it is time to move on."

"It is not time! And I will never be a party to such injustice!"

They began arguing heatedly in rapid Russian, ignoring Tiffany, forgetting that she was even there. At last Tiffany understood why Nikolai had been so hostile toward her. What she had earlier taken to be senseless antagonism had not been so senseless at all. He was under the impression that Tiffany was deliberately aiding the government in an effort to sweep Zhukov under the rug.

The pieces began fitting together. Zhukov still had a strong following in Russia and worldwide. His foreign fans could cause trouble by boycotting the Volgaya's performances in protest against Zhukov's political ouster. By producing a film that glorified Nikolai, that showed what an incredible dancer he was, Tiffany would be aiding the government in getting the public to accept the new lead dancer—and forget the old.

So that was why the government was so eager to cooperate in getting this film done! An American-made documentary would be much more influential than a Russian one, which would be viewed as biased. And that was why Nikolai had refused to cooperate.

"Nyet!" shouted Nikolai in response to something Zhukov had just said. "Never! Never!" The two of them continued arguing heatedly in Russian.

As Tiffany watched Nikolai stalking about and gesturing emotionally, his face so boldly resolute, she began feeling much more respectful of the man. Some dancers were so greedy for personal glory they would do anything to get it. Yet here was a man who, despite his love of his art, was willing to sacrifice one of the most desirable positions in the land, rather than take part in what he considered an injustice against a friend.

What strength of character he had! Tiffany felt regret at the way she had looked down on him earlier as being insufferably self-assured and obnoxiously arrogant. Of course he was supremely self-assured! He had to be to do what he was doing—to stand up single-handedly against the leadership of the ballet and the forces of government that were arrayed against him. He had to have a will of steel and a belief in himself that transcended all doubts. Arrogant? Yes, he was that—and he had every right to be!

"Nikolai," Zhukov declared, "you are impossible!" He threw up his hands in despair. He gave up trying to influence him and turned instead to Tiffany. "Do not let him make you abandon your film, I beseech you. Do it just as you had intended. If you abandon it now, the government will know that Nikolai was responsible. He will suffer gravely."

Tiffany hesitated. "But if I—"

"And it will not help me in any way," Zhukov continued. "If you abandon it or change it, it will not serve me in any way at all. Nikolai is only tilting at windmills." He turned to Nikolai again. "You deserve to be *premier danseur*. Don't fight it this way. I had my moment in the sun, and I am grateful. Now you take yours."

Nikolai began to protest anew, but Zhukov cut him short. He refused to participate. He turned away from him and folded his arms across his chest. Finally Nikolai stopped trying to argue.

After a long moment Nikolai even managed a self-effacing half grin. He shrugged. "You know, I did not come here to argue with him," he said to Tiffany. "But sometimes I am, as he says, a hothead; sometimes I get carried away."

"I think your intentions are very noble, even if, as Mr. Zhukov says, they won't really be able to help him in any way."

"So then you *will* change your film to—"

"Nikolai," Zhukov said warningly. "We will not speak of that any longer."

Nikolai shrugged.

"Besides," said Zhukov, "I have something for you." He went to an old brown cabinet and began rummaging around in a drawer. He withdrew a featherweight airmail envelope and handed it to him. "It is from Larisa."

Nikolai raised an eyebrow. He turned the letter over in his hand a few times and looked at it warily. Then he said, "Why does she send it to you?"

"Larisa is not an easy woman to fathom. Perhaps she feels that if she sent it directly to you, the government would open it first. They know how close you and she once were."

Nikolai gazed at the already opened envelope with great reluctance and uneasiness. Finally he took a deep breath, yanked out the letter and began reading. As he read, he began to smolder with anger, and his jaw began trembling. When he had finished, he crumpled the letter angrily in his fist and flung it against the wall.

Tiffany was so stunned by this she could not help asking, even though it was none of her business, "What is it? What's wrong?"

He stood there seeming deeply tormented, his jaw trembling. Then he shook his head and said in a raw tightly controlled voice, "It is nothing I cannot handle."

Whatever it was in that letter, Tiffany thought, it affected him very deeply. Instead of continuing to watch him, she decided it would be more respectful of his privacy to turn away and pretend disinterest. Zhukov evidently felt this, also, for he came to Tiffany and gestured at one of the photographs on the wall. "Three years ago," he said, "in happier times."

The picture was of Zhukov and Nikolai, smiling merrily in the royally embroidered costumes from the ballet *Sleeping Beauty*. Tiffany let her eyes travel over the other photographs on the wall. They could have served as an honor gallery of ballet greats. Legendary performers from almost every country were pictured smiling with Zhukov or shaking hands with him or dancing with him.

As Tiffany progressed along the wall, she came to one photograph that made her gasp. "Why, that's my mother!"

Zhukov frowned at her disbelievingly. Even Nikolai turned to her, divorcing himself from the contemplation of his letter. "No," said Zhukov, "you must be mistaken." Then he leaned forward and looked at the photograph closely—and looked at Tiffany closely, too. He could see the resemblance. "Your mother is Victoria Farrow?" he asked.

Tiffany nodded.

"Yes, of course. The last name—I should have realized. But. . . but that is incredible! You are Victoria Farrow's daughter, and you are not a dancer? How can this be?"

Tiffany felt instantly uncomfortable. Her skin began to feel prickly. This was a question she hated being faced with, even under the best of circumstances. From the corner of her eye she could see that Nikolai was looking at her curiously, also. Tiffany did not want to answer. To tell him the truth would only result in pain and arguments and demands. It always did.

Instead of answering, she changed the subject by asking a question. "How did you happen to dance with my mother? I don't remember hearing of it."

Zhukov looked at the photograph again. It showed a red-haired woman of great classical beauty being held aloft in a graceful horizontal lift. Both dancers wore costumes from the ballet *Firebird*. The woman's face was serene and coolly confident, as befitted a ballerina who had risen to the peak of her profession with resounding international acclaim.

"It was fifteen years ago at least," said Zhukov. "It was during a tour of America. I was guest artist for *Firebird* that performance at the invitation of the...." He narrowed his eyes, trying to remember.

"New York City Ballet," said Tiffany.

"That is right, the New York City Ballet, and your mother, Victoria Farrow, was the company's prima ballerina. She danced as the Firebird, opposite me as Prince Ivan." He smiled wistfully at the memory. "Oh, what a ballerina she was. What grace! What control! I remember it. Yes, I remember it. It was the finest *Firebird* I have ever performed." He turned to Tiffany questioningly. "How is it I never hear of your mother anymore? She is too wonderful a dancer to have faded so early."

"She...um...she had an accident. She hurt her ankle. She hasn't danced in more than ten years."

Zhukov wanted to know more. He began asking further questions. It was Nikolai who saved Tiffany. He saw her look of sharp discomfort, and he was perceptive enough to realize that for some reason this was a very painful subject for her.

"Serge," he said, stepping forward and taking Tiffany's arm, "we really must go. It is late. My visit here was not...shall we say, 'officially approved'?"

Zhukov understood; he nodded sagely. "Go. I want you to get into no more trouble than you are in already. Miss Farrow...." He bowed over her hand and kissed it. "A pleasure meeting the daughter of one of the world's finest ballerinas. My regards to your mother.''

"I'll tell her," Tiffany said.

As they were on their way out, Zhukov made one last parting statement. "Do not let Nikolai bully you into having his own way!" he said. "You continue with your film just as you started it." Then they were out the door and hurrying to the nearest taxi stand.

In Moscow taxi stands are never far away. Since few of the residents can afford cars, taxis are a major mode of transportation. When Tiffany and Nikolai arrived, though, there were no cabs present. They had to wait for several minutes. Nikolai kept glancing around cautiously. It was clear to Tiffany there was danger in his being here and he did not want to be seen in the open any longer than was necessary. Finally a taxi, with its distinctive checkered door, pulled into the stand. The green light bulb in the windshield was on, signifying that the taxi was free. The two of them got in quickly, and the cab started back to Tiffany's hotel.

She rolled the window down a bit so the balmy breeze could waft in. The night was pleasant, and the Moscow cityscape was intriguing to look at. Next to her Nikolai seemed broodingly lost in thought, much as he had looked after reading that letter Zhukov had handed him. Whatever had been in the letter had affected him strongly—and was still affecting him. He seemed much more human and emotional now than he had during the past few days.

"I didn't know your government was planning to use my film in a propagandalike way," Tiffany said softly. "I had no idea."

He turned to her and, after a moment, managed to divorce himself from his other concerns. "In that case," he said, "I apologize to you for my rudeness of these past days. I assumed that you did know, that you were cooperating knowingly. But I could see from your reaction when I spoke to Serge that I was wrong in blaming you."

"Yes, you were. I'm glad you understand now."

He smiled. It was a warm smile, and it made Tiffany feel much more warmly toward him. "To tell the truth, Tiffany Farrow, being rude to you was not so easy as you might think." He paused as if deciding whether to tell her something that was on his mind. Then he said, "From the first moment I saw you when you sat in the theater, your head so high, your expression so uncompromising as you watched me to see if I was as good as you had heard—it was very appealing. Women who have a sharp artistic sense and who are uncompromising are rare."

He hesitated. His eyes were very sensuous as they watched her. He seemed not to want to go on, to be uncomfortable speaking of this. But then he added, "It is more than just the way you carry yourself, your beauty. There is a look in those emerald eyes of yours, a look of willfulness, of intelligence. These are powerfully attractive traits to me."

Tiffany felt taken aback by his words and by the

sudden intensity she saw in his penetrating blue eyes. Until now she had had no hint he felt this way.

"It is your defiant spirit, too," he said, his voice throatier, as he moved nearer to her in the seat. "It makes me feel that—" He stopped. He deliberately cut himself short. He looked upset with himself suddenly for speaking of such things. He turned his head away abruptly and looked out the window. For some reason he clearly did not want to let himself show his true feelings. He appeared angry with himself for having done so. Tiffany could not imagine why. "No," he said finally, getting firmer control of his voice, "it was not so easy being rude to you—not at all."

"Well, for someone who had a hard time doing it, you sure did a good job."

He caught the humor in her voice, and he almost smiled, but he stopped himself. Again there was a sense that for some reason he was deliberately holding back his feelings. Tiffany had an urge to touch him gently and say, "It's all right...you don't have to be afraid to let me know the way you feel."

But then Nikolai's mood changed abruptly, as if deliberately to put distance between them. "Then you will alter your film now," he said brusquely, "so that I am not included in it. Yes?"

She sat bolt upright and looked at him. "I can't do that. You're the focal point of the film."

His eyes became dark and piercing. "Before you

had the excuse of not knowing what you were doing; now you know, and yet you intend to continue?''

Tiffany moved away from him and glared at him. His nearness had suddenly become unwelcome. She felt almost as if she had been manipulated.

"Now you listen to me, Nikolai Sharmonov. You may be a brilliant dancer, but you have no common sense at all. Didn't you hear what Zhukov was telling you? Nothing that you or I can do will get him taken back by the Volgaya. It simply won't happen. All that'll happen, if you continue refusing to cooperate, is that you'll be booted out, too. You may want to ruin your career with such a stupidly self-destructive act, but don't pretend it'll do Zhukov any good. He told you himself it wouldn't.''

"So you will do nothing any differently?" he said accusingly. "You will help to sweep him under the rug?''

This was not actually true. "I do plan to make a change in the film. I'll include a mention in the narration of how Zhukov was removed for political reasons and how the government is eager to get you accepted so they can stop the resistance against Zhukov's ouster." She added quickly, "But don't think I'm doing this to soothe your ruffled feathers. I'm going ahead because I think it's the right thing to do.''

He seemed satisfied with this—not entirely, but enough to let his hard-edged expression soften a bit. But then Tiffany said, "I have to tell you, though, that if my film is shown in Russia, your government will censor out that part during the translation."

"Then you must include in your contract, when your company sells the film to my government, that no alterations may take place."

"I'd love to, but I'm sure your government won't sign a contract like that, and you know it."

Now he became angry once again. He folded his arms across his chest. "Fine. That is very fine. And if you can find a way to make an interesting film of my back and the back of my head, I wish you the best of luck." He looked away, his hard jaw thrust forward.

Tiffany was fuming. What a stubborn pigheaded man! She turned away, too, and stared out the other window, refusing to say another word to him.

When they reached the hotel, she almost refused to go up the rear stairway with him and enter the veranda windows, as they had left. She relented, though, because she did not want to get him in trouble with the authorities. Vronsky was undoubtedly still stationed in the stairway outside her door.

"Thank you for a wonderful evening," she said sarcastically, marching across the living room and yanking the door open for him.

"My pleasure entirely," he replied equally as frigidly. He bowed, turned on his heel and left.

Tiffany slammed the door. What an infuriating man! Now how was she going to complete her project if he kept turning his back to the camera? He was going to ruin his career—and her first producing credit—out of pigheaded stubbornness. He was tilting at windmills, just as Zhukov had said.

Well, Tiffany thought, the shoot might be over sooner than she had planned. And as bad as that was, there was one thing good about it: it meant that very soon she would not have to see this arrogant temperamental Nikolai Sharmonov ever again. All she wanted right now was to get as far away from him as possible—and as quickly as possible.

CHAPTER SIX

TIFFANY TRIED to make a good film, but Nikolai foiled her at every turn. He went out of his way to make life hard for her. In the next few days the situation went from bad to worse. He refused to do any of the personal bits so necessary to turning a cold documentary into one that sparkled with life. He wouldn't fool around for the camera. He wouldn't let himself be filmed coaching the other dancers or in any informal settings. Though his director succeeded in making him face the front of the stage during his rehearsals, Nikolai still turned his back to the camera whenever he was working at the *barre* or practicing center stage. And he steadfastly refused to be interviewed on film.

The situation became so intolerable that Rolf Grayson called from New York to see what the problem was. He had been checking Tiffany's dailies—the films sent back to New York for processing—and had noticed the lack of any personal shots. He had also noticed the unusually high number of views of Nikolai dancing with his back to the camera.

"What's going on over there?" he demanded.

Tiffany dared not tell him the truth—that it was a political situation she seemed incapable of handling. She knew Rolf. He would send Langerhorn over to take control of the shoot, figuring Tiffany lacked the skill or experience to handle it herself. Tiffany detested the idea of that happening. So instead of telling Rolf the truth, she stalled him, hoping the situation would improve in time.

"I'm getting around to the personal shots, Rolf. I'll start in on them very soon. Right now, though, I just want to give Sharmonov a chance to feel less self-conscious before the camera. He's...shy." What a laugh, she thought as she said this, to accuse that obnoxiously self-assured man of being a shrinking violet!

Rolf sounded satisfied, and Tiffany figured she had bought herself a temporary reprieve. But a week later, without warning, the double doors of the Volgaya Theater crashed open behind her just as she was instructing Michael French on the camera angle she wanted for a particular shot, and she turned to see Rolf striding briskly toward her in his Ivy League suit, winking at her and grinning his usual high-energy, self-assured grin.

"Hi, kids," he said to Tiffany's crew, who were gaping at him in awe. Aside from Mary, none of them had ever seen him in person before except by sheer chance, such as when passing him in the hall if they happened to be visiting on the top-executive floor. Grayson took a seat next to Tiffany and smiled at her.

"Hello, Rolf," she said casually, in understatement, as if unexpected visitors from five thousand or so miles away were an everyday occurrence to her. "Welcome to Moscow."

"Just happened to be passing through and thought I'd drop in."

Tiffany laughed despite herself. How could you help but like a man who was so *obvious*?

"All right, kid, so what's the problem? I've got just twenty hours before I have to leave for an affiliate meeting in Barcelona. Then it's back to New York for a meeting with my board on the Foundation for the Arts benefit. We still haven't decided on a guest of honor who'll be a big enough draw." He glanced up at the stage, where several demisoloists were rehearsing in full costume. "You tell me why you're having trouble getting the personal shots, and I'll see what I can do to solve the problem. Maybe sending Steve Dunhill out here to help might be a good idea."

"It sounds like a terrible idea. I don't need any help, Rolf."

"Good, good. I'm glad to hear it. But the fact is—"

He was interrupted as the demisoloists in the second act left the stage and Nikolai came bounding on, followed by the corps de ballet. This was one of the final rehearsals prior to taking the ballet on tour, and a live orchestra was being used rather than a tape or records. The orchestra struck up the music, as Nikolai began his dance.

"Michael," Tiffany instructed her cameraman, "open on a long shot, pan across the corps, then close in on the principal for a close-up."

As usual Nikolai's performance was wonderful, a truly inspired piece of dancing that would surely win honors in Zurich—and probably top honors.

When the piece was over, Nikolai glanced at Tiffany, then at Grayson, who sat with his arm around her shoulders. From his look Tiffany could see that Nikolai realized the power he held over her at this instant. He knew who Rolf Grayson was. He also knew that all he had to do to have Tiffany removed from producer status was to show—by a scoffing remark or contemptuous stare—that his relations with her were hostile and that he would never cooperate with her.

At first Tiffany was surprised that Nikolai should be aware of all this. But then she thought, of course! Rolf would have had to make arrangements with the government before flying down. The government had undoubtedly told the members of the ballet, through Vronsky, just who was coming to visit them. So Nikolai knew who Rolf was; he probably knew why he had flown down, and he also knew that by showing a refusal to cooperate with Tiffany, he could ruin her career.

She was tense with anxiety as he continued staring at her, not leaving the stage with the other dancers as he was supposed to. What was he waiting for? What was he going to do? The suspense became so sharp it was like electricity in the air.

"Why is he glaring at you like that?" Rolf asked.

And then Nikolai leaped into action. He bounded forward in amazing *jetés* and began performing an impromptu, absolutely astonishing variation of the solo he had done earlier—directly in front of the camera. The conductor, seeing what was happening, immediately cued his orchestra, and the proper score burst forth from the orchestra pit. But the music could hardly keep up with Nikolai. He began inventing variations as he went along, throwing in bits and pieces of innovative dancing, the likes of which Tiffany had never seen before.

The other dancers in the stage wings came forward to watch him, and they stood gaping in awe. *This* was the stuff legend was made of—to perform such boldly brilliant innovative moves on the spur of the moment.... It was a skill that perhaps half a dozen dancers throughout the past century of ballet had possessed. And in the world today Tiffany could think of no other dancer capable of stringing together such awesome "traveling combinations"—so they were called—and executing them so flawlessly.

Nikolai finished his innovative performance with a bravura rendition of the second-act solo from *Giselle*, the piece Zhukov had become famous for. He did it with such panache that when he finished abruptly and bowed into the camera, the theater went wild. The applause was overwhelming. Everyone— the dancers, the director, the stage crew—was on his feet clapping zealously and shouting, "Bravo!

Bravo!'' Even Rolf was standing and applauding enthusiastically.

Nikolai bowed once more into the camera, then turned and bowed directly to Tiffany, making piercing eye contact. His blue eyes were blazing. Then he bounded off the stage into the wings.

Rolf was extremely impressed. ''That's wonderful stuff! I've never seen anything like it. That's the kind of thing that will really make your film. But tell me, why did you wait until now to have him do it?''

''Oh, well...I....''

''Never mind. Just make sure you get more of it. You obviously have the situation well under control.''

''I told you that over the phone,'' she said, trying to sound blithe.

''I should have listened to you. Could have saved me a trip.'' He looked back at the stage toward the side curtains through which Nikolai had disappeared. ''*He's* the man I'd like to have for my arts-foundation benefit. Can you imagine the draw he'd be as guest of honor?'' Then he shook his head wistfully, realizing how impossible such a thing was. ''Listen, Tiffany,'' he said, turning back to her, ''there's a man named Prokiev who's been trying to contact me about some problem regarding your shoot. I was planning to see him while I was here. But since you have the situation so well in hand, you can see him instead. It's your shoot, after all.''

''What problem does he want to talk about?'' This

was something new, and the last thing she needed right now was new problems.

"Have dinner with me tonight, and I'll tell you all about it. Then you can meet with this Prokiev character sometime tomorrow."

"I'd be happy to have dinner with you."

Rolf was about to say something, but he paused as the director, Gargarin, came up to them and bowed diffidently. "Miss Farrow," he said, "Nikolai asked me to say that he wishes to speak to you to set up a convenient time for you to interview him on camera."

She did her best to disguise her surprise. "Fine," she said in a voice only a little bit fainter than usual. "I'll talk to him in a moment."

The director left.

Rolf winked at her. "That's the stuff. You're doing a great job. Get the interview, get more of these impromptu touches on film, and we'll have a documentary to be proud of." He squeezed her arm. "I'll pick you up at eight." Then he was leaving the studio in his usual brisk high-energy strides.

Tiffany went backstage and found Nikolai in his private dressing room. The door was open, and he was standing with his legs braced apart, his hands on his hips. His expression was stern. "You're welcome," he said, not waiting for her to thank him.

"So you know how important that was to me." she said.

"Vronsky told me who your companion was."

"And he asked you to behave yourself?" That was very surprising. It was not in Nikolai's nature to do as he was told.

"Yes," he replied, "and as a result, I was on the verge of acting abominably, doing exactly the opposite of what Vronsky wanted."

"But you didn't," she said softly. "You helped me instead. Why?"

He looked at her with great intensity. Tiffany had not seen him so serious since the moment he had read that mysterious letter at Zhukov's home.

"Miss Farrow...."

"Will you call me Tiffany? *Please.*"

He stared at her. His words were clipped. "There's something I want from you."

Tiffany was disappointed. She had hoped he had helped her out of some other motive than mere self-interest. As silly as it seemed to admit, she had been wishing that perhaps there was the chance, just the slightest chance, that he actually *felt* something for her—some affection or warmth—and that he had behaved as he had for that reason only. But obviously this wasn't the case.

"I already told you," Tiffany said, trying to keep the disappointment out of her voice, "there's nothing I can do about altering the film. No matter what I put in the narration about Zhukov, it'll just be edited out when your government translates it."

"This has nothing to do with your film."

"No? Well, what does it concern?" Looking at

him standing so straight and tall, his fists on his hips, his eyes smoldering and his teeth slightly bared, an image leaped into Tiffany's mind: that of a jungle animal with powerful needs that took what it wanted.

A sexual energy seemed to radiate from him, and it was so strong that Tiffany was almost afraid to hold eye contact with him. A strange thrill surged through her. What did he want from her? She remembered his reputation as a notorious womanizer. He was said to have had relationships with the most desirable women in the world, who practically threw themselves at him in each capital he toured, casting dignity to the wind as they allowed themselves to be mesmerized by his powerful animal magnetism. Looking at him, feeling the aura radiating from him, Tiffany could see how such a thing could happen.

But it would *not* happen to her, she decided. And yet. . . why did she feel so suddenly weak, so shaky in her resolve?

Nikolai came toward her. As his lean muscular body drew very close, she involuntarily jerked back. She raised her chin in what she had intended as a gesture of defiance, but she really looked more like a vulnerable girl trying self-consciously to show that she was stronger than she actually was.

He put his hands on her shoulders. "What I want from you has nothing to do with your film," he repeated. "I no longer care about your film."

"You don't?"

"I've decided on a new course of action. It makes resistance to your film no longer necessary."

"What course of action?" she asked. The way he'd spoken, it sounded ominous.

He glanced at the door of his dressing room. "I cannot talk of it here. I want you to meet me later at your hotel room."

"At my... hotel?"

"Is eight o'clock a good time?"

"No," she said, forcing herself to think clearly. "I have a previous engagement. I should be back by ten, though, or a little bit after."

He nodded curtly. He stared into her eyes for a moment, then he turned her around and pushed her gently out the door. He did not follow her out; he shut the door and remained within.

BY SIX O'CLOCK Tiffany was becoming very edgy. She knew that part of the reason she felt this way was her anticipation over her meeting with Nikolai later on. But there was also another very specific reason for this feeling, and she recognized the signs: the restlessness, the malaise, the feeling of a deep hollowness within her.

The problem was, Tiffany had not danced in almost two weeks. Back in New York she practiced at least every other night, sometimes more often. It was an obsession with her, one that provided her with her greatest pleasure in life and gave her the serenity and peace of mind to face each new day.

Other than the ancient owner of the old ballet studio she secretly went to, no one knew she still danced. Most people thought she had quit ballet for good, since she never went to performances or classes and since no one ever saw her dance. This was the way Tiffany wanted it. If word got out that she still danced, it would revive the terrible situation that had caused her to give up her dreams of a ballet career in the first place. Tiffany could not bear the torment of having to go through that again.

The fact that she practiced alone, though, did not mean she went easy on herself. No, when Tiffany practiced, she performed extremely difficult demanding material, challenging herself constantly. This was the only way she could get the satisfaction from her dancing that she thrived on.

Shortly after she had first come to Moscow, she had stolen away one evening to the upstairs studios of the Volgaya Theater, found an empty room and practiced to her heart's content. Toward the end of her session, though, she heard voices outside the room—the voices of dancers returning from a workout. She threw on her coat and left quickly before they could come upon her. She had not gone back since.

Now she was feeling the emptiness inside her from being away from ballet far too long. Practicing in her room as she had been doing, using a chair back as stand-in for a *barre*, was nowhere near good enough. It only made her more frustrated.

Tiffany paced about her hotel room, tense and restless. She simply had to dance again. She needed the release. There was still time before she had to meet with Rolf. She made a decision. Quickly she changed into her leotard and tights, put a white blouse and long peasant skirt over them and left for the Volgaya Theater.

When she arrived, she saw that the theater was deserted, as she had hoped it would be. Later in the evening a few dancers might come in for practice, but now they were all at dinner. Tiffany hurried to the upstairs rooms and found the one she had practiced in the last time. It was a very quaint old-fashioned room, with polished wooden walls and floors and a modestly elevated gallery section built along the upper portion of the far wall. Mirrors covered the long wall opposite the door.

She turned on her portable cassette player, which she had brought. The music was by Riccardo Drigo from the ballet *Le Corsaire*. It was Tiffany's favorite ballet, about a Greek girl abducted by a pirate chief. The music from this passage was bold and lyrical. Tiffany stripped down to her leotard and put on her ballet slippers and rosined the toes at the box in the corner. She quickly did her warm-up exercises at the *barre*, then she launched into her dance.

She felt wonderful, untethered, filled with the greatest kind of freedom and joy, which only ballet could give her. She leaped, she soared, she glided. She swept about the floor *sur les pointes*—on the tips of her toes. She *bourréed* and *entrechated*, performing the most difficult steps with the greatest of ease. At the end of the piece her arms swept up in a glorious *port de bras*, her hands gracefully posed high above her head. She felt wonderful, exhilarated.

And she felt astonished, too, to hear vigorous applause from the gallery above her. Jerking her head up, she saw a figure standing at the railing, clapping enthusiastically. It was Nikolai. His expression was one of amazement—and supreme admiration. He had silently entered the gallery box from the stairway outside the room.

"Brava! Brava!" he called, still applauding. Tiffany felt shaken. She also felt shy and embarrassed and violated in some strange way. She had expected to see a mocking look in his eyes, but instead there was absolute sincerity. Obviously ballet was one subject sacred to him and immune from his usual arrogant disdain.

She hurried to where she had left her street clothes and put them on quickly over her leotard. Then she started for the door without saying a word.

"No!" called Nikolai. "Wait!" And before she could get to the door, he had leaped over the railing of the six-foot-high gallery box and onto the studio floor, blocking her exit. Only a man of such athletic ability as Nikolai could have made the leap without fear of injury.

"Let me pass," she said. "Please." Her eyes were lowered.

"I will not." Then, seeing how strangely vulnerable she looked, he frowned. He was confused. In a much more gentle voice he added, "Wait, please." He put his hand to her chin and raised her face to his. In his eyes Tiffany could see a sensitivity he had never before displayed to her. He seemed aware that she felt extremely vulnerable now, though he did not know why. He did not want to do anything to make her more uneasy, but he also did not want to let her go.

"Don't leave," he said gently. "I wish to speak to you."

"Can't we talk later? We're going to meet in only a few hours."

"Tiffany," he said. He had intended to speak quietly and in a subdued tone so as not to make her more withdrawn, but his words did not come out that way. "You are incredible!" he declared, his words bursting from him. "How can you possibly be anything but a professional ballerina? How can you possibly allow yourself to have any other career, to do anything else with your life?"

"I . . . I'm not that good, really. So if you'll just let me go—"

"Do not tell me how good you are! Remember to whom you are speaking! I am Nikolai Sharmonov!" He gestured sharply. "That was *Le Corsaire*, yes? I have not seen it danced so wonderfully since Alla Sizova performed it for the Kirov."

Tiffany said nothing. It hurt her to hear his praise,

rather than warmed her. It made her think of the career she might have had. She started to go around him, but he put his hand on her slender arm and stopped her. "Tell me," he said. "Do you also know the *pas de deux* from this ballet?"

She knew it. It was one of her very favorite pieces. "No," she said. "Now please let me go."

"Not until you tell me why you have not made ballet your life. You obviously have taken instruction for many years. Yet now you are a filmmaker." His voice became demanding. "You tell me now. Why have you abandoned your art?"

"I won't tell you. It's none of your business. Let me go."

"If only you could see yourself dance," he said, his voice strangely tortured. "You look so innocent, like a beautiful fairy princess; so determined, with your jaw set petulantly, your entire concentration focused upon your art. Your moves—they are elegant and precise. Your face is angelic when you dance, like that of a little girl wondrous at discovering the glory of her own existence."

His voice was becoming more and more tormented as he spoke, and this frightened Tiffany, for she did not know the cause. Nikolai seemed to be battling with himself to remain in control of his emotions. Then suddenly he lost control. He closed his eyes tightly and said in words torn savagely from his very soul, "Why must you be as you are? Is it not torture enough for me already having to endure your beauty, your sensitivity, when I cannot let myself become close to you? Must I now endure knowing you are a brilliant ballerina, too?''

He threw his head back and shook his fist at the heavens. ''God, how strong do you think I am? Do you think I have the self-control of a superman?''

Tiffany was astounded by the outburst and by the depth of his pain. And she was even more astounded when he glared at her with burning intensity, then flung his arms around her and kissed her with searing passion. She lost all sense of reality. Her arms were out to her sides, slightly back, her fingers clenching and unclenching. She felt his torrid crushing lips upon hers, tantalizing her, pleasuring her, sending her mind reeling. To her amazement her own lips were responding to his kiss.

She was leaning backward over his supporting arm. His lips moved to her cheek, her chin; he began kissing her all over her throat. His mouth and tongue caressed her bare skin. He kissed her impassionedly, like a man lost in a storm of forbidden desire. Then he stopped kissing her and clutched her to him, as if for dear life. His face was against her cheek, and she could hear his labored tortured breathing. After a moment he finally seemed to regain control of himself.

He released her and stepped away. ''I—I apologize,'' he said in a low, deep, tightly controlled voice. ''I did not intend that.''

Tiffany's voice was soft. ''It's—it's okay, Nikolai.''

"It is not okay! I have no right to do this! It isn't fair to you to let you believe we might—" He cut himself short. "Leave me," he said in a low growl of anger directed against himself.

She stood silently looking at him, awed by the depth of his emotions and the mystery of what was causing him such anguish. She went to him and put her hand gently on his cheek.

He pounced on her as if she were an enemy. "Leave me! Do you not have any sense, woman? Now!"

She stumbled back from him toward the door. She didn't understand him. . . she didn't understand him at all! She saw the way he was glaring at her, and she turned and ran.

CHAPTER SEVEN

SHE HAD TO CALM DOWN; she had to force herself into a different mood. She didn't want Rolf to see her upset like this. He would insist on knowing the cause, and Tiffany couldn't tell him. The last thing she wanted him to find out was that some sort of relationship—any sort, even as crazy as it was—existed between her and the subject of her film.

By the time he arrived to take her to dinner, Tiffany had showered and changed into an attractive evening gown and had changed her mood, too—or at least had disguised it enough so that her upset didn't show.

Rolf himself helped alter her frame of mind. From the moment he arrived, when she opened the door and saw him in the hall, she felt a breath of fresh air. He was dressed in an elegantly tailored tuxedo with satin lapels. Standing there so lean and tall, his long face looking more handsomely aristocratic than ever, he seemed to be the very picture of what the Soviets would consider an overbearing self-possessed American capitalist. It was not just his clothes, but the way he wore them—like a man born to wealth and power, a lord of the manor. His dynamic aura and energy were clear in his posture and expression, too.

Tiffany could not help laughing, despite her mood. "Rolf! Hardly anyone wears a tuxedo to dinner in the Soviet Union as far as I know," she said.

"I do," he replied, grinning.

"You did it on purpose, didn't you?"

He shrugged, but Tiffany knew the truth. It was part of his bullish perverse nature. If the Russians wanted to cherish their stereotype of an American millionaire, he'd show them what a "capitalist lackey" really looked like. It was typical of him. In situations where most men would take a small step backward to avoid causing antagonism, Rolf took two giant steps forward.

"You look beautiful," he said, taking in her salmon-colored gown and pearl necklace and the way her hair curled down to her shoulders in loose waves. He came into the room as Tiffany picked up the thin coat she intended to bring.

"Better take something warmer than that," he said.

"Why? Is it chilly out?"

"Not here. But we're going down the river."

"Down the river? I thought we were having dinner."

"Anyone can eat sitting in one place; there's no trick to that." He grinned as he helped her on with the fur jacket she had taken from the closet.

Tiffany understood what he had in mind when

they reached the Krymsky Bridge over the Moskva River. A floating barge was docked there, and it had been converted into an elegant restaurant called Lastochka. It was more elegant, in fact, than Tiffany had expected to find in Russia. Leave it to Rolf, she reflected, to discover a gourmet restaurant if one existed.

"Most foreigners think Russia is a land of peasants," he said, leading her up the ramp onto the barge. "They don't realize there are first-class pleasures and accommodations here for anyone who can pay the price. There's a privileged upper class in Russia, despite government propaganda to the contrary. Anyone who thinks a coalminer earns the same as a physicist just doesn't understand this country."

"I thought everyone was supposed to earn about the same."

"Most people think that, but it just isn't so. There are different pay scales for the different professions, according to how valuable a man's services are to society. For instance, doctors don't earn that much because there are so many of them—close to eight hundred thousand, which is almost twice as many as we've got in the United States." He held her chair for her while they were being seated at a table near the front of the barge. "It's the high-level government people and the scientists and technicians who make the most in this country. And they like luxury, the same as we capitalist imperialist lackeys."

There were fresh carnations in a vase on the white linen tablecloth. The table at which they sat was under the stars, though other tables closer to the center of the barge were covered by a blue-and-white, pavilion-type roof. The nighttime view of the city bordering the riverbank was exquisite. Streetlamps in the shape of teardrops lined the shoreline as far as the eye could see.

Rolf ordered for both of them. The white wine arrived just as the barge was casting off for its trip down the Moskva.

"How long does it take," Tiffany asked, "to go downriver and back?" She was concerned she might not be back in time to keep her appointment with Nikolai, assuming he intended to keep it—which was something she had grave doubts about.

"Two hours or so," he said. "Relax, kid. You're stuck for the duration." He raised his wineglass and clicked it against hers. *"Na zdorovye."*

Tiffany sipped at the chablis. It was excellent, of course. She had never dined with Rolf when the wine was anything but excellent. Still, she had wondered if he could keep up his record in a land hardly known for its vineyards.

"So how was your day?" he asked.

"Oh, it was...fine. A few minor problems." She added quickly, "But nothing I can't handle."

"There's one problem you don't even know about yet. I told you about this Comrade Prokiev who wants to see me? He's hinting around that we may have problems in Hungary regarding the use of our own crew."

"I thought that was already taken care of, that Russia and Hungary agreed to bend their rules because they were so anxious to have the film made."

"They did agree to it, but now it looks like Hungary may backpedal on the agreement. They want us to use Hungarian technicians instead of our own for the lighting, sound and camera work."

"Oh, no!"

"Oh, no is right. Their technicians aren't anywhere near as good as the people I've got working for me. I pay top dollar to my technicians to get the best in the business. That's how Grayson Productions got its reputation for absolutely first-rate quality." He paused as the beluga caviar arrived on a silver tray and motioned for Tiffany to taste some.

The bad news had taken away whatever appetite she might have had, but she tried it anyway. Thin light pancakes surrounded the iced bowl of caviar. Rolf told her they were called *blinis*. She spooned some of the black caviar on a *blini* and looked at the various condiments around the bowl: chopped egg yolk, diced onions, lemon wedges. She decided against these.

The caviar tasted exquisite—quite salty, but with a unique delicious tang. The beady-textured morsels burst in her mouth tinglingly.

"The Hungarians are also supposed to be insisting that we develop our film in-country," Rolf said, "instead of sending the exposed negatives back to New York. What do you think of that?"

"That's impossible. It doesn't matter how good the filming is if we can't control development of the prints. There isn't a single lab in eastern Europe that's as good as the one we use back home."

"Good girl, you did your homework. You're right. If we let them handle the developing, we're just wasting our film. Their technicians are probably very competent, but their standards of quality may not be what Grayson Productions considers acceptable, not to mention the special techniques my men have perfected."

The meal that now arrived looked very tantalizing and had a wonderful aroma. Rolf could see from Tiffany's expression, though, that she had lost her appetite.

"Relax!" he said in a cheerful voice. "You think I brought you all the way out here just to tell you bad news? Not a chance. There's a bright side to this. The Hungarians will do what the Russians tell them to and this man Prokiev promises he can set things straight. That's why you're meeting with him tomorrow morning."

Tiffany felt vastly relieved. "He's not helping us out of the goodness of his heart, though, is he?"

"He wants to talk to us about certain material he either wants or doesn't want included in our film. He expects certain concessions."

"What did you tell him?"

"What do you think I told him?"

Tiffany pursed her lips thoughtfully and looked at him. Rolf was such a hard man to figure. He was ruthless about doing whatever it took to achieve his ends, but at the same time he was one of the few men she knew who had real integrity. After a moment of thought she answered him. "I think you told him it was my film, and he'd have to talk to me about it."

He winked at her. "You got it, kid."

Tiffany felt like reaching out and squeezing his hand in appreciation. It was actually a brave thing for him to do. She doubted if other men in his position would have risked the entire project on the judgment of a young filmmaker handling her first solo shoot. "Thank you, Rolf," she said simply.

"I'm doing it for purely selfish reasons. You're on the payroll, and I don't like carrying people on my payroll who can't pull their own weight. If I sent Langerhorn in to take charge, that would be one thing, but since I'm keeping you in charge, you'll have to handle it. Besides," he said, shrugging, "I've got better things to do than spend my time interfering in my producer's affairs. Now eat your dinner."

The main course was a trout cooked in a fluffy pastry shell, called *forel v tyestye*. It was divine. Other dishes brought to the table at intervals included *tolma*—vine leaves stuffed with spiced beef—and a delicious cold soup made, amazingly, of boiled chicken, apples and walnuts. There was also a dish of vanilla ice cream. Russians were fanatics about ice cream, and it was impossible to walk down two city blocks without coming upon several street vendors selling from outdoor carts. Tiffany tasted a bit of each of the exotic treats, rather than finishing any one of them. Rolf ate everything and enjoyed it all. He had a hearty appetite that almost nothing seemed to dampen.

After dinner they were drinking rich, Russian tea when Rolf stood up and took her hand. "Let's take our drinks to the railing," he said.

They stood at the wooden railing of the barge and watched the city along the banks pass slowly by. The new twenty-five-story buildings along Kalinin Avenue were floodlit from the bottom, creating a very striking sight. The water of the river was a beautiful blue. As the barge made a wide turn in the river to begin its journey back, the foam left in its wake appeared phosphorescent under the giant white moon. Tiffany took in a deep breath of the night air, which was fresh and invigorating. Behind her came the soft strains of violin and balalaika music from the wandering minstrels.

As she stood looking out at the beautiful sight, Rolf put his arm around her shoulders. "You know," he said, "if Prokiev hadn't come up with this problem about using the Hungarian crew, I might have had to invent some difficulty so I could get you out here with me to discuss it."

"You wouldn't do that," she said, smiling playfully.

"I wouldn't put it past me," he replied. There was a glint of good-natured humor in his eyes, but gradually it began to fade. After a while his expression became serious. "Tiffany, I don't suppose I'd have any better luck proposing to you out in the middle of the Moskva River than I did back in the middle of Manhattan, would I?"

Tiffany lowered her eyes. "Rolf," she said softly, "you promised you wouldn't ask me that again."

"I lied," he answered cheerfully.

The way he said it so brazenly and proudly, like a scoundrel who pretended to be nothing else, made Tiffany smile. She couldn't help it. He had a way of being so darn charming sometimes.

Seeing her smile, Rolf seemed encouraged. "Come on," he said with a gleam in his eyes, "we'll do it right here. I'll flag down the captain of this noble vessel. I'm sure the captain of a restaurant barge on the Moskva is every bit the equal of an American flag liner's—as far as being able to marry people goes."

"He'd perform the ceremony in Russian," Tiffany said, going along with his joking tone. But she was blushing. She felt a little light-headed, too. That Crimean wine was surprisingly strong stuff!

"Sure he'd perform the ceremony in Russian, but you only need to know one word, and I'll tell it to you now: *da*. Just remember that. When he looks at you and asks you a question, just say *da*. It doesn't matter what he asks. Say *da* to everything. That'll do the trick."

Tiffany laughed.

He took her in his arms suddenly, surprising her. His handsome strong face was very near. "You're lovely when you laugh," he said.

"Rolf, don't," she said in a plaintive voice.

"Why not?"

"Because I. . . ." How could she say it to him? She knew he was going to try to kiss her, and she did not want that now. His kiss would be symbolic of something a great deal more important than the emotions of a moment. She didn't want to hurt him, but with a man like that there was no other way than to be brutally frank. "Because I don't love you," she said, trying to take the edge off the words.

"I love you."

"I know." Her voice was soft.

"You don't think that if you gave yourself half a chance, lowered your guard a bit, you might not learn to love me? In time?"

"I—I don't know," she said honestly. "But I won't accept your proposal on that basis." She saw the searching look in his eyes, and she wanted to make him understand, to show that she did feel affection for him. But there was no way of expressing it with a tender gesture or gentle kiss without having him think she was inviting his further attentions. He was the hard-charging type of man who never relented when he sensed there was an opening for getting what he wanted.

"Please, Rolf, I'll have to tell you what I said last

time—and I really mean it. You have to stop being romantic with me, or I can't keep working for you. And I do want to keep working for you. Can't we just be...friends?''

He released her and turned to the railing. He lighted a thin cigar and blew the smoke out in a gray stream as he stared at the glowing city lights along the riverbank.

Tiffany watched him, recalling how he had looked that first time they'd met about two years ago. She had been working for Grayson Productions almost three years then but had been too junior an employee ever to run into him personally. Then one day she was in the editing room, rough-editing a shoot she was second assistant on, when he came barging in, demanding to use her machine for a rush job. His domineering attitude had offended her, and she had refused to give up the machine. Instead she had given him a lecture on the merits of politeness as opposed to rudeness. She had had no idea who he was and had simply assumed he was some brash newly hired producer. Rolf hadn't taken the time to enlighten her, either. He picked her up bodily and carried her out of the room, then slammed and locked the door on her, refusing to open it until he was finished.

When Tiffany found out who he was, she expected she might be fired, especially when he called her into his office the next day. Instead of firing her, though, he offered her a drink and sat talking to her for an hour. (It was then that Tiffany first acquired her taste for Cointreau.) Rolf clearly admired her spunky defiant spirit, and they hit it off almost instantly. They had dinner together that night, then saw each other socially for almost two years thereafter—until the night he proposed.

That was when Tiffany was forced to confront her true feelings about him. She cared for him—there was no doubt of that. And she *was* highly attracted to him. They had spent evenings together doing far more than kissing, though she had never let him take her to bed. There had been times when it had been extremely difficult to fight down her own flames of yearning, much less to fight off Rolf. But the fact was, she did not love him. Rolf seemed so. . . so self-contained somehow, so much like a law unto himself. It was as if he had no *need* of Tiffany or her love, despite his declarations to the contrary. It was as if her love would almost go unnoticed, would merely be like water sliding off his back.

Rolf wanted to marry her whether she loved him or not. To Tiffany, though, there could be no question of marriage without love. And after turning down his proposal, there could be no question of continuing to see him, either, in the intense steady way they had been dating. It wouldn't be fair to him, because he would get the impression she was still "persuadable." And it wouldn't be fair to her, either, Tiffany knew, because Rolf was such a dynamic powerful personality, that she might find herself being persuaded, despite her intentions. So they had limited their relationship to that of employee and employer at Tiffany's insistence.

She knew Rolf had never stopped caring for her. Until now, though, he had not mentioned it again in such a blatant way, forcing her to respond. She hoped he wouldn't continue pushing the matter.

"All right," Rolf said, turning to her. "I probably shouldn't have brought this up again. I know how you feel." His eyes were steely. "But I won't apologize."

"I don't expect you to."

"I love you, and I want you as my wife. Anything I have to do to accomplish that goal is fair play. However," he added in a more conciliatory tone, "you don't have to worry about my proposing to you again. I can see it would only cause that stubborn streak of yours to become even more pronounced, and I have no doubts you really would quit, just as you say. So I won't mention it again. But Tiffany—" he put his hand to her cheek "—I won't give up."

She said nothing. What could she possibly say?

When they arrived back at her room, he did not wait to be asked in for a nightcap. "I'll let you get your sleep," he said. "I'm leaving tonight instead of tomorrow. I stayed this long only to have dinner with you." His voice became businesslike. "You're meeting with Prokiev at ten in the morning." He told her where. "I don't know what he's going to tell you to include or not include in the film, but there's only one rule of diplomacy you have to remember: promise him anything, as long as you can get out of it later. That may not sound like fair play, but he's trying to blackmail us on this.''

He looked at her with a slight edge to his expression, and Tiffany knew she had hurt him, though he refused to show it. She could see he was debating whether to embrace her in a good-night hug. She hoped he would, so she could have a chance to let him see she still felt fondly toward him. But he turned away instead and started to go.

''Good night?'' she called after him, the words sounding like a question. He started to descend the flight of carpeted stairs without turning back. But at the last moment, he turned to face her. He winked at her, then he was down the steps and gone.

CHAPTER EIGHT

NIKOLAI ARRIVED ten minutes after Rolf left. Tiffany was relieved to see him. "I wasn't sure you were coming," she said, letting him into the room.

"I told you I would."

"Yes," she said, "but that was before you got so...upset at the studio this evening."

"Upset," he said, grinning ruefully. "That is a good word to call it."

"Also," Tiffany said, "I'm a bit late. I thought I might have missed you."

He walked around the room, looking it over. He wore faded blue jeans, which were quite rare in Russia, and black cossack-style boots. His flannel shirt was open at the chest, showing a forest of curly golden hairs. The woodsman-type shirt fit very loosely over his broad-shouldered muscular frame. In his fist he carried a bottle of liquor. The way he held it so openly, not even in a bag, seemed a bit uncouth. He set the bottle down on an end table. Then, satisfied with the room, he stopped his strange reconnaissance and returned to Tiffany.

He seemed grim and serious. Whenever he had

acted gruff with Tiffany lately, there had usually been a slight hint of mischief in his eyes, showing that he knew he was playing a game. This now was clearly no game to him.

"Can I offer you something to drink?" Tiffany asked.

He shook his head. He turned the living-room radio on quite loud. Whatever he had to say, he did not want it overheard by anyone who might be bugging the room.

"Tiffany," he said. "I need your help. I wish to defect to America."

Tiffany was stunned. This was the last thing she had expected to hear. Her voice was weak as she asked, "But why, Nikolai? This is your homeland."

"It is my homeland, and I love it dearly!" he declared. His eyes were fierce. He turned away from her and began pacing the room. He ran his fingers through his shock of golden hair. "I'm sorry," he said. "My anger is not directed at you."

"Is it because of my film?" She would hate to think that was the reason he wanted to defect.

"It has nothing to do with your film." He kept his voice low, still aware of the possibility that the room might be bugged.

"Then why? Is it because of the way your government treated Zhukov?"

"I'd be lying if I said that was the reason. I have deep resentment of the way my government controls the arts with such an iron fist. But still, it is my government and my homeland, and I'd never leave for such a reason. I'd stay and fight to change it."

He was leaning forward as he paced, like a charging bull, his jaw thrust aggressively out. He shot a fiery glance at her from under a lowered brow. Tiffany was glad he had told her his anger was not directed at her, because she certainly wouldn't have guessed it from the way he was behaving.

"I know I'm not being very helpful," he said. "You want to know why I'm taking such drastic action, and I'm not telling you. I'm sorry. The fact is, I can't tell you."

She felt a little insulted. "You don't trust me?"

"If I didn't trust you, I wouldn't be here," he said, turning upon her. His face showed the depth of his anguish over his decision to defect. "Trust has nothing to do with it. It's just—I can't tell you the reason. I'm sworn not to, and I won't."

"All right, Nikolai," she said soothingly, trying to calm him. "You don't have to tell me."

"Let's just say that what Serge called me is true. I'm a hothead. I do not easily keep my feelings inside me. One day I'll speak too loudly, and my career will be ruined. I won't be allowed to dance, just as Serge is not." He paused. "That's not the reason I'm defecting, but it will have to do. If you agree to help me, that's the reason you'll give the American embassy when they ask you why I'm seeking asylum."

He said nothing further. He looked at her, his

striking blue eyes serious and searching. He was waiting for her answer.

"Why is it me you want to help you with this?" She had to know.

"You're an American. You can contact your embassy to get the information I need. You have freedom of movement, which I do not. And most of all, I trust you."

"You don't even know me very well."

"Tiffany, I may be rude and arrogant and conceited as hell. I may be as temperamental as a spoiled child. But one positive quality I do possess is that I'm a good judge of people. I know you. I've seen you dance. I know you maybe better than you know yourself."

Tiffany doubted this but didn't argue. There was one other question she had to ask him. She knew that defection in Russia was a major crime. Defectors were viewed as traitors. Those who tried to defect and failed were sent to Siberian prison camps.

"Nikolai," she said. "Yes. I'll help you. But first tell me this: are you positive you want to do this drastic thing?"

"*Want?*" he declared. "*Want?* What is 'want'? I *have* to do it." His eyes were raging.

From the way he looked at her, a thought came unbidden into Tiffany's mind. That letter he had read at Zhukov's home—it had to have something to do with his decision. She didn't know how or what. She just knew that his fierce troubled look right now was exactly like the look he'd had after reading that letter and crumpling it angrily in his fist.

"Yes," she said. "I'll help you."

He put his heels together, stood straight, bowed his head formally. Then he stalked over to the bottle of liquor he had brought. He twisted open the top and poured a splash of it into two glasses. He handed one to Tiffany. "I didn't plan on drinking this miserable stuff," he said. "I brought it and carried it openly so my coming here would seem, to whoever is watching, to be for an evening of romance, rather than something more serious." He clinked his glass against hers. "But now I find I have a bitter taste in my mouth and want some vodka to wash it away."

He threw back his head and tossed the drink down. Then he crinkled up his eyes and shaking his head, exclaimed, "Bah! That's terrible stuff!" He put the glass down. "I never could stomach liquor. I confess I am not very much of a drinker." He shook his head violently once more.

Tiffany almost felt like laughing at his comical reaction, but the seriousness of the moment prevented this. She sniffed at the drink in her hand. It smelled strangely sweet, yet also like vodka. "What is it?" she asked.

"Ashberry vodka."

"Berry vodka?" she said in amazement.

"What's wrong with that? In Russia we have many kinds of vodka. Fruits or spices are added to give the vodka a taste. Zubrovka is grass-flavored. Pertcovka is pepper-flavored. Ryabena is fruit-flavored. It's not like this in America?''

"In America we have only plain old vodka-flavored vodka."

He shrugged in a very Russian way, lowering his chin, raising his shoulders.

Tiffany was glad for this interruption, for it seemed to lighten his mood a bit. She sipped at her vodka, wrinkled her nose at the sharp taste and put the drink on an end table. She went to the sofa and sat down. Nikolai looked at her for a moment, looked at the empty place beside her, then went to an armchair near the sofa and sat in it.

"Here's what I want you to do," he said. "Tomorrow afternoon the Volgaya leaves for Hungary, the first stop on our tour. All day will be spent traveling and settling in once we arrive. It will be the same for you and your film crew. The next day, early, whenever you find a moment that you are not being watched by Vronsky—"

"He's going, too?"

"*Da*. When you find you are not being watched, I want you to go to the American Embassy. There's information I need from them. I can't go with you. I could shake off Vronsky or any of his friends, but afterward he'd find out where I had gone."

"But Nikolai, what would it matter if he found out afterward? Once you're in the American Embassy, you're safe."

He shook his head. "That's a misconception. I

know. I have a friend who defected two years ago. I learned this from her escape: not everyone who asks for asylum is granted it. She was, but most are refused.''

Tiffany was surprised. ''That sounds terrible. I didn't know people were refused.''

''It has to be this way. Many people want to live in the United States. Not everyone can be accepted. That's why I need your help. If I go to the embassy myself to seek asylum, and if they say no, Vronsky will have me picked up as I'm leaving. He and the other KGB men travel with the ballet to prevent defections.''

''That's why you want me to go to the embassy for you? So I can find out if they'll grant you asylum before you risk your life defecting?''

He nodded. ''That's all I want from you. Find out if they'll accept me. If they say yes, *then* I'll try to make my escape to your embassy.''

''Is there anything else I can do to help you?''

''Nothing,'' he said forcefully. He looked her in the eyes pointedly for emphasis. ''I don't want you involved in this. It's dangerous. Just find out if they'll grant me asylum, then forget me and forget you had anything to do with this.''

''After I get the information,'' she said quietly, ''how shall I get it to you? Will you be able to come to my room in Hungary? I won't have a private room there as I do here. I'll be sharing it with my assistant director, Mary. You've met her; she's completely trustworthy.''

Nikolai didn't even pause to think about it. He had his course of action all planned out. "There's a beautiful park in Budapest called Városliget Park. I fell in love with it the last time we toured Hungary. It's the largest in all Budapest. I want you to meet me at the bridge over the pond at the southeast entrance. If I'm not there when you arrive, wait for me. I'll have to shake off Vronsky." His voice became cautionary. "If he sees us meeting there, he'll be very suspicious. But I think I can lose him without him knowing it was deliberate."

He gazed at her, and Tiffany could see a yearning in his eyes. He seemed to be making a decision about what he would do at the moment, now that the purpose for his visit had been taken care of. Tiffany thought for a second that he would come sit beside her, but instead he stood up abruptly. "Thank you for your help," he said. "I'll leave now."

Tiffany stood, also. "Your bringing that vodka up to my room—" she said in a gentle voice, "—it was to make them think we have a romantic relationship so they won't be suspicious. Maybe to keep them thinking that you should...stay the night." She pointed quickly to the living-room sofa and forced a smile. "It's not very comfortable, but it won't kill you for one night."

Nikolai looked strangely tortured. "That's what I should do. There's no question about it. I should stay the night to make it more believable that our being together is for romance. But the problem is, I can't stay." His face became very hard, as if he were deliberately blocking his emotions. His eyes, though, held a sensitivity and longing and affection he could not hide.

He knew she saw this in his eyes, and he felt he had to counter the impression this gave. He came close to her and took her hands in his. "Listen to me, Tiffany, beware of me. I'm not as strong as you think. That incident between us earlier, after your dance—it was weakness in me. I should never have done that."

"Nikolai, maybe I—maybe I wanted you to."

"Don't want me to! You don't understand, my darling, I—" He moved away from her sharply, realizing what he had just called her. He spoke through gritted teeth now, clearly angry with himself, trying to control his emotions. "Don't let yourself become close to me. And I mustn't let myself become close to you. That's why I can't stay the night. I couldn't control myself if I remained with you now, so near to you like this. I'd weaken. I'd tell you how deeply I—" He stopped himself. "I have to leave. Now." He moved quickly to the door.

"Nikolai," she said, "*why*? Why do you have to be so on guard against us becoming close?"

He shook his head. He would not—or could not—tell her. Tiffany felt like screaming in frustration. Instead she said very calmly, "Nikolai...you don't have to leave."

He looked at her from the open doorway. Powerful crosscurrents of emotion seemed to buffet him. For an instant he appeared on the verge of going back into the room. But then he squared his shoulders, tossed back his hair and walked out through the door, closing it after him.

TIFFANY THOUGHT it rather strange that Comrade Prokiev wanted to meet her at a subway station. She had expected Moscow's underground system to look like New York's. After all, weren't all big-city subways pretty much the same throughout the world? She had been in the Paris Métro and the London Underground, and they, within reason, were similar to New York's subways.

What Tiffany beheld when she entered the street-level portal marked with a giant *M* above answered her question—and it was an answer that flabbergasted her. The Moscow Metro, she realized instantly, was no ordinary subway system. The first thing she saw was an enormous tunnel, sloping downward, that took passengers to the level beneath the street. There was no stairway in the tunnel, however. Instead there were extremely wide escalators—not just one or maybe two, but four. And they were works of art, separated by ribbons of gleaming chrome and brass studded at intervals not with bare light bulbs—or even utilitarian lamps—but with beautiful crystal-like chandeliers.

When she reached the bottom, she saw the Metro station itself. It was gorgeous. The high vaulted ceilings were decorated with mosaics and relief carvings. The floors and interior walls were of polished marble. There were majestic marble columns and magnificent sculptures. Paintings and other works of art were displayed high up on the walls. Intricate, multicolored, stained-glass panels lighted from behind adorned the base of the walls.

Tiffany was awestruck. Her first thought was that she had made a mistake and accidentally wandered into some wonderful museum. But no, that couldn't be, for far in front of her were tracks in the center of the wide crosstunnel, and travelers were anxiously milling about waiting. Soon a gleaming, modern subway train rumbled down the tunnel and came to a stop. It disgorged one load of Muscovites and picked up another. As it began rumbling away again, someone tapped Tiffany on the shoulder. She turned abruptly to see a thin sharp-nosed man wearing a gray suit.

"Miss Farrow?" he said.

"Yes," Tiffany replied. She had recovered enough from her awe to smile in greeting. "Comrade Prokiev?" She was standing under the station clock, where Rolf had said Prokiev would meet her.

"Yes. I bid you hello." He bowed slightly.

"I'm glad to see you here," Tiffany said. "For a moment I thought I'd wandered into a beautiful museum, instead of the metro."

"It is beautiful, is it not? All our metro stations are like this. 'Palatial' is a word I've heard used to describe them. In Russia we believe that work is noble and anything that touches upon the lives of workers should be as beautiful and comfortable as is humanly possible. Workers spend much time commuting by subway, so our stations are places that are pleasant to behold."

" 'Pleasant' isn't the word," Tiffany said, looking at the vaulted ceilings and gleaming chandeliers, the marble archways and stunning works of art. "But... it's hard to believe that *all* your stations are like this."

Prokiev looked offended. Tiffany had not meant to suggest he was lying, only that he might naturally be boosting his city, just as any good citizen anywhere in the world would do. But Prokiev seemed personally insulted. "Come," he said, "we go to another station. Any station. Pick a direction."

"You don't have to take me to another station," Tiffany said with a slight laugh, hoping to defuse the tension. "I believe you."

"Please. I insist."

Oh, this is just great, thought Tiffany sarcastically. She didn't even know what this man wanted yet, and here she had already started off on the wrong foot with him. She followed him as he slipped two five-kopek tokens into a turnstile, allowing them access to the tracks. "Five kopeks is less than one of your American dimes," he said. "For this price we can ride as long as we want, as far as we want." When the next train arrived, he ushered Tiffany inside. There was comfortable seating and plenty of room. They sat down as they began their journey to.... To heaven knows where, thought Tiffany.

"Comrade Prokiev," she said in as pleasant a voice as she could manage, "may I ask you why you wanted to meet with me—and why in the metro station?"

"To tell the truth, it was not you I wished to see; it was your Mr. Grayson. But since it is you, I'm certain we will get along fine. I wished to meet you in the metro because I thought you might enjoy seeing such a beautiful example of Soviet achievement."

Tiffany didn't believe him, but then she recalled that Rolf had said Prokiev wanted to talk about including or excluding certain material in her film. "Did you want me to put shots of the metro in my film?" she asked.

He laughed. It was strange to see him laugh, for he had very suspicious eyes and seemed like a humorless man. "Not at all," he said. "Not at all."

"Well, what is the purpose of this meeting, may I ask?"

He dodged the question, his beady eyes darting to the side. The train pulled into a new station, and he pointed at the main concourse, where travelers were milling around waiting to board. "There," he said. "You see?"

This station, too, was lovely, a work of architectural splendor. Carved reliefs adorned the high ceiling, and the floor was of colorful glazed mosaic tiles. Recessed floodlights bathed the scene in bright light so that one forgot the station was underground. Gleaming bronze statues were positioned about the waiting area. There was not a speck of dirt anywhere. The station was spotless and shining.

Prokiev was watching her, awaiting her approval. "Yes," she said, "it truly is lovely." The train pulled out of the station on toward the next.

"Our metro is only half the size of your famed New York system, yet it carries more passengers. The trains are not overcrowded because we have so many of them. During rush hours trains leave the stations every ninety seconds. Imagine that! And there are dozens of stations, each palatial and magnificent, with no two of them alike."

Tiffany was becoming impatient. She should be back with Mary and the others, helping prepare the equipment for the trip to Hungary, not joyriding around the Moscow Metro, no matter how beautiful it truly was. "As I say, Comrade Prokiev, it's very impressive, but can we get on with—"

"Oh, by the way," he said offhandedly, "you have not had occasion to perhaps visit any former members of the Volgaya, have you? In the company of some gentleman?"

From the way he gazed at her with such a falsely casual look, Tiffany could tell this was why he had wanted to meet her at the metro station. He wanted a busy place with loud sounds and lots to see so she'd be distracted when he asked her this question. She realized something else, too: this man was probably

KGB, despite his false title, and Nikolai was in danger.

Normally Vronsky would have asked her this question, but Tiffany would have been on guard if it had come from him, so they figured Prokiev might be able to slip it in without putting her on the defensive. Once they knew it was she who would be meeting Prokiev, instead of Rolf, they had decided to take advantage of the situation by asking her the question here in the metro.

Tiffany looked at Prokiev. "I beg your pardon?" she said innocently.

"A woman with hair the color of yours was recently seen entering the household of a Comrade Serge Zhukov. Do you know who he is, by any chance?"

"Yes."

"Was it you who visited him in the company of a Soviet citizen?"

Tiffany frowned as if bewildered. "I don't understand. Is there some law against visiting former members of the Volgaya? If I did visit him, did I do something wrong?"

"Not at all! Not at all! I was merely curious as to whether it was you, indeed, who was seen visiting him."

Tiffany didn't know what to say. Evidently the KGB suspected—but didn't know for sure—that it was Tiffany and Nikolai who had visited Zhukov. She knew she could get into serious trouble by lying, but she was also pretty sure from the way Prokiev stared so intently waiting for her answer, that Nikolai might get into even worse trouble for taking her to Zhukov.

"Miss Farrow," said Prokiev, ready to pursue his question. "I really must insist that—"

"Oh, look!" Tiffany exclaimed as the train pulled into yet another stunning subway station. She pointed to an enormous hammered bronze mural, which dominated an entire wall. "Can we go look at it?"

Prokiev narrowed an eye at her, deciding whether to press on more firmly. For the moment he decided against it. He nodded. They left the train to examine the mural. Tiffany had only one thought: she wanted to get out of there—fast. She wanted to get back so she could warn Nikolai about the situation.

"Miss Farrow," Prokiev said as Tiffany pretended to be absorbed in studying the bronze mural from up close. "There is, of course, no reason why you should not have visited Serge Zhukov if you so desired. But I would like to make you aware that any mention in your film of Comrade Zhukov would be greatly frowned upon by my government."

"Oh, really?" Tiffany replied innocently. So that's what he meant when he told Rolf there was material he wanted included or excluded from her film. Excluded was what he wanted, and the material was any interview with favorable mention of Zhukov.

Prokiev's look was stern. He was through playing

games, Tiffany could see. "Regarding any mention of Zhukov in your film—my government prefers that you, as a filmmaker, do as you stated you would on your work permit, that you do what your visa was approved for you to do."

"Which is?"

"Very simple—that you make a film about the Volgaya Ballet."

"I intend to."

"And that you make your film *only* about the Volgaya Ballet. Any people who are not presently dancers for the Volgaya are, of course, beyond the scope of the approval you received."

"I see."

"And you will cooperate?"

Tiffany continued studying the intricate metal sculpture.

"Miss Farrow, if you do not cooperate, you may find problems developing in your relations with the Hungarian Arts Directory regarding use of your crews and development of your films. Such problems might make your film difficult to complete."

She looked him in the eye. "Comrade Prokiev, are you threatening me?"

"Not at all!" He forced a not-very-convincing laugh. "I am a member of the Ministry for Cultural Affairs, nothing more. What power do I have to threaten anybody? No, I simply wish to let you know that if you did perhaps have some contact with Zhukov, and if you did perhaps decide to mention him in your film, it would not be wise. Also, it would be a breach of your stated reason for requesting permission to film in Russia."

"I understand," Tiffany said.

"We have no connection whatever with the Hungarian authorities. If something happened to ruin your chances of filming in Hungary, it would be completely out of our hands."

"I understand." She also understood how wise Rolf had been in making a point of emphasizing to her one of his main rules of diplomacy: When being blackmailed, promise anything, so long as you can get out of it later. "I assure you, I have no intention of including any mention of Serge Zhukov in my film. Does that satisfy you?"

"It most certainly does." He seemed satisfied, too. His hard-edged look had softened, and he appeared relieved and a bit relaxed.

"And I expect to have no problems whatever with the Hungarian authorities," Tiffany said.

"I, also, expect that you will have no problems."

"Now if you'll excuse me, I have to get back." She started toward the other side of the walkway to catch a train heading back toward her hotel. Prokiev came with her. "I can find my way by myself, thank you," she said.

The train pulled to a stop; Tiffany started to board. Prokiev called out her name. "I have one last question," he said. His expression showed that this was a deadly serious matter and that Tiffany had better tell the truth or she could get into trouble. "I don't care whether you were the girl who visited Zhukov the Thursday night before last, but I do want to find out this: do you know if Nikolai Sharmonov was the man? Do you know if Sharmonov visited Zhukov that night?"

"Yes," she said, looking him in the eye. "I know. It wasn't Nikolai Sharmonov. He was with me that evening. We spent the whole night talking."

She climbed aboard the train. The doors closed after her, and the train began speeding down the tunnel.

CHAPTER NINE

Nikolai was in danger. Tiffany had to warn him. He didn't realize the KGB suspected he had taken her to visit Zhukov.

When she arrived at the theater, there was much commotion and hectic activity. The finishing touches were being put on the packing of scenery and costumes by the Volgaya's stage crew. The younger dancers from the corps were prancing around, happy and playful, eager to embark on the tour that would bring many of them a small degree of glory and recognition. Boris Grechko, Nikolai's understudy, was practicing his *jetés*. The Volgaya's seamstress, lighting director and head carpenter were heatedly discussing some subject in Russian. Tiffany's crew was busy double-checking all their equipment, under Mary's supervision, to make sure everything was packed and ready for the trip to Budapest.

Nikolai stood off in a corner, but it would be impossible to talk to him, Tiffany saw, without Vronsky overhearing. Vronsky had stationed himself next to Nikolai and showed no signs of departing. When

Nikolai moved, Vronsky moved with him, in a falsely casual "spontaneous" way.

Nikolai glanced at Tiffany. She could see from his
eyes he understood she was desperate to speak to
him. He raised his eyebrows in a fatalistic gesture,
though, and shrugged. There was nothing he could
do at the moment.

Soon the bus came to take the dancers to the airport. Michael French went with them, carrying his
hand-held camera and wearing a utility pack around
his waist. His sound man accompanied him, toting a
shoulder-strap tape recorder. Everyone else in Tiffany's crew went with her in the hired van that took
their equipment to the airport.

There was no chance to speak to Nikolai privately
in the busy airport lobby or on the plane ride from
Moscow to Budapest. Tiffany glanced out the window of the Tupolev propeller aircraft, which was
much noisier than the Russian jet they had flown in
on. She watched the sprawling metropolis of
Moscow disappear as the plane climbed into the
clouds. Budapest, when it appeared, was a beautiful
sight. It was really two very different cities in one,
separated by a stretch of one of the world's most
romantic rivers: the broad, very blue Danube. Buda,
on one bank, was the ancient city, the first site of
Celtic settlements two thousand years ago. On the
opposite bank was Pest, the modern cosmopolitan
city. Together they formed Budapest, the capital of
the Hungarian nation.

Once they arrived, Tiffany was swamped in urgent matters that demanded her immediate attention. There was not a single spare moment to speak to Nikolai, even if he had been free of Vronsky—which he was not. The equipment had to be retrieved and shepherded through a scrupulous examination by the authorities; permits had to be shown; currency had to be changed into Hungarian *forints*. Then the crew and equipment had to be transported to the elegant Gellért Hotel in the old city of Buda.

Before Tiffany knew it, it was the next morning and time for her to go to the American embassy to inquire about Nikolai's being granted political asylum. She wished she had had a chance to speak to Nikolai about Prokiev's suspicions, but it had not been possible. The best thing she could do for him now, she reflected at the breakfast table of their hotel's dining room, was just to go ahead and visit the embassy as planned, then to meet with Nikolai in Városliget Park afterward.

"Mary," Tiffany said quietly, "I'm going to the American embassy this morning to check on the arrangements for using our crew instead of Hungarian technicians. I'll be back in the afternoon." Tiffany told her this falsehood so that if Vronsky did somehow learn where she was off to, she'd have a ready-made excuse to fall back on.

Mary said that was fine. She would attend to

checking out the new theater and going over the different shooting angles with Michael.

On the taxi ride to the embassy Tiffany worried that her ready-made excuse really might not be worth very much if she was seen entering the compound. In other circumstances Tiffany could have gone directly to the embassy without arousing suspicion. But at the moment, the embassy was temporarily maintaining a separate cultural affairs center; she would be expected to go there for any purposes related to filming, not to the compound itself.

The embassy was a sturdy brick building, two stories high, fronted by a brownish lawn and surrounded by a high white brick wall. When Tiffany first entered the building, she was met by a clerk whose desk was situated at the front of the foyer. The clerk asked what business Tiffany had come on. Tiffany refused to tell him. She said that it was a very delicate situation and she could reveal her purpose only to someone of high rank on the diplomatic staff.

The clerk tried to remain courteous, but he explained that if Tiffany didn't tell him what her purpose was, he wouldn't know the department to which to direct her. Tiffany said she was sorry but steadfastly refused to divulge her mission or even fill out any of the forms the clerk tried to push on her. All she would do was tell him her name. As far as she was concerned, the fewer people who knew she had come to inquire about defection and who knew Nikolai's name, the safer Nikolai was.

Finally, after a good deal of wrangling back and forth during which Tiffany remained obstinate, she won her point. A high-level official named Wharton Brand came down to see her and led her back up the stairway to his large but disorganized-looking office. Files and stacks of papers were everywhere. Brand was a serious older man who wore spectacles and looked like a rumpled university professor.

When Tiffany told him her mission, he did not seem very surprised. "People from iron-curtain countries ask to defect all the time," he said in a clipped businesslike voice. "It's not as unusual as most people think. Unless there's an overriding political reason or a person of particular note is involved, we're often forced to turn them down. Why don't you tell me who it is you represent and what country he's from?"

"I will tell you, Mr. Brand, but first I want to make sure the name won't leave this office. His life could be in danger."

Brand looked skeptical. He fiddled with a mechanical pencil, leaning back in his chair. "Miss Farrow, I appreciate your concern, but it may be an overreaction, I assure you. Especially if you've watched many low-budget melodramatic movies. Most people who want to defect choose to do so for purely economic reasons—doctors, engineers, that sort of professional. Often we have to refuse them.

They're in little danger of their nation trying to find out that they asked for asylum. The only iron-curtain countries that really cause trouble for potential defectors are East Germany and Albania. And Russia, of course."

"You don't seem very sensitive to the delicacy of this situation," Tiffany said, disturbed. At this point she felt that the United States had not taken much care to staff its embassies with very high-quality individuals. This Mr. Brand, doodling with his pencil, did not seem very sharp or alert. However, what Brand did next changed Tiffany's impression about him entirely.

He was not doodling, as she had thought. He was writing names on a pad of paper in block letters. He held the pad out to her. There were three names on it. "As of today, Thursday, there are only three renowned foreign nationals in Hungary who might conceivably want to defect and who truly would be in danger if their intentions were known."

Tiffany looked at the list. The very top name was NIKOLAI SHARMONOV. "Suppose the person I represent is one of these three?" she said.

He took the pad back. "Then I would say there's an excellent chance we'd take your man."

"I want to be sure before I tell you his name, if I can be."

"Miss Farrow, I appreciate your caution. But around me it's not necessary." He smiled and held his palms out to show he wasn't hiding anything.

"I'm on your side. Besides, I have great respect for Mr. Sharmonov. I wouldn't want to see him in undue danger."

Tiffany was astounded. "How did you know that's who I came about?"

"You're speaking of a 'he.' That leaves out Ludmila Prosek, the Polish physicist on the list. And as far as which of the two men it is, I had your visa information pulled when you gave your name to the clerk downstairs. I know you're in Budapest in connection with your job as a filmmaker. The marine biologist on this list is certainly not a likely candidate for a documentary that takes you from Hungary to Austria to Zurich, as your itinerary does. The Russian dance troupe, however, would be. The only prominent male member of that troupe who might lean toward defection, who doesn't have family ties in Russia to keep him in line, is Sharmonov—of whom, incidentally, I'm a great fan. I loved his performance as Mercutio, which he danced here last year as second lead to Zhukov's Romeo."

"All right," Tiffany said. "Can you help Niko—can you help Mr. Sharmonov?"

"What reason does he give for wanting to defect?"

"He's in danger in the Soviet Union. He's afraid that he may speak out too openly on some sensitive matters and the government will punish him severely." She paused. "Also, there's some other reason, but I don't know what it is. He's very closemouthed about it.''

Brand held the mechanical pencil in both hands and studied it. ''The first reason is sufficient. Sharmonov is important enough that we can accept him on those grounds. I don't have to meet with the ambassador. You can tell him the answer is a definite yes.'' He lowered the pencil and looked at her pointedly. ''The question, Miss Farrow, is how Sharmonov plans to get here. He's undoubtedly under constant surveillance by the KGB men assigned to the troupe. If *I* know he's a potential defector, as I just told you I do, you can be sure the KGB is aware of it, too. I don't think he'll be able to reach the embassy here on his own.''

''Can you send anyone to help?''

''Absolutely not. We're guests in this country. We have sovereign rights within our own embassy compound but none at all outside it. It would be a breach of international relations of a very high order if we tried to help him reach the embassy. No, he has to enter the compound of his own free will, without our assistance.''

''Well, how is he to do that?'' she asked in frustration.

''I can give you a very good suggestion—don't do it here. It's an extremely dangerous thing to try— and an unnecessary risk. He'll be traveling to Austria and Zurich on this tour after Hungary. In both those places he'll be able to reach the

American embassy with a lot less danger. The KGB has no power to interfere with a defection in a non-Communist nation. Oh, they sometimes try anyway, but it's much easier to stop them. In a Western or neutral nation all your man has to do is walk into a police station and tell them he wants to defect. The police will protect him from the KGB and guarantee his freedom to travel wherever he wants to go inside that country. And of course the first place he'll travel to will be the US embassy."

"But he can't just go to a police station here in Hungary?"

Brand shook his head. "The police here are an instrument of the state, just as they are in all Communist nations. They'd do nothing but put him in a cell and contact the KGB agents traveling with the troupe."

Tiffany sighed, realizing she should have known this. "Well, thank you very much," she said as she stood to leave.

Brand rose, too. "My pleasure. I wish him luck. If there's anything else I can tell you, feel free to ask." He paused. "Austria is the next stop for the Volgaya, isn't it?"

"That's right."

"I'd suggest your man make his move there. When he's out walking, have him stroll into the nearest police station. Although few people realize it, it's really that simple—in a non-Communist country."

"Thank you," she said. "I'll tell him."

As she was leaving, she felt slightly relieved. So Nikolai's defection would not be as dangerous as she had thought, as long as he did it later in the tour in one of the non-Communist countries. She was sure Nikolai would be relieved to hear this and to hear that the arrangements had been made for the United States to accept him as a defector.

This is what she was thinking about as she walked out of the embassy gates onto the city sidewalk, where she was instantly confronted by the bearish figure of Vronsky. He stepped directly in front of her, blocking her way, making her gasp in surprise. "Good morning, dear lady," he said quickly. "Are the arrangements made?"

She was so surprised at his presence there and at his question that she didn't know what to say. "No!" she blurted out, trying to put him off the track. "They're not! I mean, what arrangements? I don't know what you're talking about!" Her panicky voice betrayed her. She hated herself for responding this way, but everything had happened so quickly that she hadn't had a chance to collect her wits.

Vronsky tipped his hat as if nothing unusual had been said and as if he had learned nothing from her voice. "You ask, 'what arrangements?' Why the arrangements you make to use your own film crew instead of the Hungarians, of course. What arrangements did you think I meant?"

Tiffany forced herself to regain her composure and speak very calmly. "None," she said. "I just didn't know you were aware I was asking about that particular matter."

He shrugged. "I asked your assistant director where you were. She told me."

Tiffany frowned. She had considered telling Mary to keep her destination secret but had decided that that would only make matters worse. If Vronsky found out she had gone to the embassy and also knew she wanted her trip kept secret, he would suspect her true reason for being there.

"The embassy gave me just the information I need," she said, attempting to stride by him. He let her pass but then began walking with her, matching her brisk pace as she tried to move away down the sidewalk.

"That is very good," he said. "I'm surprised, though, that you did not go to your American cultural center for such information."

"I made a mistake. The embassy was kind enough to contact the cultural center for me and get me the information. And the fact is, the arrangements are all made—" she looked at him pointedly "—for me to use my own crew."

He tipped his hat and smiled at her. "Naturally I was only curious."

"Naturally."

"I bid you good morning." He dropped back as she continued her rapid pace.

Tiffany walked on for several blocks, then hailed a cab and had it drive her in the wrong direction long enough for her to make sure no one was following her. Finally she gave the driver the name of the park where she was to meet Nikolai. She sat back in nervous anticipation, biting her lip. She hoped she had not betrayed too much to Vronsky. She hoped she had not put Nikolai's life in even greater danger!

VAROSLIGET PARK WAS LUSH AND GREEN, with tall trees and grassy rises. Part of Hungary was forested, and this park was like a small forest in the midst of the city. A quaint cobblestone path led Tiffany to the plank bridge over the pond where she was to meet Nikolai.

She saw him standing alone on the bridge, his elbows on the railing, watching the swans in the water below. His expression was sullen—and, as usual, extremely sensual. The weather was a bit nippy today, with clouds overhead, and his attire reflected this. He wore a gray Windbreaker over a black shirt. A blazing red scarf was draped around his neck, its ends hanging down in front and back. His black wool trousers were similar to sailors' pants but were far more form-fitting.

He looked up when he heard her approaching and grinned at her. Tiffany, too, was dressed for the chilly weather. She had on a pale blue cashmere sweater over a cotton shirt. Her tweed skirt came down to cover the tops of her high leather boots.

"*Dobraii utro,*" Nikolai said as she came up to him.

"And good morning to you, also. I hope you haven't been waiting long?"

"Not too long. You have good news for me, I hope?"

"Not so good. Well, part of it is good." She glanced around to see that no one was near them. This corner of the park was deserted. "The man at the embassy," she said in a low voice, "told me the United States will definitely grant you asylum, meaning that once you defect, you'll be accepted. But here's the bad news...." She told him about her conversation with Prokiev the day before and about how she had been surprised by Vronsky after leaving the embassy just a few minutes ago.

Nikolai listened to the news impassively. When she had finished speaking, though, he turned his head down to gaze at the swans in the pond again, and she could see from his expression that her news was just as bad as she had thought.

"About Prokiev," he said, "it is not such a problem. So they know I took you to visit Serge. That doesn't matter so much. There's no law against it, even though they frown on it. They can't take strong action against me for it."

"And they don't really know for sure," she said. "They just suspect it."

"No. They know."

"But they asked me if it was you and I who visited him—they weren't sure. And I denied it."

He smiled at her in a tolerant way, the way one might smile at a naive child. "That's why they asked you. To see if you'd deny it, to see if you would lie for me." Tiffany was startled, and her face showed it. Nikolai took her hand and squeezed it. It was a gesture of reassurance and gratitude, not of romance. But the way he grinned at her with such natural unconscious sensuality, his cobalt-blue eyes so smolderingly sexy, she could not help but feel a tingling excitement.

He released her hand and started to walk down the bridge, indicating for her to walk alongside him. "About Vronsky confronting you outside the embassy," he said, "that is very bad news indeed. It means he most certainly is suspicious of me—suspicious that I might be planning something drastic." He saw the look on Tiffany's face and, because he was sensitive, realized how she felt. "Don't be angry with yourself that your voice betrayed you when you spoke to Vronsky. It's not your fault he came upon you so suddenly. He's trained to do that. You had no way of knowing it would happen."

Tiffany still felt responsible. "What's going to happen now?" she asked.

He looked thoughtful. They were walking down the cobblestone path through the fragrant forested park. "I don't think your visit to the embassy and the way you spoke to Vronsky afterward will be enough to confirm their suspicions about me. If anything else happens, it could be very bad. But just that alone, I don't think—'' He broke off his words abruptly. His expression was alert. Tiffany noticed that his gaze had shifted. He had been looking at her; now he was looking past her shoulder, beyond her, down the winding path.

"What's wrong?" she asked.

"Don't be alarmed." He put his arm around her shoulders casually as they continued walking. Tiffany started to turn her head in the direction in which Nikolai had been peering. "Don't look yet," he said. "I don't want him to know we've seen him."

"Who?"

"There's a KGB agent on the path to the side of us."

"That's not possible!" she protested. "I made sure I wasn't followed here."

Again he smiled at her in that worldly tolerant way. "What do you know of shaking off a man who's following you? You are a young American girl. KGB men are highly trained, highly experienced creatures of the shadows. They have more cunning tricks than you could ever dream of. Vronsky just had another agent follow you here, knowing that if he himself came, you'd recognize him."

"How can you detect them?"

"I've seen this one before. Besides, the way they

dress is a joke throughout Russia—the ill-fitting gray suits, the black shoes and white socks. They look like American gangsters from the thirties." Nikolai led Tiffany over to a tall grassy area half-surrounded by a hedgerow of small bushes. They sat down on the lush green grass. From her new position she could see the man who was following them out of the corner of her eye. He was dressed as Nikolai had described and, in addition, had on a battered old brimmed hat. In his hand was a sack with bread crumbs, which he casually tossed to the birds as if he were nothing more than a kindly old man taking a pleasant stroll through the park. Now that they had stopped, he stopped, too, and stayed well behind them. He was far enough back on the winding trail that he probably didn't realize they had spotted him.

"What can we do?" Tiffany asked. She turned to Nikolai and saw that his eyes were intense, his face serious.

"Tiffany," he said, "their seeing you at the embassy—that alone might not have made them suspicious that I'm planning to defect. But this on top of it—their seeing you meet me right after you go to the embassy—this makes it look very bad for me. There's only one thing we can do to lessen their suspicions."

"What is it?"

"We have to make them think our meeting here was for some purpose other than to discuss your embassy visit." He paused, then added with strong significance, "and we must make them believe that beyond any doubt."

She could see what he wanted. It was clear in his eyes. And it was not such a surprise to Tiffany. Hadn't he used just such a deception against Vronsky before by bringing that bottle of vodka to her hotel room their last night in Moscow?

He leaned forward until his face was very near and brushed his parted lips against hers, barely touching them. Then he looked at her again.

Tiffany hesitated, but then she nodded, so slight a nod as to be almost imperceptible. Nikolai's arms went around her, and he lowered her down to the ground with him. She lay on her back. He was on his side, leaning over her. His lips came down on hers in a kiss that started out quite coldly and stiffly, as if he were fighting back any emotion that might creep into it. He seemed to be making a desperate effort to deny his feelings, to stifle them.

Why was it so important to him not to let her see how he felt about her, Tiffany wondered. What a mystery that was. He seemed anguished even now as he pulled his head back and looked at her. There was such deep affection in those eyes, and yet, at the same time, such agony! Tiffany could tell his anguish was not over being forced to subject her to his advances. No, he was anguished because his own powerful emotions were on the verge of escaping his tight control—and that he didn't want. But by being in this situation where he was forced to kiss her, he was in danger of revealing how much he truly desired to do so, despite his warning that they must not become close.

There was such torment in his eyes that Tiffany felt she had to say something or he would not go on. And if he did not go on, the KGB man would sense they were putting on an act for him; he would realize their true purpose for being there.

"Nikolai," Tiffany said softly, "it's...all right."

Their eyes locked. She leaned forward and kissed him gently on the lips.

Suddenly it was as though a great dam had burst inside him. Emotions surged through that overwhelmed Tiffany. He began kissing her passionately, hungrily. He was like a starving man who had fought back his hunger for far too long. His will to resist was crumbling.

"Oh, my dearest!" he declared, losing control. His hands began moving over her shoulders and down toward the front of her sweater.

Tiffany's heart raced. Had he really said that?

His hand came to rest on her sweater over her breast; he caressed her. His lips were on her throat and chin and cheek, kissing her hotly. Tiffany felt herself responding to him and to her own pent-up longing for him. His hands roamed over her breasts freely, lighting fires of sensation everywhere they touched. "Oh, Nikolai,"

Tiffany heard herself moaning, the words escaping her lips.

The situation was so crazy! The man in the gray suit was far down the path, undoubtedly trying to watch them. The row of bushes surrounding them formed a natural secluded enclosure, but he would be able to see them partially especially since he knew they were in there. The strange thing was that if it were not for the KGB man, Tiffany would surely have stopped Nikolai. But now she couldn't stop him. If she didn't let him take these liberties—if they just kissed a little, say—the KGB man would know they were playacting for his benefit. By letting Nikolai go this far she was making it believable that they had rendezvoused there because they were passionately involved.

Tiffany was doing this to create a credible deception. Nikolai had started out doing it for that reason, but now, Tiffany knew, his deep feelings for her had run away with him. His will to resist had crumbled. She could tell this from the look in his eyes, from his kisses and caresses.

How strange fate was, Tiffany thought, even as her body was being inflamed with sensation at Nikolai's increasingly bold touches. She couldn't stop him, and he couldn't stop himself. Both of them were trapped in this strange situation where they were forced to reveal their true feelings for each other, even though Nikolai was fiercely against doing so. But there had been a small crack in the dam, and now the crack had rent the dam asunder. His feelings and passions burst through in a torrential outpouring.

"My darling, my darling," he whispered hotly, probably not even aware he was speaking the words. His hands were on the hem of her pale blue sweater, jerking the sweater up above her bosom. He did not unbutton her cotton blouse; he ripped it open. Her pert firm breasts lay bare before him and his mouth lowered. Suddenly her nipple was captured in his warm wet mouth. The sensation was so shockingly delicious that an involuntary moan broke from her throat. He licked her breast tantalizingly and teased her nipple gently with his teeth. His hand was on her other breast, stroking it, caressing it.

Tiffany was breathing shallowly and rapidly, quivering beneath his touch on the tall lush grass, feeling sensations she had never felt before with any man. Rolf was the only man who had ever seen her unclothed and touched her in this fashion. And in the entire year they had been intimate, Rolf had never made her feel like *this*, the way Nikolai was making her feel in only minutes...seconds.

His body was atop hers now, pressing torturously against her, though both were fully dressed below the waist. The tingling throbbing yearning that surged through her was excruciating in its pleasure. Tiffany felt lost; her mind was reeling. She was overwhelmed by the sensations her body was feeling. Her fingers were in his hair with a will of their own, running through the thick golden mane. Her other hand was under his Windbreaker, under his shirt, touching the bare skin at the small of his back.

Nikolai was lost to his passion now. He ripped open his own shirt so that his hard muscular chest pressed searingly against her naked breasts as he lay atop her. His mouth was against her cheek, his tongue licking teasingly at her ear. He shifted position and looked at her. Tiffany felt awash in deep emotion as she lay on her back, gazing up at his incredibly handsome sensual face, his heavily lidded eyes and long golden lashes. She could see the unmistakable tender look of love in his eyes.

She knew she should not say what she was feeling. She knew how defensive he was about not showing his emotions, how strangely insistent that they not let themselves become close. But Tiffany could not restrain herself. She was weakened by the deep emotions rushing through her. "Oh, Nikolai," she said. "I—I love you."

Instantly it was as though a chill wind were descending upon her. He looked at her, then shut his eyes tightly. For a long moment he did not open them, did not move. Then abruptly he rolled off her and rose to his feet. He pulled his shirt closed and zipped up his jacket. He looked at her again, saying nothing.

Tiffany was startled by his sudden coldness. And as he gazed at her now, his face so tightly closed, she suddenly felt shamed and deeply embarrassed. She turned away from him while she pulled her sweater back down into place. Her skin was burning, but not with passion. It was burning with embarrassment—and anger.

Nikolai glanced up the path to where the man in the gray suit had been. He was gone now. Apparently he had become fearful of being conspicuous if he remained too long. He might still be around, though, farther down the path.

"What I did, I did because it was necessary," Nikolai said. "Do not believe I did it out of any...feelings for you." His expression was icy.

"I hate you for this," she hissed. She started to rise to her feet. Nikolai offered his hand, but she slapped it away.

"There were no personal feelings involved in this at all," he said. "I think I may have said words of...endearment. I think some words may have escaped my lips that I—that I did not mean...and do not mean. I assure you, I did what I did only because it was necessary."

"Oh, well, pardon me for suggesting you might actually have *enjoyed* it. I thought you *would* enjoy having me in such a disadvantaged position."

For an instant Tiffany thought she saw a hint of emotion in his eyes, but then it vanished abruptly. "I warned you," he said. "Don't let yourself get close to me. And I must not let myself get close to you." He added in a cool formal tone, "Thank you for helping me. I say this to you now because I probably won't see you again.''

Tiffany was surprised but said nothing.

''Vronsky will be too suspicious of me now, even though the report of our...playacting here will probably make him less so than he would otherwise be. But I can't wait until Austria or Zurich to defect. He'll have his agents stick so close to me when we reach those places that defection will be impossible.'' His voice was low so he couldn't be overheard. ''It has to be tonight,'' he said, ''during our performance in Hungary. He won't guard me so closely while we're in a Communist country.''

''And for good reason,'' Tiffany replied frostily. ''I told you what Mr. Brand said—about how dangerous it is to try to reach the American embassy here.''

''I have no choice.''

Tiffany was angry and deeply hurt by his sudden coldness, especially since it came so soon after the strong affection he seemed to have displayed only moments ago. But she had been wrong about all of that, she now realized with a terrible sinking feeling. What she had thought to be love for her had really been nothing more than sexual passion. The affection she had seen so clearly in his eyes—had not really been there at all! It had been only her imagination, letting her see what she had wanted so dearly to see.

Nikolai took her arm. "Let's leave the park together," he said.

Tiffany tore herself away from him. "You play your silly games without me!" She was surprised to find her eyes tearing. "If that man is waiting down the path, it won't change the impression he got to see me leaving alone like this. I'm sure I'm not the first girl you've ever made cry."

And so saying, she rushed off down the path, hating herself for being so gullible and naive. *You silly little fool,* she cursed herself as she ran, tears streaming hotly down her cheeks. *Believing he could really love you....*

CHAPTER TEN

TIFFANY DIDN'T WANT to go to the performance that evening—the first performance of the Volgaya's tour. She didn't want to see Nikolai. She went, however, because it would have been unprofessional of her not to go to such an important highlight of the tour she was filming. If there was one thing Tiffany prided herself on, it was being professional.

Nikolai didn't glance in her direction during any part of the first two excerpts from different ballets that the Volgaya was presenting this night. Tiffany felt tense and anxious as she watched him dance from the wings. She assumed from what he had said earlier that he would make his move at the end of tonight's performance. But how? What could he do? The KGB men were present in great force in the theater this evening. After the ballet they would make it impossible for him to leave.

The Budapest National Theater was a quite large auditorium—four thousand seats—with gilded bronze walls and decorative red pennants. It was filled to capacity with a rapt crowd, for Hungarians took their ballet very seriously, almost as seriously as Russians.

Nikolai's performance during the first two excerpts was wonderful. If he was experiencing the same tense anticipation as Tiffany, it certainly didn't show in his dancing. Now the third and final excerpt of the evening was beginning. It was from the ballet *Firebird*, and the dancers wore full-face masks until the last moments of the scene. The *Firebird* is the story of a simple prince who stumbles into the eerie garden of a monster named Koschey and falls in love with, then rescues a beautiful maiden held captive by the monster.

The orchestra struck up the lyrical ringing score composed by Igor Stravinsky especially for the work, and the corps de ballet swept onto center stage and began dancing, several of them wearing the masks of the subservient monsters. After a moment Nikolai sprang onto the stage, too, in front of the corps. He had on the mask of Koschey, the king of all the monsters in the garden. On his head was a spiked crown of burnished gold. He flourished his dark red cape as he began dancing, imparting an ominous presence to this monster king he was portraying. The audience watched intently, completely absorbed. From the orchestra came the sound of low throbbing strings and baleful trombones, giving a hint of darkness.

After an instant of watching the performance, Tiffany felt jolted by a small shock. Something was wrong, she realized. It took an instant for her to fight through her sense of disorientation to realize what it was: the lead dancer in the mask of the monster king was not Nikolai. The dancer was very good, whoever he was, and very talented. But he was not brilliant, and that meant he was not Nikolai Sharmonov.

Tiffany knew this because ballet had been her life. She could no more fail to tell the difference between a great dancer and a world-class dancer than she could between a glass of water and a glass of chablis. Those in the audience were not so discerning, not even the balletomanes. Of course it had been a full year since they had seen Nikolai dance, while Tiffany had watched him almost every day of the past month.

Who was this dancer in the monster king's mask, Tiffany wondered. She watched his quite respectable *jetés* and his precise turns. Then it came to her: it was Boris Grechko, Nikolai's understudy. It had to be— no one else had so similar a build or knew the part so well.

Tiffany gasped, realizing that Nikolai's escape attempt had already begun! Did the others in the company know he was not playing the lead? Probably they did. Gargarin, the director, certainly must. But where was Gargarin? From Tiffany's vantage point at the side of the stage she should have been able to see him backstage, but he was nowhere in sight.

Tiffany turned to look at Vronsky, who was seated in the farthest left-aisle seat, near the orchestra. He was clearly unaware that the dancer he was watching

was anyone other than Nikolai. Vronsky was a true
Russian, completely enthralled by his ballet. His fist
moved snappily from side to side in time with the
rousing Stravinsky score. His head nodded sharply
with each downbeat. He was clearly enjoying the performance. Onstage the entire company was dancing
now, "Nikolai" and his partner in the foreground.

Tiffany bit her lower lip, anxiously hoping
Nikolai's escape would be successful. He would be
on his way to the American embassy at this very moment, rushing alone through the night. If he was
lucky, he would reach the embassy gates just as the
ballet was ending and the dancers were taking their
bows. They would all remove their masks at that
time, and Vronsky would see that he had been deceived. But by then it would be too late.

Tiffany's heart was racing. No matter how deeply
Nikolai had hurt her earlier, she still prayed for his
success. She couldn't lie to herself; she cared about
him deeply. *Merde,* she wished him silently—the
ballet dancer's word for "luck." The expression was
really a French curse. It was used by dancers only
because it was considered bad luck actually to say
"good luck."

Suddenly something was going very wrong. Tiffany sensed it coming. One of the younger security
men came hurrying down the side aisle toward Vronsky. Behind him was Gargarin, his gray hair frizzy,
his hangdog expression now exchanged for one of
desperation and panic. Tiffany left the stage and hur-

ried to where they were congregating aroud Vronsky. The people near that corner of the hall were distracted and upset by the low-voiced urgent conversation now taking place. Some tried to hush the talkers, but Vronsky ignored them totally. The thunderous music drowned out most of them.

"He tied me up!" declared Gargarin, his expression fearful and pleading. "I couldn't help it!" He held out his wrists, one of which still had a loop of rope around it. "After the second excerpt he held a gun to me, hidden under a cloth! He said he'd kill me if I didn't tell Grechko he was ill and order him to go on in his place. Then afterward he tied me up and gagged me and left me in his dressing room."

"You fool!" raged Vronsky, his beefy face turning red and his jowls jiggling with his movement. People around him started to shush him angrily. "Shut up!" he roared at them. Then he began speaking rapidly in Russian, browbeating the director. Though Tiffany could not understand him, she could guess what he was saying. He was probably telling Gargarin that Nikolai did not have a gun, could not get one and had almost certainly tricked him by holding something else under the cloth and pretending it was a gun. And the director—the fool—had fallen for the ruse!

Vronsky gave rapid-fire orders to the younger security man, who left immediately to relay the message to others. Vronsky turned abruptly to leave. Only now did he notice Tiffany standing within earshot. His mind was on more urgent matters, though. He scowled at her for an instant in passing, then hurried out the side emergency door. Onstage the ballet continued.

Oh, no! thought Tiffany. This was terrible! Nikolai hadn't had time yet to reach the embassy. KGB men near the embassy would now be alerted to stand outside the gates. Vronsky would close in on Nikolai from the direction of the theater. The police would be notified to hunt him down. He didn't stand a chance! They would catch him for sure, closing in on him from both ends. Unless. . . .

Tiffany rushed out of the hall. She hailed a taxi and ordered it to go to the American embassy on Szabadsag Street. During the entire ride, as the cab sped through the chilly nighttime streets, she was filled with anxiety. What would she find when she got there? Nikolai, in chains, being beaten and shoved into a police van?

When she finally arrived in the vicinity of the building, the sight she saw was at least a little bit heartening. KGB men in overcoats stood near the embassy gates, their faces impassive, trying to look inconspicuous. Vronsky was waiting off to the side, extremely watchful, a harried look on his face. Good, that meant they hadn't caught Nikolai yet, otherwise they would have departed.

"Stop here," Tiffany said to the driver when they were a short distance from the gates. The man didn't understand her and kept going. Tiffany almost panicked. If Vronsky saw her there, he would suspect she was involved in the escape. And Tiffany didn't know any Hungarian. *"Stoi!"* she almost screamed at the driver, saying "stop" in Russian. It was one of the few useful words she had picked up in Moscow.

That did the trick; the cab came to a halt in the middle of the street. Tiffany used hand motions to get the driver to turn the car around. Before they could drive off, though, two men approached the taxi. They were obviously KGB. They had been seated in a Russian-built Volga sedan, situated halfway down the block. They peered into the taxi, making no pretense about their interest. Seeing that the passenger was a woman, they prepared to let the taxi go. They said a few words to the driver and he said a few words back in Hungarian and pointed to his head, his hand describing a circular motion. Then he jerked his thumb back toward Tiffany. The usual crazy American tourist, he seemed to be saying.

When the two men had departed, Tiffany gave the driver the address of the theater just to get the cab moving again. Once it was on the road, she racked her brain trying to think. Where would Nikolai go? He was a fugitive now and knew it, with no place to run to, no place to hide. He must have been on foot, at least during the last part of his trip to the embassy. He couldn't have risked having a cab take him directly up to the gates. It would have been too obvious a sign to have it turn around and speed off if KGB men were present.

Where could he go now? Tiffany thought of him wandering the streets helplessly, constantly glancing over his shoulder, fearfully awaiting the dawn.

Suddenly an idea came to her. It was a long shot, but it was the only hope she had. She gave the driver the name of a street near Városliget Park. When the taxi arrived, she paid the driver, then hurried the few blocks to the park on foot, constantly checking to see if she was being followed.

The night was cool, and Tiffany was without a coat. She was wearing the beautiful, slinky, modestly low-cut black evening gown she had dressed in for the theater. It took several minutes to reach the park, then several more to find her way down the winding paths, unfamiliar and ominous in the moonlit darkness. Soon she began to near the bridge over the pond, which Nikolai had said was one of his favorite places in Budapest. The pond came into view.

"Nikolai?" Tiffany called quietly.

No answer.

She continued forward nervously. If rushing through the dark city streets had made her nervous, being here in this deserted park made her even more so. At least in the city streets she could scream if she were attacked. Here no one would hear her cries for help.

"Nikolai?" she said a bit more loudly. Fear was in her heart—fear that he was not here. She did not know where else to look for him. A thrashing noise made her jerk to the side, terrified. No one was

there.... It must have been an animal in the under-
brush, the noise magnified by her imagination to
sound like a potential rapist or mugger.

She moved forward and called his name once more.
Again no answer. Now she was becoming horribly
frustrated at the realization that her hopes of finding
him were to be dashed. He wasn't here. She could do
nothing to help him. His doom was practically sealed.
She nearly screamed it this time, "Niko—"

A hand clamped over her mouth, and a strong arm
went around her chest, dragging her backward into
the bushes. She began to scratch at the hand fiercely.

"Ow! Is that why you came here? So you could
maul me to death?"

"Nikolai!" she said with immense relief, turning
to face him. She saw his strong chiseled face illuminated by the moonlight, his golden hair falling
over his forehead. He wore a thick blue turtleneck
and dark trousers. "Oh, Nikolai!" she cried, throwing her arms around him. Then she remembered how
he had acted so coldly to her earlier. She took her
arms away and composed herself. "I was worried
that they... that you were...."

"Captured? Not yet. Soon I will be, I'm quite certain, having endless faith in Vronsky and his
minions. But not yet."

They knelt near the hedge in the tall grass, and it
felt moist and cool. "Why did you put your hand
over my mouth like that?" she asked, rubbing her
tender lips, which had almost been bruised.

"You spoke too loudly. Do you think you're the only one who realizes I might come here? The police may realize it, too."

Tiffany looked around at the darkened park. It seemed safe enough at the moment. "What are you going to do now?" she asked. "You saw the KGB men at the embassy gate?"

"Yes. It was foolish of me to think I could deceive Vronsky. Don't even tell me how he found out." He glanced at the bridge. "I have to think of a way to escape." He looked back at Tiffany. "You have to go now," he said almost gently. "I can't let you get mixed up in this."

"Go? Do you know how much trouble I went to to get here, to find you?"

He looked at her, and it was a very warm sincere look. He took her hands in his, his expression becoming serious. "I cannot tell you how much this means to me—that you've come here to help me. Thank you, Tiffany. Truly, it means very much to me." He raised her hand to his lips and kissed it. "But now you must go. I can't let you get mixed up in this; it's too dangerous."

"I helped you earlier when I got information from the embassy."

"This is different. I'm a fugitive now. If you're caught in my company, it would be very bad for you, very serious."

"If you don't let me help you," she said, looking him straight in the eyes, "you'll end up in Siberia."

He scowled at the possible truth of this observation. He didn't retract his words, though.

Tiffany's face set in stubborn protest, and her voice became willful and frank. "Nikolai, I don't know what's going through your mind right now, but I do know this: if you want to get out of Hungary alive, you'd better let me help. You have no freedom of movement, and the police are looking for you. I do have freedom of movement; I can get you what you need, visit whomever you need."

She saw that her words were getting through to him, but still he hesitated. Tiffany had an intuition. "Are you afraid," she said, "of our being close together during your escape, of being constantly next to each other?" From his look of sudden alertness, she could see she had hit upon something important.

"I don't know why you're so afraid we might fall in... we might become close," she said. "But I can tell you this, Nikolai Sharmonov, you don't have to worry about it. I didn't like what you did to me this afternoon. In fact, I don't like your whole attitude. And I know now you're *not* the kind of man I could ever fall in love with."

"Good," he said nodding grimly. "Then on that basis I'll accept your offer. And I'm grateful. I'll let you help me. I don't like putting you in such danger, but as you say, I don't seem to have any choice."

"Well, that's settled," Tiffany said. "What do we do now?"

"We have to get out of the city. Every policeman

in Budapest will be looking for me soon. We'll have to get to the outskirts of town, where it's safer."

"How do we do that?" A taxi was out of the question. Taxi drivers were always the first to be alerted by the police when a fugitive was in the area.

"In the morning, when it gets light enough so we won't seem suspicious, we'll—how do you Americans say it—we'll hikehitch a ride."

"Hitchhike," corrected Tiffany.

"I do not have such a good command of the Hungarian language, either, barely enough to say the address we need."

"Should I go back to my hotel room in the meantime to get some provisions? Things you'll need during your escape?"

Nikolai reached behind him and held up a knapsacklike shoulder bag. "I put a few things together before I left my room this evening, and I hid this outside the theater." The bag wasn't very big. "It isn't much," he said, "but it'll have to do. If you went back to your hotel to gather supplies, you wouldn't be able to reach me again without leading them to me. Vronsky will be suspicious of you by now because of your disappearance from the ballet. No, the only thing to do is try to get some sleep. We can't find a ride at this time of night without arousing suspicion, and the streets will be practically deserted, except for people who are out looking for me." He leaned against a tree. "Try to get some sleep; at daybreak we'll start."

Tiffany settled back against a nearby tree and hugged herself. She was shivering. It was cold for that time of year, and she had on only the thin slinky evening gown she had worn to the performance. She had not even brought her wrap, having left the theater too quickly to fetch it. Nikolai gave her a wool shirt from his shoulder bag, but it did not do much good. He looked at her and saw her tremble. "Come here," he said softly.

She came forward and looked at him questioningly. He made a motion to put his arm around her, but she backed away quickly. "You'll freeze," he said.

"It's not that cold."

He shrugged and pretended to be unconcerned, but then he said quite stiffly, "This isn't for romance. It's for warmth. You're cold, and it's my fault. Now come here and let me warm you."

She looked away from him and refused to come forward. She rested against the tree, still shivering. The night became colder. After a while she cautiously moved forward and let him put his arm around her shoulders and pull her close to him. He lay in the grass, his back propped up by the tree trunk. Tiffany lay beside him; her head and shoulders against his chest. His strong arms were around her, cradling her. She could feel the hardness of his torso through his thick blue sweater.

He said nothing. She said nothing. She tried to get to sleep but knew it would be impossible. As the night wore on, she lay sheltered warmly in his arms, listening to the chirping of the crickets and breathing the fragrant moist forest air.

AT THE FIRST RAYS of morning sun they moved to the edge of the park where it bordered the street and stood far back, cautiously eyeing the early-waking traffic. Tiffany gave Nikolai back his wool shirt, which he returned to his shoulder bag. Soon he spotted a vehicle that looked like a safer bet than the others. It was a rickety old flatbed truck, with a few bales of hay visible in the back.

"A farmer," Nikolai said. "In the direction he's heading, he's leaving the city, probably for his farm." He moved out into the street and held out his thumb—the universally recognized sign, even in Communist countries. This was risky, but Nikolai had no choice.

The driver peered at him closely. He looked more like a hoodlum than a farmer. He was big and burly and unkempt. He smiled, showing a missing front tooth. He nodded at Nikolai and pulled over to the side.

Nikolai motioned Tiffany forward. The farmer looked at her in surprise but said nothing. He leaned over the seat and pushed open the door for the two of them to enter. As they got into the truck, he put something under the seat, apparently to make more room for them.

The truck started away, rumbling and jolting. It had terrible shock absorbers. Nikolai said something to the man, using the very few words of Hungarian that he knew.

The farmer laughed at him. "You're foreigners, yes?" he said in halting, choppy English. "Americans, maybe?" He saw Tiffany's look of alarm and laughed again. "The lady's dress and hairstyle—that's how I know. Decadent American imperialists, without a doubt." His laugh showed that he was making a joke and that he had nothing against American tourists. "And you," he said, looking at Nikolai, "is that supposed to be Hungarian you were speaking?" He scowled in mock disgust. "Gibberish!" he declared. "An insult to my language."

"We're going to Szentendre," Nikolai said, naming a town not far from the city. "Can you take us anywhere near there?"

The farmer nodded happily, but Tiffany didn't trust his happy expression.

After a few minutes of driving, the farmer's gaze began drifting down to Tiffany's modestly low-cut neckline. She pulled her dress up as far as she could, but this didn't stop the farmer from continuing to stare hungrily at the bare top of her bosom. She became nervous. Nikolai was too busy scanning the streets for the blue-and-white Lada police cars to pay any attention to the farmer's lecherous glances.

After they had been driving for several minutes, the traffic began thinning out as they neared the city's outskirts. Suddenly a police car appeared at a cross street in front of them. Tiffany could sense

Nikolai tensing. The police car passed on to their left, though, ignoring them. Tiffany let out her breath slowly in relief.

Suddenly the farmer cut his wheel sharply to the left and picked up speed, turning the corner and following the police car. "Two fine Americans like you," said the farmer in a mean voice, "you would not want to meet the police, now would you? Especially when one of you Americans happens to be a Russian defector." He grinned at them in an unsavory, almost sadistic way, showing his missing front tooth. His hand was poised over his horn threateningly to prevent Nikolai from making any aggressive move. With his right leg he kicked out the morning newspaper he had shoved under the seat when they had first entered the truck.

On the front page were photographs of both Nikolai and Tiffany. Tiffany didn't have to be able to read Hungarian to know what the bold black headline said.

CHAPTER ELEVEN

THE FARMER did not honk his horn to attract the police car's attention or speed up very close to it. Instead he stayed a reasonable distance behind.

"All right," Nikolai said to him harshly. "You obviously want something from us. What is it?"

"You are very smart for a Russian," said the farmer, smiling unpleasantly.

"Money?" asked Nikolai, eyeing the police car with concern. "How much do you want to keep your silence?"

"Oh, only all that you have. And there is something else I want, too." His hand left the gearshift knob and wandered down to Tiffany's knees.

Tiffany slapped his hand away, almost nauseated with disgust. Nikolai's face seethed with rage, and he tried to move forward. There was no way he could easily swing at the farmer, though, for Tiffany sat directly between the two of them.

"You stay still!" warned the farmer menacingly. He brought his hand down close to his horn again.

Nikolai froze in his seat.

The farmer looked nasty. He said to Tiffany, "If I

honk my horn or speed up on top of that *rendör auto*—that police car—your handsome Russian friend will soon become a handsome Russian icicle. Is that not what happens to traitors who are sent to Siberia?''

Tiffany turned to Nikolai desperately, not knowing what to do. Nikolai's teeth were bared, his eyes burning with fury.

The farmer's hand alighted on Tiffany's knee once more. She sucked in her breath sharply, and her body tensed, but she did not push his hand away. The big rough hand became bold. It slowly pulled the folds of her skirt up to her knee and slipped in under the skirt. She felt his hand slowly sliding along her silken panty hose up her leg. The horrible vile sensation made her flesh crawl. What could she do?

"Do not be foolish, Russian," the farmer warned Nikolai, sensing his murderous rage. "You would be risking your life—and for very little. If you let me have what I want, I will let you escape from the police. If you do not, then it's Siberia for you—and death."

Tiffany knew it was true. Any move Nikolai made to stop the farmer would be taking his life in his hands. Their seating position alone made any aggressive move impossible.

Nikolai's voice was low and dangerous, but his words were strange. "What *can* I do?" he said. "My situation is as helpless as Swanilda's in act 2 of *Coppélia*."

"What's that?" the farmer asked sharply in bewilderment. His fingers inched farther up Tiffany's leg.

Tiffany knew what Nikolai meant. In the second act of the ballet *Coppélia*, the doll maker lunges at the beautiful Swanilda. Swanilda eludes him by quickly ducking, so that her pursuer grabs only thin air. Tiffany looked at Nikolai expectantly.

He returned her look, his face hard. "Now!" he yelled.

She ducked quickly in her seat.

"Hey!" shouted the farmer.

It was too late, though. Before his hand could hit the horn, Nikolai leaned toward him, now that Tiffany was no longer in the way, and hit him in the face, throwing the full strength of his mighty shoulders and arms into the blow.

The farmer's head sank down on his chest; he was unconscious. The truck began careening wildly. Nikolai grabbed the steering wheel and steadied it. "His foot!" he shouted. "His foot!"

Tiffany pulled and shoved until the heavy man's leg was off the gas pedal. She remained low in the seat so as not to interfere with Nikolai's steering. She raised herself up just enough to peer over the top of the dashboard. The suspense was agonizing. Had the police noticed the veering truck? Had they seen what had happened in their rearview mirror?

A wave of relief washed over her as she saw the police car continuing down the road. Nikolai maneuvered himself until he could put his foot on the gas pedal. He drove to the first crossroad, onto a deserted dirt road, then pulled over to the side.

He turned instantly to Tiffany, a look of deep concern on his face. "Are you all right?" he asked.

She was still quite shaken. She could barely trust herself to speak. "I-I'm okay," she said in a trembling voice.

He pulled her to him and held her tightly, so tightly that it seemed he would crush her. His hand stroked her hair. "Oh, Tiffany, Tiffany...."

"I'm all right, Nikolai," she said softly.

After a moment he relaxed his grip and held her away from him so that he could look at her to see if she truly was all right after such a harrowing experience.

"Thank you for...stopping him. You risked your life by—"

"Don't *thank* me!" he declared in fierce self-disgust. "You should curse me for ever allowing you into such a situation!" He climbed out of the cab and crossed over to the driver's side, where he opened the door and yanked the farmer out onto the dirt. From his raging expression it seemed as if he wanted to beat the farmer to death. Instead, though, he picked him up, slung the heavy body over his shoulder and carried him into the golden wheatfield alongside the road. Then he dropped him to the earth, out of sight. It would not be long before he regained consciousness, but it would not matter if they could get away quickly.

Nikolai came back to the truck and got in. He drove back toward the city, instead of away from it. He stopped at a busy junction. "It's time for you to get out," he said.

"What?"

"You must leave me now. It was a mistake to take you. I can't endanger your life like this any longer."

"Nikolai, I can't leave you."

"This isn't a request! It's an order!"

She bridled with defiance. "I don't care what you call it. I can't do it. Here, look!" She pointed to the newspaper that bore both their pictures on the front page.

Nikolai gazed at the photographs. "Damn!" he cursed, slamming his fist on the dashboard. He understood.

"They know I'm with you," Tiffany said. "They'll be looking for me now, too. And when they find that farmer, he'll tell them you and I are together voluntarily, so even the American embassy won't be able to help me. Nikolai, I'm a fugitive now, too, just like you."

Nikolai shook his head in agitation. He put the truck in gear and started away toward the hills on the city's northern outskirts.

Tiffany watched him as he drove, looking at his hard high-cheekboned profile and lean muscular torso. She reflected on how she was about to escape into the hills with this glowering, fierce, enigmatic man and how they would be forced to spend several days and nights close together—never leaving each other's side—as they escaped into Austria in a desperate flight for survival.

As she thought this, she felt a mixture of fear and apprehension—and a strange undeniable thrill that surged all through her.

THEY WERE SEVERAL MILES into the mountains north of the city when the truck finally ran out of gas. Nikolai coasted over to the side of the mountain road, jerked the wheel sharply and rammed the truck into a clump of tall bushes. He had Tiffany help him cover it with loose branches and brush until it was no longer visible from the roadside. Then they began their trek into the hills.

Several miles to the west lay the last outliers of the Austrian Alps, but here, where they were now hiking, the terrain was rolling and hilly, rather than mountainous. As in the park, it was much like a forest, covered with tall trees and lush green undergrowth. Tiffany could not hike in her high heels, so she went barefoot, feeling the moist tall grass beneath her feet. She was not at all dressed for this kind of activity. But how could she have known, when she was dressing for the ballet yesterday evening, that she would end up in the mountains, fleeing from the state police alongside one of the world's great ballet dancers?

Soon the terrain became too rugged for Tiffany to

continue walking barefoot. Nikolai took his wool shirt from the shoulder bag and tore it in two, then wrapped Tiffany's feet in the material to protect them. He tied the wool in place with strips he sliced from the hem of her slip.

"How far do we have to go?" she asked as they hiked along a slightly sloping ridge.

"Not far—two days and two nights, maybe. We're on our way to the place where the Danube curves westward into Austria. This section is far different from the part of it that cuts southward through Budapest. It's more of a wilderness area there. The boatmen who travel the Danube along the river's great curve are notoriously independent and anti-government—and corrupt, too. We'll be able to bribe them to take us upriver into Austria. Either that, or I'll have to steal a boat."

"Well, meantime, what'll we eat?"

Nikolai surprised her with a full open smile. "Did you know that my father was a woodsman in the Urals? I was a woodsman's son and I can live off the land."

They were hiking alongside a cool flowing stream. The sun was becoming high, the day hot. Nikolai pulled off his sweater and stuffed it into his shoulder bag. He was walking slightly ahead of Tiffany, barechested now, his muscular shoulders and back rippling with his stride.

Tiffany sensed the change in his mood. He was more at ease, much less tense and serious. For a change his natural charm and a refreshing boyishness were allowed to show through his usually formidable masculinity. "Hiking through the mountains seems to agree with you," Tiffany said. "Or is it being pursued by every policeman in the state that turns you on so?"

He smiled at her. "Being here in the open air in such a lovely forest does agree with me. But, also, to be truthful, my mood is caused partly by relief. For a time I didn't think we would make it. It looked very grim. Now it looks not so grim."

"How can you say that? We're fugitives. That farmer must have gone to the police. There'll probably be a statewide manhunt for that truck starting any minute."

"We hid it well, and by the time they do find it, we'll be halfway through these hills on the way to the Danube. They'll look for us, of course, but this range of hills covers a very large area, so as long as we keep up our pace, they won't be able to catch us. They'll have to be on foot. Horses or trucks would never work in this terrain."

"Don't they have any helicopters in Hungary?"

"With this dense foliage to hide us, what would be the use?"

Tiffany had to play the devil's advocate. It made her feel much more secure to have him destroy an objection each time she raised one. "They could wait for us on the banks of the Danube, couldn't they? To grab us as we leave the mountains?"

At this he actually laughed. "The Danube, my dear Tiffany, is the second longest river in all Europe. It's over seventeen hundred miles long, with a fair portion of that distance running through Hungary. That is quite a long bank for them to watch." He shook his head. "No, my advice to you is to relax and enjoy the view. There is danger, yes, but it is not so great as long as we keep moving. The threat comes from pursuers who will be behind us, not in front of us."

They took a few rest breaks along the stream, but these were quite brief, due to the need to keep up their pace. Each time they stopped, Tiffany drank from the cool rushing water. The scenery was very pleasant, and Tiffany felt her own tension receding.

Nikolai was a totally different man here in the wilderness. The hardness and hostility he had displayed so often in Russia seemed to have been left behind. It was so refreshing to see him relaxed. His attitude was very carefree—except for the one time Tiffany asked him what he planned to do when they reached freedom in the West. Then he shut his lips and became sullen and quiet. He clearly did not want to speak of his future plans, or even to think of them.

In the late afternoon Tiffany fell and twisted her ankle. Nikolai went to her as she lay in the grass. He inspected her ankle, squeezing it gently in a few places.

"Ow!" She grimaced against the sharp pain.

He set her foot down gently. "It's not broken; it's sprained."

"I'll have to rest it awhile. I'm sorry, but I don't think I can walk on it like this. I should bathe it in the cold stream so it doesn't swell."

"That's what you should do, yes, but we don't have the time." He frowned as he looked at the horizon and the sun, which was nearly down. "We have to travel farther inland while we have the light. We can't travel in darkness."

Tiffany suspected that what he really meant was *she* couldn't travel in the darkness, though he probably could do it quite nicely, thank you very much. But he said nothing about this. Instead he slipped his arms under her and raised her up without warning. To avoid falling, she put her arms around his neck.

She looked at him as he looked at her. She could see that the effect of his having her slender body in his arms pressing against his naked chest was not lost on him. The humor and carefreeness went out of his expression as he carried her through the forested hillside.

From the set of his jaw and the look in his eyes Tiffany could tell he was becoming tormented by her physical closeness. An air of sexual tension sprang up between them, making Tiffany feel terrible. It had been so nice to have him untroubled and relaxed! She tried to think of something witty to say to take the edge off the suddenly tense situation. Nothing came into her mind, though—except the way his naked broad shoulders felt beneath her palms. To avoid having to look at his face, which was only inches from hers, she turned her eyes down. And now she had the golden hairs of his powerful chest to look at. She shut her eyes. *Don't become close,* she thought to herself, repeating his warning to her over and over in her head. *Remember how he treated you yesterday in the park.*

They continued moving over the hillside, she in his strong arms, both of them tense with the effort of trying to fight down their feelings.

WHEN IT BECAME DARK, Nikolai made a campfire from branches and leaves.

"Won't it give our position away?" Tiffany asked.

"No. The forest is too thick for the fire to be seen," he replied.

He wanted to leave her by the fireside while he foraged in the woods for small game. Tiffany asked him not to go, though. She didn't want to be left alone in this unfamiliar environment, which really was quite forbidding now that it was dark. So instead he gathered fruits and berries for their dinner, and they shared a loaf of bread from his shoulder bag. All around them were the chirping and rustle of forest animals and the fragrance of the greenery. The air was crisp and a bit chill.

A strong sexual tension still existed between them. Tiffany wished she could draw Nikolai into conversation to ease the situation, but each time she tried, he answered with only a word or two, and the conversation died away. He sat by the campfire, the illumination making his brooding face appear golden.

After a while he looked up and spoke to her, but only briefly. There was something about which he wanted reassurance. "Remember when I danced impromptu for your camera the day your Mr. Grayson came to see you?"

"Yes. It was wonderful."

"It was also something I regret deeply—or at least part of it. The first part of the dance I don't care about. You can keep that on your film. But the last part was a variation from the second-act solo in *Giselle*. That's Serge Zhukov's famous solo. I do not want you to keep that part in your film."

Tiffany understood. That particular solo was Zhukov's *pièce de résistance*, and yet Nikolai's performance of it had put Zhukov's to shame. If she used it, it would indeed show the world that Nikolai was a better dancer than Zhukov. "I won't use it," she said, "if it's that important to you."

"It's very important to me," he replied. Then he fell silent again, his expression somber. For a long time he did not speak. Finally he did look up and ask another question. By this time Tiffany was eager for almost any subject that would draw him out of his silent shell. This particular topic, though, was the last one in the world she wanted to talk about, and she almost recoiled at his mentioning it.

"That time I saw you dance," he said. "You were

so wonderful, so magnificent. How is it you don't dance professionally?''

"I—I don't want to talk about that," she said.

His eyes, which had been alive for an instant, now closed down again. Tiffany watched the flicker of interest go out of his face. She didn't want that. She wanted to get him talking to her, instead of withdrawing back into his silence. She had the feeling that if she could get him talking, perhaps she might find out why he was so strongly opposed to any relationship developing between them.

So now, though she had never spoken of this to anyone, she heard herself saying in a soft voice pained with memory, "It was my mother's doing. She was once a major ballerina in the United States, but then she got hurt and never danced again." Tiffany glossed over this part quickly. There was something emotional here that she didn't want to tell Nikolai. "When I received an offer from the NBT, she... 'persuaded' me to turn it down."

"From the National Ballet Theater?" he said in amazement. "How could you possibly turn it down? I'm familiar with Julian Temple's NBT. Everyone in ballet is familiar with it. It's the best company in the United States."

"I didn't want to turn it down," she said quietly, reflectively. "It's just that mother was so dead set against it, so bitter about ballet. Even when I was in school she tried to make me give it up, telling me it was such a hard life, so filled with heartache and disappointment.''

''It is a hard life! It is filled with heartache! But that only discourages those who do not truly have ballet in their blood. I saw you dance; you have it in your blood.''

Tiffany listened to the crackling of the campfire and felt its warmth. She remembered the night she made the decision to turn down the NBT's offer. ''I didn't let her stop me when I was going to ballet school. I kept going despite her constant attempts to make me give it up. But then when I got selected by NBT, well, the pressure just got so intense. It was as if mother went crazy with desperation to stop me from joining.'' She glanced down, then looked at him from under her lowered brow. ''You have no idea how overwhelming she can be when she wants something badly. In ballet circles she was sometimes called Dame Victoria. She's such a strong woman.''

''I don't understand,'' Nikolai said. ''Why did she become so desperate when you were selected by NBT, though she wasn't that way when you were simply going to classes?''

Tiffany hesitated. She knew she shouldn't be telling him this; she had never told anyone. But he seemed so sympathetic now, and—maybe because of the golden orange firelight, maybe because of his physical nearness—she wanted him to understand. It had been pent up inside her for so long—for five long years—and she had not confided it to a single soul.

She took a deep breath, then said, "I think it's because she was afraid I'd outshine her—though she'd never admit it. I think she was afraid I'd get better than she was, even in her prime. She knew how good I was. She couldn't have stood that—having me become more famous, more acclaimed." Tiffany felt guilty for saying this. She added quickly, "But don't get the wrong idea. She's a wonderful woman, and I love her dearly. It's just that she's vain about her talent."

"I don't get the wrong idea. I know about vanity and talent. In ballet it's almost necessary to be vain to endure all that must be endured to reach the top. The vanity carries you over the bad spots when you must make your sacrifices."

"I'm glad you understand," Tiffany said, feeling better.

"I do understand. I understand so completely that one thing is absolutely clear—you must return to ballet."

"No," she said, looking at him. "I won't do that. I made my decision a long time ago."

"You must. You will. Your happiness is at stake; I can see that clearly."

"No," she said more sharply, looking him in the eye to make it plain she didn't want to discuss this any further.

"Yes."

"*No!* Now leave it alone. Can't you see I don't

want to talk about it? I shouldn't even have told you this much."

She was amazed he refused to obey her wishes on this, despite her strong feelings about the painful subject. He gazed at her with deep intensity and said emotionally, "Tiffany, you must not be allowed to abandon your art—no matter how hard it may be for you to confront your mother. You're living an empty shallow life away from ballet. I can see that, even though maybe you cannot. I saw it from the way your face lighted up when you were dancing."

"Stop it!"

"You must go back to ballet! Make it your career! You must confront your mother!"

She became so incensed that she found herself shouting, "It's none of your business! Never mention this to me again. Never!" She stood up and moved away from him, favoring her hurt ankle, which was much better now than it had been before. "And besides," she demanded, "why should you care?"

"I care," he declared, "because I—because I—" But he stopped himself in midsentence. He looked at her for an instant. Then he shut his lips tightly. "That's right. Why should I care? You are none of my business. I...do not care."

His words hung in the air. There was a moment of silence, with the crackling of the fire and the chirping of the forest creatures the only sounds. They stared at each other, worlds of meaning in their eyes. Then he lay back and turned his face away abruptly. "Get some sleep," he said flatly. "We have a long hike tomorrow; by evening we should reach the Danube."

Tiffany gazed at his broad back for a long time. Then she went and lay down close to the fire. He made no move to take her into his arms tonight, not for warmth or for any other reason. Slowly she drifted into a deep exhausted sleep.

CHAPTER TWELVE

IT WAS SO STRANGE the way it finally happened...so
unexpected....

The day started simply enough. At daybreak they
resumed their hike. Tiffany's ankle was almost completely better now, and she could walk unaided. By
evening they crested a final hill, and looking down
they could see the beautiful, very broad Danube
River, whose banks in this region were very grassy. It
was a majestic sight. Far off to the west a small pier
was visible, with a few motorboats and fishing
dinghies tied up to a wharf.

They went down to the shoreline, a good distance
away from the pier. Nikolai had Tiffany wait there
while he traveled to a small encampment. Several
hours later, after night had fallen, he returned with
news that arrangements had been made. A fisherman
with a motor launch had been bribed. He would pick
them up in the morning and take them into Austrian
waters, with no questions asked.

The news was good, but Nikolai's attitude was the
same as it had been all day long: impersonal, chilly
and distant. Tiffany found his silence unbearable.

Though Nikolai had not mentioned it, she knew there was a chance of betrayal by the fisherman he had bribed. In the morning, instead of a boat that would carry them to safety, they might be greeted by a Hungarian police patrol. Tonight might be their very last night together—ever—and yet Nikolai was treating her so coldly.

Finally Tiffany could bear it no longer. As Nikolai stood stiffly with his back to her, gazing out at the magnificent river shimmering under the full moon, she grasped his arm and pulled him around to face her.

"Why do you hate me so?" she blurted out emotionally, unable to restrain herself.

Nikolai frowned. "Hate you?" he said in a disbelieving voice. "How could you think such a thing?"

"You've gone out of your way to show it! You've treated me with nothing but hostility and coldness ever since last night."

Nikolai stared at her, seemingly shocked by the look of pain in Tiffany's eyes and the understanding—which was slowly dawning on him—that he had hurt her deeply. Watching his expression, Tiffany saw changes taking place. It was as if he had erected some barrier, some sturdy wall of insensitivity, to keep himself from showing his true feelings. The barrier had lasted this long, but now, seeing how much he had hurt her without even realizing it, his wall seemed to crumble. His eyes became gentler and filled with feeling.

Slowly, haltingly, his hand moved to her face and tenderly stroked her cheek. He opened his mouth to speak, but his words became choked with emotion. He closed his mouth.

"You don't hate me?" Tiffany asked hopefully.

Suddenly his brows furrowed, and the words burst from his lips as if torn right from his heart. *"Hate you? My darling, I love you!"* He threw his arms around her and embraced her tightly, crushing her against his lean hard body. "Oh, Tiffany, Tiffany." His voice was filled with anguish. "Forgive me, my darling. Forgive me for ever letting you believe such a thing."

Tiffany was too startled and overwhelmed by his reaction to speak. For an instant she resisted letting her guard down.

"I shouldn't be telling you this now," he said. "I shouldn't let you know how deeply I love you. I tried not to let you see it. I did everything I could not to let you see it! That's the reason I was so cold and hostile that day in the park. I reacted too strongly, trying to deny my feelings so you wouldn't know."

"But why, Nikolai?"

"It's not fair to you. Even now it's not fair to let you know how I feel. I shouldn't be telling you this. But. . . ." He shook his head helplessly. "My darling, I can't go on pretending any longer!"

He gazed deeply into her eyes. "I love you, Tiffany. *Ia tebia liubliu.* Almost from the first time I saw you I felt an excitement inside me; I knew you were special—your beauty, your defiant spirit. But back then I thought you were part of a propaganda crew. Later, when I saw that you were not, it became harder to pretend I didn't care, especially when each time I saw you, I saw more that made me fall in love with you—your sensitivity, your enchanting smile, your incredible talent. Tiffany, you are the woman I've been searching for all my life.''

His lips touched hers, and he kissed her gently, but soon his restraint deserted him, and the gentleness gave way to burning passion.

"Why were you afraid to tell me how you felt?" Tiffany asked, bewildered. "And why do you say it isn't fair to me now to let me know you love me?" Her heart was soaring with such joy that she could barely speak. But she had to know. "Didn't you know I wanted to hear it? You knew how I felt about you, didn't you?"

"Don't tell me," he said almost desperately.

"I love you. I'm not afraid to say it. I love you, Nikolai." If only he knew, Tiffany reflected, how long she had been looking for a man like him—a man of strength, who was sensitive, as well; a man of fierce pride and great talent, who could still be compassionate and caring. There was a magical "chemistry" here that affected her deeply. His looks, his talent, his creative genius, even his flaring temperament—they all added up to strike a chord deep within her. He had said she was the woman he had been looking for. *He* was the man *she* had been looking for—and never expected to find.

"I love you, Nikolai," she said tenderly. "I've never loved any man before. But I love you."

Cradled in his arms, she felt him shudder slightly. He seemed to be waging that strange battle within himself, the nature of which she could not imagine. But then he sighed resignedly, surrendering to the powerful emotions he felt—to the realization that they were in a foreign hostile land where capture might await them in the morning and to the knowledge that this might be their last chance ever to be together.

His fingers went to her hair and stroked it. He kissed her cheek. He pulled the fabric of her gown down low and kissed her bare shoulder. He looked at her. There had been anguish in his face only moments ago as he had struggled with that private battle he was waging. Now there was anguish no more. Now there was nothing but a look of powerful overwhelming love that thrilled Tiffany to her very soul.

"My love," he said in a throaty voice. "*Moia dorogaia.* I love you so deeply I feel I'll explode with my love of you. I love you, Tiffany. You're the only one I'll ever love. And I'll love you always." He seemed overcome by the deep feelings he had kept locked inside himself for so long. He picked her up and carried her to a thick grassy area under a shade tree and set her down. It was an unusually warm night. Even the grass was warm beneath her. He lay down beside her. His hands began roaming over her body as his blue eyes held hers transfixed in a look of deep emotion.

His hands went to the back of her gown and unzipped it. Then he gently pulled the front of the gown past her shoulders, taking the straps of her silk slip with it. He lowered the gown and slip until they were at her hips, leaving her breasts bare. Tiffany felt her body tingling all over under his loving gaze. Her breathing became shallow and rapid.

She had a strong urge to jerk her hands up to hide her nakedness. She resisted the urge, though. *This is the man I love,* she thought, *the man I've searched for all my life. This great man who is becoming a legend is the man who loves me. . . . He loves me. . . .*

His hands moved gently over her shoulders, down her arms, across her slightly rounded belly. They traced over her soft fair skin in circles and arcs, tenderly, as if worshiping her body. They did not touch her shapely breasts, though. Soon her breasts were tingling with desire, aching with yearning. And only then did Nikolai smile at her very slightly, very lovingly. . . and lower his face to touch it against her breasts. He moved his forehead, his nose, his chin, tenderly against her, savoring the feel of her soft skin and excited nipples against his face. To Tiffany the sensation was wickedly sensual but also a telling act of love. "Oh, Nikolai," she moaned, her voice filled with tenderness.

She wanted to—but found she was afraid to—touch him. Her hands lay rigidly at her sides, her fingers clawing the moist green earth. When Nikolai removed his sweater, though, baring his powerful torso, she tentatively moved her fingers up to touch his naked stomach, then his lean sides.

She was very shy at first, her fingers touching only lightly. But then as his own hands began caressing her thighs and his lips and tongue began assaulting her ear with maddening probes and kisses, her hands became bolder. She was swept up in the beauty and passion of the moment. Her hands closed over his powerful shoulders and stroked the flat planes of his brawny chest.

Nikolai was trying to be gentle, but his passion soon overwhelmed him. "I love you," he whispered in her ear in a low voice thick with desire. "I love you more than I've ever loved anyone. I love you more than life itself. My darling, my darling, how dear you are to me!" He kissed her in a way that was searing, shattering—deeply impassioned. Tiffany felt herself responding to his kiss, her mouth opening wider beneath his. She had never felt anything so wantonly wonderfully sensual in her life as the way he caressed and kissed and loved her now. He loved her with his eyes, his lips, his hands—his very soul.

After a rapturous eternity of touching and kissing, she felt his hands return to her gown and slip, which now were bunched up around her waist. When he began tugging the clothing down, Tiffany tensed. Her hands jerked automatically to his wrists to stop him. He did stop. But he also gazed deeply into her eyes, his expression filled with love. Slowly, hesitatingly, Tiffany removed her hands from his wrists. . . .

Soon she was completely naked before him. She felt the soft moist grass beneath her shoulder blades and the backs of her legs. She had never thought she would be in this position of leaving herself open to be taken by a man who was not her husband. She had always thought that when she would give this great gift to a man, it would be to her husband, after her wedding.

The world had been less complicated then. Now she was on the banks of a foreign land, where brutal men were searching to find the man she loved and take him away from her to some horrible place. She might never see him again. There might be no tomorrow. But there was now, and the man she loved was here beside her.

She looked at Nikolai, who was towering over her, gazing down at her with worshipful eyes. He undid the buckle of his pants and then stepped out of them. Tiffany sucked in her breath at the sight of him and bit her lower lip. When he came down to her, it was like a blanket covering her that warmed and thrilled her. He kissed her gently as he gazed into her eyes. There was a moment of pain, then later an eternity of warmth and pleasure. His love surrounded her, washed over her, overwhelmed her with its richness and fullness. She heard his whispered words of endearment in her ear, partly in English, mostly in Russian. Her hands moved over his hard back.

"Oh, Nikolai," she cried, tears of joy streaming down her cheeks. "Nikolai, I love you. I love you." Her heart soared higher and higher, her spirit reaching for the brilliant stars above. She was filled with rapture. In her ear she heard Nikolai whisper over and over, "My love...my true love...*moia dorogaia....*"

CHAPTER THIRTEEN

At DAYBREAK the boat arrived and transported them up the Danube to freedom in Austria.

Things happened very quickly once they reached Austria. They were whisked away to the American embassy, where they were both heartily welcomed. Even the people outside the embassy, the Austrians, cheered them as the State Department car took them through the city streets on the way to the compound. Unbeknownst to Tiffany and Nikolai their escape had become front-page news throughout Europe and America. During the two days and nights the massive manhunt for them had been going on, Europeans had been silently cheering for them, praying for their success. Now that they had finally reached freedom, they found they had become celebrities.

Nikolai had been a celebrity already due to his fame as a dancer, but his defection and the dramatic escape from Communist Hungary made him even more famous. Tiffany was applauded as the American filmmaker who had helped him in his defection and who, it was widely believed, had made his escape possible.

There wasn't much time to enjoy their newfound celebrity status in Austria, though. After a preliminary debriefing by embassy personnel, they were whisked off to the airport and put aboard an American jetliner bound for New York. A more comprehensive debriefing session was to take place at the State Department offices once they were home.

There wasn't much opportunity for them to be together on the trip back to the United States, for Nikolai was seated between two State Department escorts, and Tiffany sat a few rows in front of them. She wondered why Nikolai didn't come forward for a few minutes to be with her and say a few words, to share the joy of their having succeeded in such a dangerous undertaking. She didn't let this bother her, though. He was probably too tired from being hustled from one place to another all day long.

"I love you now, and I'll love you always," he had said to her as they made love on the bank of the Danube. Tiffany basked in the glow of the memory, letting it warm her. She had no doubt at all that once they arrived in New York and had a few unhurried moments to themselves, he would propose to her.

And so, having lowered her emotional defenses, Tiffany was completely stunned when the TWA jet landed at Kennedy International and upon disembarkation she saw a beautiful black-haired girl rush forward from the customs area into Nikolai's arms. His arms were open to receive her, and he embraced her tightly.

A throng of reporters and photographers closed around him to snap pictures and shout questions. One reporter asked above the din of all the other shouted questions, "And how does it feel to finally reach the land of freedom, Mr. Sharmonov, and the arms of your loving fiancée?"

No, it can't be! thought Tiffany, her mind reeling. *He'll tell them it isn't so. He'll tell them it's all some horrid mistake. That girl is his... his relative. That must be it. A cousin, perhaps. Or a...a.... Tell them it isn't so, Nikolai! Tell them it's not true!*

"It feels wonderful to be in the United States," Nikolai said in a voice that sounded hollow. His arms were still around the beautiful petite girl, who was beaming at him and at the photographers snapping their pictures. "And it feels wonderful to be reunited at long last with my lovely Larisa."

Larisa rose up on tiptoes to kiss him. She had a dancer's posture. Tiffany watched in shock as Nikolai's head lowered and his lips touched Larisa's. The crowd of enthusiastic onlookers who had gathered for his arrival burst into cheers and applause. Tiffany stumbled backward, her face ashen. "Are you all right?" asked the State Department man who had been her escort. Tiffany could not speak. She felt queasy and on the verge of fainting.

IN THE FOLLOWING DAYS Nikolai sent her letters and tried to reach her by phone, but now she understood why he had told her he didn't want her to become involved. She was so shattered she sent the letters back unopened and refused his calls. He would only tell her more lies, she was sure, and she could not bear to hear them. She was too emotionally devastated already from listening to his lies. "I love you," he had said that night. "You're the only one I'll ever love. And I'll love you always."

The only news she had about him she received from the evening television news, just as millions of other Americans did. He was a major celebrity now. Tiffany saw him being greeted by various public figures. She saw him being courted by the directors of the major ballet companies. Finally she saw him shaking hands with Julian Temple after signing an agreement to join the NBT as its new *premier danseur*. Most of the broadcasts showed Larisa at Nikolai's side, her arm possessively through his, smiling at the camera.

None of the broadcasts mentioned Tiffany as anything other than "the young filmmaker who helped Mr. Sharmonov in his escape to freedom." There was no mention of any personal relationship between them. Obviously Nikolai had not seen fit to say anything about that. Tiffany had not, either. Reporters were constantly coming around asking to interview her, to learn more details of their escape— and of any possible relationship that might exist between her and Nikolai. Tiffany refused all such requests and went into seclusion.

The reporters had gathered around her New York

apartment so relentlessly that she finally was forced to abandon it and move in with her mother for a few days until the publicity storm blew over. Another reason for the move was that Nikolai had come to her door twice already. She had refused to open it both times, pretending she was not home.

She didn't want to see him—not even for a brief moment. The State Department officer, a man named Aaron Aronson, had wanted to debrief them together—ask them questions about their escape for intelligence purposes. Tiffany had refused. She told Mr. Aronson she'd be happy to answer his questions, but *not* if Nikolai was in the room. As a result Aronson had had to arrange two separate sessions.

Victoria Farrow was pleased to have her daughter home again. She was an imposing woman of regal bearing, who had been one of the great beauties of her day. In her youth her hair had been flaming red. Now it was tawny, with streaks of gray. This complemented, rather than detracted from, her patrician looks and mature beauty.

Victoria Farrow had begun her formal ballet training at the age of eleven in London, where her family lived, at the celebrated Downy Academy. Right from the start her outstanding talent had shone, and she was singled out as an exceptionally promising student. Soon she fell under the personal tutelage of Marion Downy herself. By the time Victoria was nineteen, she had been selected by the famous Sadler's Wells ballet troupe. She made her triumphant professional debut in Antony Tudor's *Pillar of Fire*. For a decade thereafter she was the toast of London ballet society and then, when she married Tiffany's father and moved to the United States, of New York society.

Tiffany's father had been an international maritime-law attorney. When Tiffany was eight, he had died on a big-game safari in Africa, gored by a charging rhino. The fact that he had provided extremely well for his wife and young daughter in the event of his death did not lessen the tragedy. Then, only a few years later, a second tragedy befell Victoria Farrow. At the age of thirty-one, at the height of her creative powers, her career came to an abrupt end in an accident that left her ankle permanently weakened. Tiffany had been "involved" in the accident—the word she used in her own mind. And even to this day Tiffany could not think of the incident without feeling immense guilt.

Victoria was happy to have Tiffany living with her again—even temporarily. She welcomed the chance to try to improve her relationship with her daughter. For the past five years, ever since Victoria had caused Tiffany to turn down the NBT offer, their relationship had been extremely rocky. Shortly after Tiffany had given the NBT her answer, she had left her mother's apartment and moved into one of her own, which she shared with a roommate. Aside from Tiffany's infrequent, dutiful, but not very warm visits, she and her mother did not see much of each other.

Now Tiffany needed a place to stay where she could sort out her emotions and get her life back in order without the constant harassment of reporters demanding to know things about her "relationship" with Nikolai that she herself did not even know. Her mother was a willful woman who excelled at running interference for Tiffany during this period. She screened her phone calls and answered the wall buzzer with a firm no to anyone who wished to visit her daughter.

Tiffany was in somewhat of a traumatized state, and it was comforting to be able to lean on her mother's strength for a while. If there was one trait Victoria Farrow had in abundance, it was strength. She was such a strong woman that Tiffany often felt inadequate in her presence.

"That was Mr. Grayson," Victoria now said to Tiffany, hanging up the phone. "He called to wish you well. He said to tell you he knows what an ordeal you must have been through during that escape and for you to rest up and relax as long as you want—so long as it's not more than just one more day. Those are his exact words. He said he wants to see you tomorrow to talk about your continuing with the film."

"I'll see him when I'm ready," Tiffany said from the sofa, where she was watching a TV news broadcast. The broadcast was running a feature of Nikolai as he visited Paramount Ballet to see his fiancée, Larisa, rehearse for Paramount's upcoming production.

Victoria noticed Tiffany's expression as she watched Nikolai on television. "Dear," she said, "I don't suppose you'd care to tell me what went on with you two during those days and nights you were escaping together?"

"I didn't say anything went on, mother. And besides, I don't want to talk about it."

"Well, whenever you're ready."

Tiffany would never be ready. She did appreciate her mother's sensitivity to her reluctant mood, though. Sensitivity was a very rare trait in her mother. Usually her manner was one of domineering determination that refused to take no for an answer. Now, however, as a result of the past five years of bad feeling between them, her mother was making every effort to reestablish harmony in their relationship.

Seeing Nikolai's face on the screen as he smiled at the accolades of an adoring public, seeing him so obviously untouched by doubt or misery, Tiffany felt even more betrayed than she had earlier. How could he have lied to her this way, she wondered bitterly. And that's what it was almost—an outright lie. By not telling her that he was engaged, that the reason he was defecting was to join his fiancée, he had deceived her in a cruel and brutal way. What possible explanation could there be for such behavior? There was none, she was convinced, other than the obvious one: that Nikolai Sharmonov was a coldhearted man who had no scruples. His reputation as a womanizer was true. Oh, if only she'd had the sense to pay attention to that reputation of his!

He *had* told her there was a secret reason for his defection, but by deliberately and mysteriously refusing to tell her what that reason was, he had only made himself more appealing to her.

Oh, he had planned it all so well! He'd manipulated her so perfectly! He knew that if he told her the truth—that he was defecting to the States so he could marry his fiancée—there would be no chance in the world of his ever making love to her. So instead he had acted reluctant about wanting to seduce her, pretending he was tormented, warning her to stay away from him, playing exactly the right role he knew would win over her trust and love. And then, when he succeeded, he took the only thing he really wanted from her. . . before returning to his fiancée.

TIFFANY FINALLY AGREED to see Rolf Grayson after having her mother answer his calls for several days with word that she was feeling ill. They met at the Four Seasons for lunch. Since the season was now summer, the decor of the dining room emphasized cool blues and pastels that fit in well with the dining room's lovely reflecting pool. Aside from its exquisite and astronomically priced cuisine, the Four Seasons was known for its custom of revamping its decor four times a year to suit each of the four seasons.

After talking to her for a few minutes in a testing

way to make sure she was emotionally fit enough to
take it, Rolf hit her with a verbal barrage designed to
get her back on the job without further delay.

"Look, Tiffany, I don't know what the situation is
with you, but whatever it is, snap out of it, kid.
You've been goldbricking long enough. I know you
had a hard time during that escape from Hungary,
even though I don't know the details, since you
refuse to enlighten me. But that's over with! Look,
whatever it is that's got you down, I sympathize. And
if there's anything I can do to help, you just name
it."

"Thank you, Rolf," she said. "But there's
nothing that needs doing."

"Good. And to tell the truth, you look healthy
enough to me."

"I am healthy."

"Then what the hell are you doing holed up with
that palace guard of a mother of yours—bless her
soul—when you should be out covering this story for
me? It's only the biggest story of your career and
probably the biggest story in the arts for the entire
year. You're letting me down."

"I'm not letting you down, Rolf. I'll give you a
full report on all I know that's...that's relevant...so that whoever continues with the film
can—"

"Cut it right there! We'll have no talk about
'whoever continues with the film.' It's your film, and
you're going to finish it. I sent Kent Langerhorn out

to Europe to take charge of the crew that's continuing to film the Volgaya during its tour and the Zurich competition. And I'm putting you in charge of the crew down here that's covering Sharmonov's upcoming debut with the NBT. For now this film about Sharmonov and the Volgaya has been split into two parts, but it's still your film, and you're still the one who's going to cover the dominant aspect of it."

Tiffany lowered her head. "I'm not sure I want to do that," she said softly. The truth was, she definitely didn't want to do it. It would be too painful to have to see Nikolai again for purposes of interviewing or filming—or any purposes at all. Besides, she had lost her objectivity as a filmmaker. She could no longer produce a documentary from an unbiased point of view.

Rolf put his finger under her chin and raised her head to make her look at him. "What is this? Something new? You've turned into some kind of weakwilled coward all of a sudden? That's the last thing I'd have expected from you."

"I'm not a coward!" she declared. "I just—"

"Turned into a coward, that's what you just did. I don't know why. Beats the hell out of me. One thing that could always be said of you, as far as I was concerned, was that you had backbone—and spirit. Oh, you may have lacked a few of the finer points of filmmaking—"

"I certainly did not!"

"But at least you always stood your ground. You

weren't afraid to do anything necessary to bring in a good shoot. And you wouldn't take guff about it, either, not from me or anybody else.''

"And I still won't," she declared. "Not from you or anybody." *No* one could insult her professional competence.

"Then why are you afraid to continue with this project? And don't tell me it's not fear. What else could it possibly be?" He held her stare, his eyes challenging.

It was then that Tiffany realized, again, one of the reasons she liked Rolf. Aside from his ruthlessness and occasional insensitivity, the fact remained that he knew how to bring out the very best in the people who worked for him, how to nurture them in whatever way they needed nurturing. He had a sharp eye for detecting obstacles in the way of his getting what he wanted from his people, and he didn't hesitate to smash those obstacles to smithereens—by whatever means, fair or foul, necessary.

"Come on, Tiffany," he said, smiling in a comradely yet taunting manner, "you're stronger than this. Whatever it is that's got you down, you can overcome it. You're a big girl now. And if I do say so myself, you're becoming one heck of a fine filmmaker."

"Don't try to flatter me."

"Now would I do that?"

She saw him try to hold the look of righteous indignation for a moment, but a tiny smile cracked through. Tiffany laughed. Rolf laughed, also. "All right, so I'd flatter you if that's what it took to get me what I wanted. Aside from that, the truth, is you're too strong to let something like...like whatever this problem is get you down. You don't really want to risk stunting your career by passing up an inside story on the biggest assignment you've ever had, do you?"

No, she thought, she did not. Rolf was right again. She was being cowardly. She was letting Nikolai triumph over her in a way that was almost as bad as the first way, for now it involved ruining her self-confidence. Was she going to let herself be cowed by that heartless manipulative man? So far she had been. She had been on the verge of giving up the choicest assignment of her career simply because she was repelled by the thought of seeing Nikolai again. Well, no sir, mister! She was no weak-kneed spineless little girl. She wouldn't let her career be ruined just because some insensitive Russian playboy had tramped all over her feelings. It was her own fault for being so naive in the first place, for believing him when he told her his reputation as a womanizer was false and undeserved. Well, so she had learned a lesson.

"All right, Rolf," she said. "I'll get back on the story."

"That's my girl. I knew you would."

"Did you?" she asked softly, eager to know that he did have confidence in her strength of character,

even if she did not. It bothered her to realize she was
so eager to have him believe in her, but still, the
eagerness was definitely there.

"*Did* I?" he exclaimed, disbelieving her doubt.
"Here," he said, yanking open his leather-and-gold
attaché case and pulling out a stack of material.
"You heard about the party Temple is throwing
tonight to celebrate Sharmonov's signing with the
NBT?" Tiffany nodded. "Here's your press pass,"
he said, handing her a card bearing her name, the
date and the embossed logo of Grayson Productions.
"Here's your schedule for tomorrow's screening of
the dailies shot since you were away. And
here's...." He continued giving her everything she
needed to start back on the project immediately, including reservations for the screening room that bore
the next day's date.

When he finished, he grinned at her. "I never
doubted you for a second, Tiffany. You've got too
much spunk to let yourself get down for too very
long."

"Rolf...." She put her hand on top of his.
"You're a good man, Rolf." The look on her face
was one of gratitude—and a lot more.

His eyes became serious. "You know how I feel
about you," he said in a low voice. "You're still a bit
shaken up now, so I'll take that into account and
won't hold you to this look you're giving me now.
But after you have a few days to bounce back, if you
give me that look again, it's going to be no quarter

asked, no quarter given, kid. Old 'show-'em-no-mercy' Grayson is going to take you up on it.''

"I might want you to.''

His eyes were steel. "You take a few weeks. You get this assignment done. That'll bring your confidence back to where it should be.'' He leaned close, across the table. "Then you say that to me again—and things will happen so fast it'll make your head spin.''

CHAPTER FOURTEEN

TIFFANY DIDN'T HAVE TO use the press pass Rolf gave her to get into the party that evening. As the woman who had helped make Nikolai's escape possible, she had received her own engraved invitation in the mail.

The party was hosted by the Gallaghers, wealthy patrons and supporters of the NBT, at their Fifth Avenue apartment. When Tiffany arrived, the large living room was swamped with glitterati—celebrities from the worlds of society, dance, fashion and the arts, including various rich and powerful patrons of the New York ballet scene who helped fund the NBT. Tiffany recognized many of the most famous names in ballet among the crowd: dancers, choreographers, directors. There were also two US senators in attendance, several famous movie actors and other luminaries. All had come to celebrate Nikolai's defection and his signing with the NBT.

A maid took Tiffany's coat at the door and ushered her into the room. She saw Julian Temple standing near her, talking to a wealthy businessman, trying to get him to underwrite the costumes for the

NBT's upcoming production of *Romeo and Juliet*. The room was filled with wealthy members of the society set who supported ballet, and the executives of NBT were not letting pass this opportunity to try to cajole them into donating for various projects. Few people outside of ballet realized it, but donations were usually requested for specific items, such as the lighting for one ballet or the sets for another.

Julian Temple noticed Tiffany and seemed surprised by her presence. From his expression she could see he wanted to come talk to her but could not easily disengage himself from the businessman he was speaking to. The man was on the verge of agreeing to Temple's request.

Tiffany moved off toward the fringes of the crowd. She searched for Nikolai. Various waiters in their cutaway livery circulated through the multitude, bearing trays of drinks and delicious-smelling hot hors d'oeuvres. The women at the party wore bejeweled gowns, their fingers and wrists and necks glittering with diamonds. Most of the men had on dinner jackets or expensive sports coats, and their cuff links and rings, too, attested to their formidable financial stature. There was the clatter of laughter amidst the sound of scores of jumbled conversations. A long black Steinway piano was in one corner, the centerpiece of a group of guests congregated around it. The furniture was mostly Danish modern. Oak tables were adorned with cut flowers in delicate *cloisonné* vases. A display case built into one wall glowed softly with pearly recessed lighting, illuminating priceless *objets d'art*. On the walls Tiffany saw an authentic Renoir and an early Picasso. The room was filled with gay conversation, motion, action.

Tiffany was about to move through the crowd to try to look for Nikolai when Julian Temple came up to her. "Tiffany Farrow!" he said happily. "I'm delighted to see you. I had my secretary send the invitation, but I really didn't expect you to come—not after the way you've been hiding from publicity lately!"

"I'm surprised you even recognize me," Tiffany said.

"Recognize you? I do more than that. I remember you. You auditioned for me several years ago."

This astounded Tiffany. She had not expected her dancing to have impressed him enough that he would remember her after all these years. Probably it was reading her name in the newspaper accounts of the defection that had jogged his memory, she thought.

Temple wanted to announce her presence to the guests at the party. She was, after all, supposedly the key figure in Nikolai's defection. Tiffany asked him to please not do so, though. She didn't want to call attention to herself. She felt exposed enough as it was. Temple reluctantly agreed not to. He seemed to want to talk to her for a few minutes more, but he had caught sight of an oil magnate from Texas who had underwritten the expensive sets for the previous year's production of *Sleeping Beauty*. He said a quick goodbye to Tiffany, then headed over in the direction of the Texas millionaire.

Tiffany moved through the crowd in search of Nikolai. She was here, after all, to observe him in these new surroundings, to take mental notes that would come in handy when she wrote the narration to her film. Soon she saw him standing near a carved jade icon. She felt a jolt seeing him in person again...a strange weakness. Except for television, she had not seen him since that horrible day in the airport lobby. She moved off into a corner quickly before he could notice her.

He was dressed in a blue velvet dinner jacket and the kind of frilly lacy white shirt English noblemen had worn during past eras. He looked very handsome. He also looked very uncomfortable, as if he wished he were someplace other than here at the party. His fiancée was at his side. She was a svelte, quite lovely, dark-haired, dark-eyed woman of about Tiffany's age. Tiffany found herself secretly wishing the woman were too gaudily dressed or made up for the occasion, but this was not the case. Her hair was pulled back in a chignon at the nape of her neck. She wore a simple lime gown that accented her slender figure and not too much makeup.

Larisa almost projected a shy demure image—except for the conceited way she held her chin lifted a shade too high and her manner of speaking. At the moment she was talking in an aggressive, almost shrewish way, gesturing with the champagne glass in her slender hand.

"How perfectly dreadful of you to repeat such gutter rumors," Larisa was saying to a man in the group congregated around Nikolai and her. Her voice bore a Russian accent. "Those responsible for spreading that vile rumor are the ones who can't hope to equal my achievement in dance, and so they have to invent false reasons for their own failure and my success. My achievement is based on skill and talent as a dancer and nothing else." She turned to Nikolai. "Isn't that right, darling?"

Tiffany wished she knew what the conversation was all about. All she could tell now was that Nikolai looked even more uncomfortable than he had a moment ago. And strangely, he didn't seem to be at all fond of this woman who was looking at him so demandingly—and whom he was soon to marry. But that could be Tiffany's imagination.

He shrugged. "It has been a long time since I've seen you dance," he said.

This clearly was not the answer Larisa was looking for. A frown creased her forehead, and she fumed for a moment. But then someone in the crowd said something complimentary to her, and her expression became benign and friendly once more.

"I say, darling," said someone to Tiffany, making her turn to the side as he approached, "how good to see you. You're one bird I never expected to find standing alone at a bash like this."

"Hello, Ellsworth," Tiffany said, smiling. The man was Ellsworth Crown, an English journalist who had accompanied Tiffany and her producer on their Egyptian archaeological shoot. Tiffany liked him. He was witty, friendly and thoroughly English—and one of the few men on the Egyptian shoot who hadn't bothered Tiffany with romantic overtures. He had a wife whom he adored and by whom he was completely captivated.

"Why do you say it's unusual to see me standing here alone?" she asked him.

"Well, the most obvious reason, of course, is that you're so absolutely ravishing. But aside from that you are, after all, partly responsible for our guest of honor appearing here tonight, as opposed to putting in a star performance in some Siberian labor camp."

"That's all exaggeration, Ellsworth. I didn't help in his defection that much."

Ellsworth took two glasses of champagne from the tray of a passing waiter and handed one to Tiffany. He sipped at his own drink in a way that made Tiffany almost want to laugh: his pinkie was extended straight out. He was such a correct fastidious man, with his short red beard and short meticulously combed hair. His evening wear tonight was impeccable. Even during the sweltering days in the hot desert, he had been impeccably attired. His unrelenting aplomb had dictated that he bring an entire two-dozen identical safari suits so that he could change several times a day.

At the moment he was noticing the way Tiffany was gazing at Larisa across the room. "Terribly dull lady," he said. "And quite gauche, too. Did you hear what she was just discussing?"

"No, I came in the middle of it, but it sounded interesting. What was it?"

"She was denying the rumor, which has become quite persistent, that a secret deal was made before Sharmonov agreed to sign with NBT. She left her position with Paramount Ballet to join Sharmonov at NBT, and in the process of moving her status seems to have improved significantly. The rumor is that she insisted Sharmonov not sign with any company unless they also agreed to take her on, too, as one of their prima ballerinas."

"But that's—that's not ethical!"

Ellsworth laughed. It was a warm laugh of pure enjoyment. "Tiffany, I love you. You're so innocent. Of course it's unethical, darling. It's an absolute abomination! And as you heard, she was denying it to the high heavens. Of course old Julian would deny it, too, even more vigorously. But the fact is, I don't think she could have got this part without using Sharmonov as leverage, without having him refuse to sign unless she was taken, too."

He sighed. "Sharmonov's defection was about the best thing that could possibly happen to revive dear Larisa's sagging career. Now Julian will be able to promote it as the romantic reunion of the century when they dance together in his next production. You did know they were dance partners at the Volgaya years ago, didn't you, as well as lovers?"

Tiffany tried to make her voice sound calm and composed. "No, I wasn't aware of that."

"Until her defection to the States two years ago, she and Sharmonov danced some wonderful *pas de deux*. After her escape she disappeared for seven months. No one knew where she'd gone. Then suddenly she popped up at Paramount, doing some very good dancing in some very good roles. But recently her career's been declining steadily. Word has it she couldn't even get guarantees of principal parts—that is, until Sharmonov defected."

He took a sip of his champagne and raised an eyebrow cynically. "Now the press is playing up the romance element of a *pas de deux* between the two former lovebirds of the Soviet Union, reunited at last in spiritual bliss on the NBT stage."

Tiffany hadn't known about Larisa Zamyatin's career being on the skids because she had so pointedly ignored anything having to do with ballet these past few years. And she hadn't known that Larisa was a former flame of Nikolai's in Russia, either, though now that she thought of it, she should have known. Nikolai *had* once mentioned that he had a woman friend who had defected. And also, when Zhukov had handed him that letter from Larisa the night Nikolai took Tiffany to visit him, Tiffany should have guessed, from the depths of Nikolai's violent reaction, that this woman meant something to him—or at least had at one time.

Ellsworth took an hors d'oeuvre from the silver tray of a passing waiter, ate it in one swallow and grimaced. "Stay away from the salmon paté." He shuddered. "Dreadful stuff."

Tiffany was looking at Larisa, now surrounded by a crowd of eager fans and admirers and clearly enjoying it. Nikolai was not at her side at the moment.

Ellsworth saw where she was looking. "It's curious, though, isn't it?" He frowned.

"What is?"

"Oh, how she manages to have such leverage over Sharmonov that she could make him propose an odious deal like that to Julian Temple. I mean, how could a woman like her," he said with clear disdain, "have such a hold over a man like Nikolai Sharmonov?"

Tiffany said nothing.

"You know, when you two were in the process of defecting, it was Larisa who called a press conference and announced to reporters that Sharmonov was coming here to marry her and that they were deeply in love. No one had any inkling of it up to that time."

This made Tiffany really mad. So the entire world had known of their engagement—everyone except Tiffany. So while she had been thrashing around the bushes for two days and nights with Nikolai in a desperate escape, he knew—and the whole world knew—that he was on his way to the United States to marry Larisa. And he had not even told her. He had refused to tell her.

She raised up her eyes to look across the room at Nikolai, but he was not there. He was not with the group gathered around Larisa, nor with the group farther off to the side, gathered around the black Steinway. Where had he gone? She turned around and practically bumped into his chest. He had come up behind her and now stood staring down at her.

Ellsworth saw the way Tiffany glared at Nikolai and the way Nikolai looked back with demanding urgency. "Excuse me," Ellsworth said diplomatically, realizing that his presence was now an intrusion. "I simply must find that waiter and get some more of that *divine* salmon paté."

Tiffany looked Nikolai in the eye for a moment, then turned and started away.

"Don't go," he said. "I want to talk to you."

"It takes two to have a conversation, and I'm not interested."

He put his hand on her arm, stopping her. "Why have you refused my phone calls? Why have you sent back my letters unopened?"

"Nothing you could say to me over the phone or

in a letter could be of the slightest interest to me—nor anything you could say in person, either, for that matter. I have no desire to hear any more lies from you.''

''I never lied to you.''

She laughed in his face. It was a harsh laugh of pain and disappointment. Nikolai glanced around at the people who were turning to look at them. ''Come, let's go,'' he said, starting to guide her forward. ''We'll find a quiet place where we can talk.''

She shook off his hand almost violently. ''I'm quite happy right where I am. I came here to watch the party, not to disappear into some quiet room with you, where you can tell me more *lies* and play me for a fool *again*.'' This last sentence came out in an extremley bitter voice. Tiffany had not intended it that way. She had hoped to keep her composure, to keep her words to him light and airy to show that he meant nothing to her, that he was not even worthy of her contempt. But she failed. Her words and the way she was looking at him now showed how deeply he had hurt her.

''Please, Tiffany,'' he said, his voice softer. ''I can't have you believing this. I don't care so much that you think badly of me, but for you to think that what I said to you on the bank of the Danube was a pack of lies, was deceit—that I can't have. I see how it affects you.''

''It's none of your business how it affects me!'' she declared so fiercely, so tormentedly, that the attention of a quarter of the room was turned on them.

Nikolai, seeing that they could not continue their discussion here, like this, took her arm and guided her forcefully toward the exit. She tried to resist, but he refused to take no for an answer. She had no doubt whatever he would have picked her up and carried her, if necessary. When they were out of the main living room, he led her off into the first empty room he saw—a guest bedroom—and shut the door. The room was small. A white fur bedspread adorned the four-postered bed. The dim lighting came from candles floating in baccarat bowls on the bureau.

"All right," Tiffany said, straightening up rigidly, trying to keep her emotions in check so she would not be such easy prey for him. Seeing him so close, though, his expression so apparently sincere, was having an undeniable effect on her, despite her resolve to never let herself be taken in by him again. "All right, so you've dragged me off into a quiet room. Now what is it you've been wanting to tell me so badly?" She glanced at her watch, feigning cool disinterest. "Say it and let me go. I've got far more important matters to attend to."

He was definitely disturbed by her coldness. He did not know how to proceed, as if what he wished to tell her could almost not be said while she was so hard-edged and defensive. "Tiffany," he began, emotion in his voice, "all I want to tell you is this:

the words I spoke to you on the riverbank—they were true, every one of them. Don't doubt that I care about you deeply.''

''How can I help but doubt that?'' she shot back fiercely, anger and hurt overwhelming her desire to remain cool and detached. ''I understand how much you *cared* about me back on the bank. You cared about me enough to take me for your pleasure, wantonly, lying to me about how you loved me, while all the time you kept your precious little secret to yourself, knowing there could be nothing between us because you were on your way to marry the woman you *truly* love!''

''It's not like that at all!'' he protested.

''Oh, what a fool I was, falling for your lies,'' she said, tears suddenly streaming down her cheeks. She hated herself for crying now, for letting him see how deeply he had hurt her. ''You must have loved that—seeing how naive and gullible I was. You must have been laughing to yourself the whole while. You knew I'd never have let you make lo—you knew there never could have been anything physical between us if you'd told me the truth. So you let me believe something else instead—that you really cared for me, that we could really be together, that for once in my life I could have something I truly wanted and needed and—''

Seeing her cry, Nikolai's own expression became deeply tortured. He came to her and tried to put his arms around her to comfort her, unable to bear viewing her in such agony.

Tiffany tore herself away from him and flung herself back against the bureau. "You stay away from me!" she cried. "Haven't you done enough already? Haven't you hurt me and humiliated me enough?"

He stared at her, his eyes so sincere and tormented, Tiffany felt shaken. "It's not like that," he said. "If only you could believe in me. Oh, my dearest, if only you could trust me."

"Don't you dare call me that! I'm not your 'dearest.' I'm not anything but foolish, gullible and used!"

He shut his eyes tightly. Then, after a moment, he opened them. There was such intense emotion in the way he looked at her it almost made her believe he was sincere. "Please," he said. "Is there nothing I can do to show you how much I care?"

Tiffany found herself wondering if maybe, just possibly, there was more to the situation than she realized. She wanted to believe him so badly, to believe that a man like him *could* care for her, that there could be some love and affection for her in this world.

But just as she was on the verge of becoming vulnerable to him once more, she remembered how cruelly he had deceived her that night, letting her fancy they could have a life together when he knew such a thing could never be. And here he was, trying to make her think he cared for her even now, though he was an engaged man and his fiancée was in the other room. *Oh, how little respect he must have for me,* Tiffany thought. "You don't care about me," she said sadly, facing the inescapable truth, "not at all, not even a little bit."

Seeing her despair, hearing those words from her, something seemed to snap in Nikolai. "I'll show you how much I care!" he declared. He came to her and grasped her tightly, clutching her to him. Tiffany tried to resist, but Nikolai seemed consumed by the desperate need to make his feelings known. His eyes burned with deep emotion. It was as if he were leaving himself totally open and vulnerable to her now, lowering all his defenses so she could see how profoundly he cared for her. Realizing that his words had not worked in convincing her, he now trusted to the only alternative left to him—letting her know how he felt through his actions.

He tried to kiss her. She resisted fiercely. Finally he overpowered her and forced his lips down on hers, kissing her searingly. Tiffany tried to pull away, but his arms around her were too powerful. She felt the heat and hardness of his body pressing against her through the fabric of their clothing.

When at last he released her, he gazed at her openly, lovingly, his defenses down. Tiffany reacted to the pain and shame he had forced upon her, certain that he was only trying to deceive her again, to manipulate her emotions once more. She slapped him stingingly. "You think you can toy with me like a plaything? I hate you! You mean nothing to me! You're dirt beneath my feet! I never want to see you again! *Ever!*"

She jerked open the door and rushed out of the apartment, unable to stop the torrent of tears.

CHAPTER FIFTEEN

NIKOLAI STOPPED TRYING to contact her after that. The way Tiffany had slapped him, had refused to believe in him, had been irrevocable. A bridge had been crossed that could not be uncrossed. No more letters came for Tiffany to return unopened, no more phone calls for her to refuse.

Tiffany's mother was unusually cheerful after the night of the party, and this grated on Tiffany. Victoria Farrow didn't know exactly what had happened at the party because Tiffany refused to tell her. She did know, though, from ballet friends who had been there, that Tiffany had burst out of the bedroom in tears after shouting at Nikolai loudly enough for it to pass through the closed door.

"Well," Victoria said cheerfully one evening, "your friend seems to have finally got the message. The phone hasn't rung in two days."

"You sound very happy about that, mother."

"Dear, of course I'm happy. That man wasn't right for you."

"I know why you think that," Tiffany said bitterly. "It's because he's a dancer, and you don't want me to have any contact with anyone who has anything to do with dance. You're afraid it might tempt me into wanting to go back to ballet." She never would have spoken so bluntly if not for her taut nerves.

Her mother looked at her in stony silence. "Tiffany, there is no question of your going back."

"Oh, isn't there?"

Her expression was iron. "No. There definitely is not." To emphasize the point she brought up a weapon she had used against Tiffany before, which had never failed to win her point. "If not for you, I would have continued in ballet myself. If not for your rushing into the studio that day and surprising everyone, causing my partner to—"

"Mother, please!" Tiffany couldn't bear hearing of that again, not in the painful emotional state she was already in.

The incident her mother referred to was the one that had cost her her ballet career. Tiffany had been only a child at the time. She had rushed into the studio and seen her mother and shouted happily, "Hello, mother!" But her presence was unexpected, and her shout caused Victoria's partner to miss catching her as she hurled through the air in a climactic *pas de poisson*. Victoria landed badly on her left ankle, permanently disabling it for dance.

"You'll never let me live that down, will you, mother?" It was her mother's relentless emphasis on that incident during the night Tiffany had been offered the NBT position that had caused the girl to break down and agree to decline the offer.

Victoria touched her shoulder gently. "Dear, I don't mention it to hurt you, only to remind you of how fickle ballet can be, how much heartache you can suffer if you give yourself to it completely."

Tiffany was not in the mood to argue. She couldn't bear having to relive that horrible incident yet again. So instead she quickly got up and fixed herself a cup of coffee. After a moment she took her coffee to the table and said, "You know, it's strange about Nikolai. I have this feeling that there's something out of place, like a puzzle that fits together perfectly except for one small piece."

"What piece?"

"The way Nikolai acted toward his fiancée at the party. He didn't seem to even like her, much less love her. I could see it in his expression. And even though he had his arm around her, it seemed more out of duty than affection."

Victoria seemed disturbed at the direction the conversation was taking. She didn't want Tiffany talking about Nikolai—or about any other dedicated dancer. "Not all marriages are made in heaven," she said shortly, dismissing the subject.

"Yes," said Tiffany thoughtfully, "but if he doesn't really love her, why did he defect to marry her? And why did he wait so long to do it? Larisa Zamyatin has been in the States for two years now."

"I'm sure there was a very good reason," said her

mother. "Tiffany, forget the whys and wherefores. Really, dear, you'd be so much better off just pretending the man never existed. If you have to wonder about something, wonder about how long that fine Mr. Grayson is going to put up with your indifferent attitude toward him. Now there's the kind of man you'd do well to think seriously about."

Tiffany had been scanning the notes she had written for the ballet documentary's narration. She slammed her pencil down on the tabletop. "Mother, I'm twenty-three years old. Will you please stop trying to run my life for me?"

"Run your life? I'm doing no such thing. I'm only trying to give you the benefit of a clearheaded view of reality—which you at times seem to lack."

"Well, please stop it."

Victoria shrugged in a way that said "I'd be happy to; it's nothing to me." But then she announced, "I never found out what went on between you and that dancer during those days you were traveling through the Hungarian countryside together—you never saw fit to tell me. However, I do know this: a girl like you has no business thinking in any way whatsoever about a soon-to-be-married man, particularly one who doesn't even treat her properly. It's so unbecoming, dear! And you have so much to offer, if only you'd offer it to the right man. For instance, Mr. Gr—"

"I'm glad you brought that up again," Tiffany interrupted quickly, rising to her feet. "It reminds me that my roommate is getting tired of watering my plants by now, and I really should be getting back home.'' She began gathering her papers and putting them into her suede briefcase.

''You don't have to leave,'' her mother said, for once showing emotion. She didn't want Tiffany to go. She had looked forward to this chance to get closer to her daughter and was saddened that the opportunity might slip away.

''Really, mother, I do. Thank you for letting me stay this long, but the reporters are no longer knocking at my door, and Nikolai is no longer phoning, so there's no need to stay away any longer.''

''Tiffany,'' her mother said firmly, ''don't leave now. Leave in the morning if you must, but not now.'' At this point Victoria simply wanted to have the last word. She realized Tiffany wouldn't stay, but when she would leave was to be Victoria's decision, not Tiffany's.

''Mother, I'd really like to get home.''

''Tomorrow.'' Her eyes were steel.

Tiffany sighed. She had never been able to stand up to her mother's will. She wondered if she ever would be able to. ''All right, mother. I'll leave in the morning, if that will make you feel better.''

''Thank you, dear.'' Her voice was pleasant again.

Tiffany knew her mother loved her and only did what she thought was in Tiffany's best interest. Still, if only she'd leave her alone to live her life the way *she* wanted to live it!

Lying in bed that night in her mother's guest room, Tiffany could not stop thinking about that tiny insignificant piece to the puzzle that just refused to fit. If Nikolai did not love Larisa, as he seemed not to, why had he defected?

She tried to force the issue from her mind, but it would not go away. Then she remembered something else from the party that made the situation even more puzzling. What was it Ellsworth had said? "God knows how a woman like her can possibly have any leverage over a man like Sharmonov."

Tiffany sat up in bed. How *could* a woman like Tiffany assumed Larisa to be have any sway over a man like Nikolai? It didn't make sense. Nikolai was so strong and independent that he acted the way he wanted even when it put his life in danger. So what was he doing letting that woman pretend there was a love relationship between them when he didn't even seem very fond of her?

Tiffany set her jaw firmly. She would look into this question the first thing in the morning. She nodded. Then, satisfied with her decision, she lay back and tried to fall asleep.

SEVERAL WEEKS LATER Tiffany was in the editing room, going over the different options for the arrangement of sequences for her film, when her secretary came in. "Here's the letter you've been waiting for, Tiffany," the secretary said. "You told me to let you know as soon as it came."

"Thank you, Jaynie." Tiffany turned to the film editor she had been working with at the viewing machine. "Mark, I'll be back in a minute. Meantime, I think we should go with these two dance sequences in order and insert some of the human interest material in the middle to break them up." Her editor gave her the thumbs-up sign without raising his head from the film viewer.

Tiffany could barely contain her anticipation as she entered her office and shut the door. The letter in her hand—a small manila envelope, actually—was postmarked Russia. It was from Serge Zhukov and was in answer to the letter she had sent earlier, asking if he had any information about Nikolai's reasons for defecting. Tiffany didn't expect much in reply. At best she hoped for some response that might put her onto the right track. As she opened the manila envelope and looked inside now, she saw that Zhukov had sent her more than she had ever hoped for.

It was a wrinkled sheet of paper. At first she looked at it in bewilderment, not understanding what it was. Then she remembered—it was the letter from Larisa that Zhukov had given to Nikolai that night Tiffany and Nikolai had visited him, the letter that had caused Nikolai to seethe with anger as he read it, then crumple it in his fist and fling it violently against the wall.

The paper was faintly perfumed. The letter was handwritten in ink and signed Larisa. And it was entirely in Russian. Tiffany looked in the manila envelope again and saw with gratitude that Zhukov had provided a translation, along with a brief note to her:

Miss Farrow, I worry that I break a confidence by showing this to you. I do so because I believe, from your letter to me, that what you do will be in Nikolai's best interest. That is good, for he is a temperamental man and needs looking after.

Tiffany took a deep breath to steady herself, feeling growing excitement. Then she plunged ahead and read the translation of Larisa's letter.

My dearest Niki, It's been months since I left you and our homeland. During this time I did not ask you for help in any way. Now my situation has changed, though, and I must—not for my own sake, but for our beautiful baby, Dmitri.

Tiffany was shocked. She jerked away from the letter, but then she quickly returned to it.

Dimi is in a foster home, and I hate to tell you, but he is not being treated well; he is being treated terribly. I tried to get him back, but the agency says that as a single woman I cannot do so.

Niki, I need you here to marry me, so we can get Dimi back and give him a good life. I'm sorry to impose on you, especially now that I see you have made such a good career for yourself as *premier danseur*. But Dimi needs you desperately. He needs the father he has never seen.

You asked me to marry you once when you learned I was pregnant. I said no then. Now I wish to say yes, for Dimi's sake. Please come soon.

Don't tell anyone of your reason for coming—I must insist on this. I put you on your honor. I need to handle the announcement in my own way. If you reveal it, it will ruin our chances of helping Dimi, I warn you.

All my love, Larisa

Tiffany looked up from the letter, her heart racing. So Nikolai hadn't lied to her after all! He did have a secret reason for defecting, which he couldn't reveal to her. And he had withheld the news of his engagement not because he wanted to deceive Tiffany, to seduce her, but because Larisa had insisted on it, telling him his child's welfare was at stake.

Oh, so many things were clear now: the reason for Larisa's mysterious seven-month disappearance after her defection; the reason Nikolai had warned Tiffany not to become close to him; the reason he had acted so coldly to her, so she would not see how much he himself truly cared for her. And he did care...he did! That's what he had tried to tell her at the party as openly and honestly as he could. He did care for her, and his words and actions that night on the river-bank had been straight from his heart.

Tiffany cringed at the memory of the party. He had made himself completely vulnerable to her, had kissed her in such an open heartfelt way, begging her to trust him, to believe in him—and she had slapped him stingingly in response. He had bared his soul to her, and she had trampled it underfoot. Oh, how she must have hurt him! It hurt *her* to know about this part of his past, but he had acted honorably in offer-ing to marry Larisa, and he was acting honorably now.

Tiffany grabbed her coat and purse and started for the door. There was nothing she could do about Nikolai's having to marry Larisa and being con-demned to a joyless marriage to a woman he did not love. But there was certainly something she could do about his belief that Tiffany despised him. He had suffered too much already due to his love of her and her refusal to believe in him. At least she could let him know the truth—that she understood everything now and still loved him deeply.

She told Jaynie she would be out for the after-noon. Then she left for the NBT theater, where Niko-lai was rehearsing for his first American performance with his new company.

CHAPTER SIXTEEN

WHEN TIFFANY ENTERED the NBT building, she saw
Larisa in the hall outside the main theater where
Nikolai was rehearsing. The petite dark-eyed woman
was getting a drink of water from the water cooler.
She wore a lavender leotard and leg warmers and
pink tights. She was dabbing at her sweating face
with the towel draped around her neck. Her black
hair, pulled tight and tied in back, was also glistening
wet, showing she had just come out of a vigorous
practice session.

Larisa looked surprised when she saw Tiffany approaching. The last time she had seen Tiffany was at
the party. The two of them had never been formally
introduced. There was no doubt, though, that Larisa
knew Tiffany was the person who had helped Nikolai
during his defection. The whole world knew that.

"What are you doing here?" Larisa asked as Tiffany marched by her.

"That's none of your business," Tiffany replied.
As far as she was concerned, Larisa was a selfish
woman. Tiffany had expected her to look shocked or
to say something nasty, which she would ignore as

she continued on to the theater where Nikolai would be rehearsing. What Larisa said instead, though, made Tiffany turn back to her at once.

"You poor naive girl," Larisa began with a hint of sadness and no sarcasm at all. She shook her head sympathetically. "My Niki has you wrapped around his little finger, hasn't he?"

"He has not," declared Tiffany, facing her. She was anxious for a fight. She was convinced that this woman was not a good person—not after what she had done to Nikolai. "And I may be a 'poor naive girl,'" Tiffany said, "but at least I'm not a selfish opportunist."

Larisa's eyebrow raised in interest. "Oh? And I am?"

"You made Nikolai defect for the sake of boosting your career, and you exploited the matter of his child's welfare. You used his love for his son as leverage against him, as something to hold over his head!"

Larisa was clearly surprised Tiffany knew about her child.

"I don't care that you know I know," Tiffany said. "I'm going to tell Nikolai that I know, too, and that I'm sorry for the way I treated him and sorry I didn't believe him when he said that he lo—" She stopped herself abruptly. There was no need to speak of such fine sentiments to a woman like Larisa, who Tiffany was sure was cruel and insensitive.

Larisa's voice was surprisingly soft, not vindictive

as Tiffany had assumed it would be. "You were saying?" she prompted, urging Tiffany to continue her interrupted sentence. Tiffany said nothing. "You were saying you're going to tell Niki you're sorry you didn't believe him when he said he loved you? Is that it?"

"I don't have to talk to you."

"Forgive me for saying so, but you're going to have to talk to someone—to help you get your head on straight. Do you realize what Niki is doing to you, what a fool he's making of you?" Surprisingly, she did not look hostile but simply concerned. "My Lord, don't they teach you girls anything about life, here in the United States? Do you really believe everything a man like Niki tells you?"

"You're not going to make me doubt him," Tiffany said. "I've been fooled enough already into doing that, thanks to your self-serving demand for secrecy about your engagement."

Larisa was clearly curious about where Tiffany had learned these things she was speaking of, but instead of asking about it, she became more concerned with something else. She shook her head sadly. For a moment her expression looked so sincere in its sympathy it surprised Tiffany. "Tiffany Farrow," said Larisa sadly, "how much you have to learn. My friend, I don't want to fool or deceive you. Why should I? But I would like to tell you some truths that you're overlooking. You're only hurting yourself by not knowing them." She saw the wary look on Tiffany's face and added softly, "But if you're afraid to know the truth about Niki...."

"I'm not afraid!"

"Then let's go sit down, and I'll make some things very clear to you."

Tiffany was suspicious. She thought, *she just doesn't want me to stand here in the hall where Nikolai will see me when he comes out. She wants to stall until she has a chance to tell me her lies.* She was about to decide against listening to Larisa when the Russian woman said something that shook her up, making it impossible for her not to listen.

"You know about my baby," Larisa said in a soft but firm voice. "Do you also know about the other little boys and girls running around the world without a father, thanks to the irresponsible Nikolai Sharmonov?"

"That's not true!" Tiffany said with emotion. She realized as she said it that she was saying what she wanted to believe. She really had no evidence one way or the other.

"Please. Let's sit down. It'll take only a minute, and it may save you from making the same mistake many girls like you have unfortunately already made."

Tiffany wanted to protest but realized she had no real knowledge of Nikolai with which to dispute Larisa's words. She had thought that the letter from Zhukov had explained everything. Now she was no longer sure. She still distrusted Larisa and believed her own feelings about Nikolai, but when Larisa left the hall to go into an empty practice room, Tiffany followed.

Larisa sat down in one of the folding metal chairs near the wall. Tiffany remained standing.

"Let's start at the beginning," Larisa said. "You somehow found out that Niki is the father of my baby, and you've become indignant about how I'm using the child as leverage against Niki to achieve my selfish ends." She paused and let her eyes penetrate deeply into Tiffany's. "Dear," she said, "have you ever given any thought to what happens to the children of those girls who *aren't* strong enough to put some demands on Niki regarding his responsibility to his children?"

"I don't believe he has any other children," Tiffany said coolly. Her voice, though, betrayed her uncertainty.

"Well, I'm delighted you have such faith in human nature, but I must say, being a lovely girl, as you are, I'd think you would be much better served by a more realistic outlook." She touched her hand to Tiffany's arm and looked so sincere that it took all of Tiffany's willpower to remind herself that this woman was not to be trusted. "I don't want to hurt you," Larisa said. "But I do want you to know the truth. In Russia Niki has a reputation as what you Westerners call a Don Juan."

"I know about his reputation," Tiffany said. "But I don't believe it."

Larisa sipped at her paper cup of water, her eyes still focused on Tiffany. "You can see how handsome he is. You surely know the effect he has on the ladies. Are you aware that women actually throw themselves at him in public, or write their phone numbers on their unmentionables and have them delivered to his dressing room after performances?"

"That doesn't mean he takes them up on their offers."

"No," she admitted softly, "it doesn't." She looked down into her lap sadly, as if miserable over the pain Tiffany was letting herself in for by her inability to accept reality.

Tiffany folded her arms across her chest. She was suspicious of Larisa's look of sadness. She believed it to be phony and calculating. "You haven't told me a single thing yet that makes me distrust Nikolai," she said triumphantly. "Just because people say a man is a playboy doesn't mean he—"

"No, no, you're right. It doesn't mean he really is one." Larisa sighed deeply. Suddenly she declared in a surprisingly emotional voice, "Oh, if only I could make you see without having to tell you this, without having to tell you the real truth and hurt you as I know it will."

"I'm not afraid of you," Tiffany said. "Tell me whatever you want. I'll decide whether to believe it or not."

"This is going to wound you, and I don't want to do that, despite what you think of me, but I must.

I'm going to tell you something that will prove how well I know our friend Nikolai Sharmonov." She paused. "Without knowing anything about you except that you are so pretty and so naive, I tell you now, without any doubts whatever, that I know Niki made love to you." Her eyes were all-knowing suddenly and piercing. "He did, didn't he?"

Tiffany said nothing.

"You don't have to answer. I know the answer already. Because I know Niki." Her voice became harsher. "And I know how he eats up girls like you without the slightest scruple. Let me tell you how he did it, too, shall I?"

Tiffany could not speak, could not move. She felt frozen in place, wondering what Larisa would say next.

"He did it probably by...yes, I bet he used this one on you: I bet he told you he was a lonely orphan with no one to love him, no one to offer him any comfort. Was that it? That's one of his favorite— how do you Americans say—'lines.'"

Tiffany felt much more confident now. "No," she said with a hint of victory. "Nikolai is not the kind of man who would use a line like that."

"No? Then it must have been his other famous line, the one about how a KGB agent is watching, and if you don't let Niki take liberties with you, the agent will know your meeting is political and then Niki's life will be in danger."

Tiffany was shocked speechless.

"Of course, he would not try to make love to you right away with that one. First he would pretend for a while that he was not interested in loving you, to put you off guard." Larisa saw Tiffany's expression and added, "Do not feel too badly if you fell for that line. It only sounds as ridiculous as it really is when you look at it in the light of reason. But when your head is filled with romance and your eyes are filled with that *so* sincere blue-eyed look of his, it's hard to keep aware of how absurd the line really is."

How could she know about the incident with the KGB man in the park, Tiffany wondered agonizingly. Nikolai would never have told her. It was too personal. So how had she found out, unless it truly was a...a line that had been used before with other girls? Tiffany shut her eyes.

Larisa reached out a hand to touch her supportively. Tiffany jerked away. "Don't you touch me! I don't believe you! I don't believe any of your lies!"

Larisa hung her head. "Then there's nothing else I can say. Go to him. Go make even more of a fool of yourself over him than you already have. If you do confront him, though, don't let him avoid answering you by pretending rage. That's one of his favorite tricks."

Tiffany rushed out of the room. She had to get away from this horrid woman and her horrid lies. That's what they were, she was sure—lies!

She ran down the hall to the main theater and burst inside. She came in with such force that everyone stopped what they were doing to look at her. Nikolai was onstage with the corps, coaching them on the finer points of the particular movement they were rehearsing. The director was standing back, deferring to Nikolai. It was Nikolai's reputation that would be at stake during the performance of this ballet. Instead of falling back on the traditional choreography, which he had mastered, Nikolai had chosen to challenge himself with a much more demanding version of the ballet. It was the most difficult choreography he had ever danced, and the pressure on him was enormous.

Tiffany stopped just inside the door, disconcerted by all the eyes focused on her. Even the rehearsal pianist had stopped playing. Nikolai frowned at her.

After a moment of silence Nikolai said to the pianist, "Pick it up again. *One* two three, *one* two three." He emphasized the beat with his hand in the air. The pianist resumed playing; the dancers returned to their rehearsal.

Nikolai excused himself to the director and walked across the theater to Tiffany. "Yes?" he said to her coolly. "What is it you want?"

Tiffany was disturbed by his harsh look and tone of voice, but then she remembered their last meeting at the party. She had slapped him and declared she hated him. She had told him he was dirt beneath her feet. She had trampled on his emotions when he allowed himself to become vulnerable, asking her to trust him. What else could she expect from him now?

"Nikolai," she said quietly, wishing they were not in the same room with all those other people. "I'm so sorry about the way I acted at the party. I realize now that I was wrong, that I should have believed you."

His fists were on his hips. The anger in his eyes did not seem to lessen. "I no longer care what you believe," he said.

"Nikolai, I know about Dmitri. I know now why you had to keep your engagement secret from me and why you left me at the airport to go to...to Larisa."

Nikolai looked surprised. "I don't know how you found out these things, but it doesn't matter. After your words to me at the party I spent much energy and pain forcing myself to believe what you told me—that it was over, that you did not care for me. It was very hard, but I have finally accepted it."

"Well, don't accept it! How can you be so cold to me when I'm telling you I still love you?"

People were starting to stare. Nikolai glanced at the dancers, who had once again stopped dancing. Then he looked back at Tiffany. He took her by the arm and led her through the double doors at the rear of the theater till they stood on the sidewalk in the building's shadow.

His harsh expression had eased slightly but was still wary. He had been burned once, had convinced himself to stay away from fire and was now uncertain whether he should let himself be lured back to a situation where he might be burned again. When he spoke, his voice was almost, but not quite, friendly. "Is that what you came to tell me?"

"Yes," she said. She lowered her eyes. "And there's something else, too." She knew she should not say this, but Larisa's lies had had an undeniable impact. She had to ask him this question now, so that he could laugh at the lies to show how ridiculous they were.

"Nikolai, don't get angry, but I have to ask you this. Dmitri—he's your only child, isn't he?"

Nikolai exploded. "Don't get angry, you tell me? Don't get angry! And then you ask me something like *this*? How can you insult me in such a way?" Tiffany had never seen him in such a state. "Do you think I make love to every girl I see and have babies by them? Is that your very high opinion of me?"

"I didn't say that. I asked only if you had any other children." She was shaken but made up her mind not to be so intimidated by his rage that she would let the matter drop. "I have a right to know," she said.

There could be no doubt about it. Larisa's words had affected her more deeply than she realized. The fact was, she did have her doubts about Nikolai's honesty. Because...how could Larisa have known about that KGB "line" unless it truly was a line, unless Nikolai had used it before with other girls? Tiffany felt used and hurt and shamed.

"If I'm wrong in thinking of you this way," she said, "if you don't have any other children, all you have to do is tell me."

"Tell you?" he exploded. "Who are you to de-mand such an explanation from me?" He began gesturing agitatedly. Though his words were angry, it seemed as if he were talking to himself rather than her. "I fall in love with you—for the first time in my life I truly fall in love—and when I tell you how I feel, you slap me down. When I ask you to believe in me, to trust me, you revile me. And then, after I finally force myself to realize you don't care about me, after I finally succeed in convincing myself I will never see you again, you come here. And what do you do? You insult me! You accuse me of being a common playboy!"

"It needn't be an insult unless it's true!"

Nikolai slapped his hands to his forehead in frustration and raged, "What have I done to deserve such an opinion of my character?" He began cursing in Russian, as if cursing fate for the situation in which it had placed him.

Tiffany was so caught up in her own feelings now she could not bring herself to believe his denials. Instead she was beginning to believe the poison Larisa had planted in her mind.

"Nikolai," she plunged on, unable to stop herself from asking the fateful question. She had to know the answer; she just had to! "Was that man in the park in Hungary really a KGB man? Or did you just pretend he was, so you could take advantage of me?"

He stopped pacing. He stopped cursing himself in Russian. He stared at her, squinting, not really believing she had asked him that. For a long tense moment the world seemed to stop completely. He did not breathe. He did not move. He only stared at her.

Then his body seemed to deflate, and he sighed a long weary sigh. "Go," he said in a deathly quiet voice. "Leave me."

"So it is true!" she declared, overcome with pain. "You refuse to deny it! And the truth is, you never cared for me at all, did you? It was all just an act, so you could get the one thing you wanted from me—the only thing. And it worked! You got it!"

They stared at each other—in two different worlds.

Then she turned and ran, feeling sharper agony than she had ever in her life experienced. She ran down the street thinking only one thought: *I'll make him pay*. It was more than a thought; it was a burning obsession. *I'll make him pay if it's the last thing I do!*

CHAPTER SEVENTEEN

TIFFANY STORMED into the cutting room of Grayson Productions and went up to Mark Pernell, her film editor and audio technician. Mark was still busy working on the sequence sheet Tiffany had prepared, which showed the order the various scenes.

"Here, Mark, I brought you some new footage. You haven't seen this before. Look at it and tell me what you think."

Mark was sitting in front of his editing machine. He took the reel of film Tiffany handed him and walked over to the viewer on the other side of the room. He put the film in and looked at it in silence. Tiffany watched Mark's face and saw it light up, first with astonishment, then with professional appreciation. "This is a beaut," he said. "Isn't that Zhukov's great number that Sharmonov is doing here? The *Giselle* second-act solo?"

"That's right."

Mark whistled. "He's brilliant—this Sharmonov. No wonder he's becoming such a legend. This almost puts Zhukov to shame."

Tiffany wasn't surprised by Mark's reaction. He

was a balletomane and knew how to appreciate the art form. "Where would you want to insert it?" Tiffany asked.

He thought a moment, his hand under his chin. "Right before we show the troupe preparing to leave on its tour. Let the audience see what Sharmonov is capable of, so they'll know they're following a winner. That'll make it more exciting when they see the first two excerpts from his Hungarian performance right before he defects. They'll be rooting for him then."

"I think so, too. All right, loop it in. I'll revise my text for the narration to match it." She turned to go.

"Hey, Tiff."

She turned back.

"You had this footage all along and you're only now giving it to me? Why? You know this is the kind of stuff that can really make your film."

"You don't think maybe I just didn't realize how good it was?"

"Not you. Some of the other producers we've got running around this zoo of a film factory might have made that mistake, but not you."

"Did anyone ever tell you you're too darn perceptive for your own good?" She tried to force a smile but it didn't come. "Don't answer, Mark. Just loop it in."

Several days later Tiffany, Rolf Grayson, Mark and key members of the crew were seated in the darkened screening room, ready to view the rough cut of their documentary. The footage from the Zurich competition was all in. The competition had ended a week ago, with the Volgaya taking high, though not top, honors. All that remained to be shot was the stateside portion of the film, including Nikolai's upcoming premiere performance with the NBT.

The lights faded to darkness. Rolf spoke into the microphone connected to the projection booth behind them. "We're ready, Candy. Go ahead and roll it."

Suddenly the door burst open and slammed back against the wall. Standing in the doorway, silhouetted by the light from the hallway, was Nikolai. His legs were braced apart, his hands held low, clenched into fists. Tiffany would have recognized his lean, muscular form anywhere, even though his face was in darkness. The film began rolling now, and the illumination lighted up Nikolai's face. It was angry and seething; his nostrils were flared.

No one had invited him to this screening. Tiffany had let it leak out, that the screening was taking place, through Steve Dunhill, who had taken over filming of the NBT's rehearsals at Tiffany's request. Tiffany had also let it leak out that the documentary would include footage of Nikolai performing Zhukov's famous solo.

Rolf recognized Nikolai instantly. He saw the expression on the Russian's face, so he didn't bother attempting to shake his hand. "I'm Rolf Grayson, Mr.

Sharmonov," he said, standing. "We don't usually invite the subjects of our documentaries to view the roughs, but since you're here, you're welcome to stay."

Nikolai said nothing. He stalked in like an angry panther and sat down. His fingers gripped the sides of his seat as he glared at the screen.

"Candy," Rolf said into his microphone, "back that up for us, please, and roll it again."

The film was darked out, reversed, then run again from the beginning. The initial shots were of the ballet troupe as a whole, performing in various rehearsals. Next came shots of the lead performers—Nikolai and his ballerina, Boris Grechko and others. Interspersed during the next few scenes were intimate close-ups of the dancers talking to the off-camera interviewer, who was Tiffany.

Then came the footage that made Nikolai and Tiffany, seated apart, both go tense—Nikolai's variation of the *Giselle* solo. Tiffany observed Nikolai's face as he watched himself performing this piece on-screen. It was murderous. At the end of the sequence several crew members applauded. "Wonderful!" declared Mark Pernell. "A wonderful performance! I'm sure Serge Zhukov would be proud to see—"

"Shut up!" shouted Nikolai, leaping to his feet. The applause in the room died instantly. The film was stopped and the lights turned up. Nikolai came to where Tiffany sat and glared down at her.

Rolf, not knowing what the situation was but

sensing that Tiffany might be in danger, rose quickly and stood ready to take any action that might be required.

Tiffany looked up into Nikolai's eyes, which were burning in ferocious accusation. Her voice was cutting. "Did you think you were the only one who could lie to get what he wanted?"

Nikolai glared down at her as he towered over her. His fists were clenched in rage. His eyes were filled with the bitterness of betrayal. Finally he turned and stormed out of the screening room.

All eyes were on Tiffany now, including Rolf's. She stood up and left the room without a word to anyone.

In her mind's eye was the image of Nikolai's expression—an expression of betrayal and agony. She had done this deliberately to hurt him, to strike back at him for the hurt he had caused her. But now that she had done it, she didn't feel at all good about it. She felt cheapened, as if she had descended to a horrible petty level far beneath her.

SHE DIDN'T SEE Nikolai again. There was no doubt in her mind it was over between them. He had hurt her terribly. She had hurt him terribly. And there was no hope of reconciliation. Under no circumstances would she approach him, and she was certain he would not approach her now, either.

It was inevitable, Tiffany reflected, that the relationship had to end, since Nikolai was soon to marry. But it was too bad it had to end so savagely.

Nikolai spent his time now intensely locked in rehearsals with his new partner, Larisa, and his new company. The premiere was only a month and a half away, and the material he intended to perform was extremely difficult. A rumor drifted back to Tiffany via Steve Dunhill that Larisa was not considered good enough to perform as star ballerina and there was resentment within the company over her selection. Tiffany knew that NBT was a perfectionist company. Larisa would not be kept if she failed to meet its exacting standards, regardless of whatever ultimatum Nikolai might have given.

Tiffany spent her days putting the finishing touches to her documentary. There was much to do: supervising the insertion of "opticals," such as fade-outs and scene overlaps; rehearsing the announcer she had chosen to do the narration; overseeing the creation of the musical score and visual titles that would be appended to her film. She made a point of keeping very busy, filling up every free moment, so there would be no time to think—or feel.

After working on the film during the day, she spent several nights a week busily researching the new project Grayson had assigned to her. It involved filming a tribe of Inca descendants in Lima, Peru, and Tiffany would be a full producer again. She was glad the new project would take her far, far away from New York. She looked forward to the day of its start, which would be soon now. She had only to finish up her current work on the ballet film and add the footage from Nikolai's NBT debut when that occurred. Then she could begin the new project.

Dancing took on a new importance to Tiffany during this difficult period. Previously she had been in the habit of sneaking off to Midland Studios to dance two or three nights a week. Now she found she was going five nights a week. And on the nights she didn't go, she deliberately had to force herself to stay away. She needed the emotional and physical release of ballet. Her body craved the grueling physical exertion and the joy of performing a difficult piece absolutely perfectly. She realized her dancing was becoming an obsession, but there was nothing she could do about it. Some people turned to alcohol because they had a craving they could not fight. Some people turned to profligate love affairs. Tiffany had always loved and needed ballet—and now she needed it more than ever.

The nights she skulked away to the old nearly abandoned studio, to the practice room she had reserved, she kept telling herself this was only a temporary diversion for her, that it did not really mean anything significant in her life. She knew she was lying to herself, though. It was impossible not to see it. Ballet was in her blood, in her heart, in her soul. It was what she turned to for joy and gratification. It calmed her and put her at peace with herself. It was all she lived for now.

The time she spent dancing or working at the *barre* was the only time she felt truly alive. The music from the tape player suffused her body and soul; her lithe form merged with the music, and she lost herself to the rapture of her art. Then, afterward, she would go home to a life that seemed unbearably bleak and gray.

When the film was nearing its final stages, Tiffany made an international long-distance call to Serge Zhukov in the Soviet Union. She placed it through the overseas operator. Zhukov had earlier told her it was okay for her to use the *Giselle* sequence in her film, that he in fact gave her his blessing on it. But Tiffany wanted to check with him one last time to be absolutely sure before the film was finalized and could not be changed.

It took several minutes to make the connection. Even when she did get through, the line was broken by intermittent static. But the voice of Zhukov came through quite clearly, though a bit scratchily.

"Tiffany Farrow," he said in a delighted tone, "how good of you to call me. You brighten up my evening. It is evening over here, you know. It is—what—morning there in America?"

"Yes, Serge. I'm calling now because if I waited until later, I might wake you."

"You can wake me any time you like! How can I be of service to you?"

"Serge, my film is almost finished now, and I wanted to ask you again—one last time—if it's all right to use that sequence I have of Nikolai dancing your famous solo from *Giselle*."

"Yes, yes, yes! I want you to use it. I told that to you weeks ago when you called to ask if it was all right to give the piece to your film editor. The world needs to see how brilliant Nikolai truly is. And that piece is one of his best." His voice took on a warm tone as he asked, "Tell me, how is Nikolai? You know that he is like a son to me. The papers here, *Izvestia* and *Pravda*—they do not print any news of him."

"Nikolai is fine," Tiffany said, her voice hollow. "He's getting ready for his first performance in New York, and he's quite busy, but I'm certain he's doing very well."

"The two of you see each other often I'm sure. Is that not right?"

"Well, actually, Serge, he is quite busy with his rehearsals, and I'm spending a lot of time finishing my film. So...." Her voice trailed off. She did not like lying. She was not very good at it.

"Who is he partnering in his first performance?" Zhukov asked eagerly, anxious to know everything there was to know about Nikolai's ballet life in the West. "Is he partnering Makarova? She would be a brilliant match for him. Or maybe Natasha Panova?"

"No, not Makarova or Panova. Actually, his partner is Larisa Zamyatin."

There was a moment of silence on the line, filled only by the subdued static. It went on for so long that Tiffany began to wonder if the connection had been broken. "Serge? Are you still there?"

"Larisa," he said in a suddenly harsh tone. "She is not a good ballerina—certainly not one worthy of partnering Nikolai." He was upset. "How could this be? Do they not have any sense in the United States? How could they even put someone of the caliber of Nikolai Sharmonov, trained by me, Serge Zhukov, on the same stage with that floormaid of a ballerina?"

Tiffany did not know what to say.

"It must be more of her treachery and scheming," Zhukov said. "She is a brilliant schemer, probably one of the best in the entire world. I had experience with her lies myself. I was on the verge of having her expelled from the Volgaya when she got drift of it and decided to defect before I could do so. Let me give you advice, Tiffany Farrow, do not trust that woman; do not trust anything she says or does. She is more of an actress than Bernhardt and more malicious that Rasputin."

"Serge," Tiffany said slowly, "I heard Larisa say on a newscast that she and you were the closest of friends."

"Ha!" he laughed bitterly. "Friends? The woman is a witch! That letter I sent you—did you not read it? Did you not see the way she tried to twist Nikolai's arm into doing something that clearly was in her own interest and not in his? When I sent you that letter, I was hoping you might have been able to see from it the position Nikolai was in—and perhaps help him out of it."

"Serge, what could I possibly do? If he has a child, and if the child can be removed from a foster home only by a married couple, then he and Larisa must—"

"What is the matter, you do not like marriage?"

The question brought her up short and actually made her stutter momentarily. "I—I—Serge, I'm not the mother of the child."

"That makes a difference in the United States regarding adoption?"

She paused. "Well, to tell the truth, I don't really know. But that's beside the point. There is no question of marriage between Nikolai and me."

"Why not?"

"*Serge,*" she said, becoming flustered, "this is *not* what I called you to discuss."

There was a pause. Then, "I'm sorry. You're right, it is none of my business. I just hate to see a woman like Larisa have her way at Nikolai's expense."

Tiffany told him she understood his feelings, and she thanked him for the information he had given her. Then, after the conversation ended, she sat with her hand still on the phone, looking off into space.

So Larisa *was* a deceitful lying person, just as Tiffany had first thought. Even the woman's words about how she and Zhukov had got on so famously were lies. And if that were the case, how could Tiffany trust what she had told her about Nikolai?

Tiffany thought back, trying to recall exactly what

Larisa had said that made her so convinced she was telling the truth. There had been only one thing really—Larisa's mention of how Nikolai had a line about the KGB. Well, how else could she have known about it unless it truly were a line, unless it had been used by him so often with other girls that it had become a source of amusement among the insiders who knew him well? Certainly Nikolai would never have told Larisa about that incident in Városliget Park unless he truly was a reprehensible rake. It had to be a line; there seemed to be no other explanation. Unless....

Tiffany had a thought that made her sit bolt upright in her chair. *Unless....* Her eyes brightened at the possibility. She stood up and left for the State Department office where she had been debriefed after returning from Hungary.

CHAPTER EIGHTEEN

AARON ARONSON WAS SURPRISED when his secretary came in to tell him he had an unscheduled visitor who insisted on seeing him. He had only just arrived at his office and had not even had his morning coffee. He was even more surprised when his secretary told him who the visitor was.

He stood to receive Tiffany after telling his secretary to send her in. He was a businesslike man with horn-rimmed glasses. "I certainly never expected to see you again," he said cheerily, offering her a chair. "Though I'm not complaining. Anytime a beautiful woman wants to help me start out my day with brightened spirits, it's fine with me. Would you like some coffee?"

"Yes, that would be nice, Mr. Aronson. Thank you."

"Aaron," he corrected. "I'm only Mr. Aronson to bill collectors and solicitors."

Tiffany watched as he gave the order to his secretary. A moment later the tray arrived bearing the coffee service. Tiffany took hers black. "Aaron," she said when he was settled back with his cup, "I need some information. Can you tell me exactly what you do when you debrief someone?''

"Well, you were debriefed. Doesn't that tell you what you need to know?''

"No, I need information on how you debrief someone who's defected from Russia. I'm talking about Nikolai Sharmonov, as I'm sure you know.''

"Of course.''

"When I was debriefed it didn't last very long, and you didn't ask me many questions other than what the escape actually consisted of. But Nikolai's debriefing took a lot longer. I remember you scheduled two entire days for it.''

"It took longer because he's the one who defected. We needed all the information we could get from him about his situation in Russia and about everything leading up to the actual defection. Partly that was necessary in order to act on his request for political asylum. With you the debriefing was short because there was no concern over the issue of asylum. Also, you're already a citizen.''

"Can you tell me what he talked about during the debriefing?''

He shook his head. "I'd like to, but I really can't. A debriefing involving a defector from an iron-curtain country is strictly confidential. No one's even allowed into the room with the subject and the debriefer, except in rare cases, such as when a member of the immediate family, say, is needed to make the subject feel less nervous, more comfortable.''

"Immediate family? Is that the only exception?"

"Pretty much. In Sharmonov's case we bent the rules a little to let in that other dancer, Miss Zamyatin, who—"

"What? Larisa Zamyatin was in the room when Nikolai was being debriefed?"

Aronson looked surprised by Tiffany's strong reaction. "That's not so unusual," he said. "She's almost immediate family, after all. They're going to be married. You knew that, didn't you?"

"I knew they were going to be married, but I didn't know she was in the room with him."

"Why should that matter?" Aronson asked, leaning forward with interest. His face became businesslike. He seemed to sense that something relevant to the State Department might be involved.

"It's nothing that concerns politics," Tiffany said hastily to lessen his sudden interest. "It's strictly personal." She wanted to reassure him of this. The last thing she needed was for him to contact Nikolai to ask what Miss Tiffany Farrow had in mind when she was inquiring about his debriefing. "I just want to know... well, could you tell me how specific he was regarding events that led up to the defection?"

Aronson removed his glasses and pinched the bridge of his nose. Then he looked at her in a way different from the way he had earlier—a fatherly way. "Let me guess what you're trying to ascertain here. You want to know if he made mention of any personal relations between you and him that might have taken place during the planning of the defection in order to facilitate it.''

"Yes," Tiffany said shyly. "That's what I want to know."

"Well, I can't tell you specifically what he said— that would be a breach of security. I think I'm safe enough in telling you this, though: when I debrief a man, I insist that he be absolutely specific about any and all incidents relating to his defection." He saw that this did not answer Tiffany's question clearly enough. She still looked uncertain. "Let me put it this way," he added gently. "If a KGB man were involved, such as perhaps spying on him in a public park, I'd insist Sharmonov tell me all about it." He looked at her in a kind way. "Does that answer your question?"

"Yes," she said, feeling a bit embarrassed. "Thank you very much, Mr.—Aaron. You've been very helpful." She stood up to leave.

"Wait a minute. Let me tell you something else, too, just so you don't leave here with the wrong impression. Mr. Sharmonov did not volunteer that information we're speaking of. I had to drill it out of him. I just don't want you thinking he's the kind of guy who...kisses and tells. He most definitely is not. I had to put on my tough-guy act and actually threaten him with refusal of asylum before he agreed to talk about the matter."

"And Larisa Zamyatin was there in the room when he talked about it?"

"She was there. But I wouldn't worry about her blabbing, if I were you. She understands that her presence in the room was privileged and that everything said was strictly confidential. I made that clear to her when she came to me asking to be admitted to the debriefing. Also, she remembers my insistence on strict confidentiality from when I debriefed *her* two years ago."

"You were the one who debriefed her after her defection?"

Aronson nodded. "I've been in charge of the Soviet desk at this office for more than four years now." He smiled abstractedly at a dim memory. "You know, I was the one who suggested to her that she 'disappear' for a few months after her defection. I told her to keep a low profile, to stay out of the public eye. It's a good thing she did, too, because 'moral turpitude' is a valid reason for denying asylum, and an affair with a married American did not look good." He shrugged as though he realized he had said too much and intended to say no more.

Tiffany thanked him for his time. "You've been more help to me than you can imagine," she said. And it was true. As she traveled back to the Grayson Building, she reflected on what she had learned. Her heart was racing with excitement.

So that's how Larisa knew about the incident in the park, she thought. It wasn't because Nikolai had used a well-worn line. It was because Larisa had been right there in the debriefing room when Nikolai was forced to talk about it.

Oh, that bitch! Tiffany cursed. Serge had been so right about her.

As Tiffany watched the midmorning traffic through the taxi window, she reflected on something else she had learned from Aronson, something completely unexpected. Larisa had disappeared during that seven months following her defection not only so she could have her baby in secret, as Tiffany had assumed, but also because she was having an illicit affair with a married man.

Tiffany frowned at a sudden thought. How attractive could Larisa have been to a married philandering man while she was pregnant? Somehow it didn't seem to make much sense. Tiffany pondered this with such concentration that her temples began to throb. She massaged them as she sorted through a variety of seemingly unconnected thoughts: Larisa was a schemer and liar, capable of anything; her career had been on the skids before Nikolai defected; it was Nikolai's defection that had saved her; a truly ruthless woman would lie about almost anything to force a man to do what she wanted him to do.

"Here we are, lady," said the cabby. "The Grayson Building."

"I changed my mind, driver. Take me to the municipal office building on Lafayette Street—to the entrance nearest the office that handles papers relating to . . . to the placement of children in foster homes."

When she arrived at the building, she hoped she would not have to stand in a long line or spend half the day here trying to find the information she wanted. There were crowds of people everywhere, and most of the offices she went past had lines at least fifteen people long. When she reached the particular office she wanted, after being directed by a security guard, she was pleased to find there were only a few people there and that the office was not very large.

She saw all this at a glance while looking through the plate-glass front of the office from the corridor outside it. When she entered and looked around more closely, she saw something that surprised her greatly—or rather, she first heard something that surprised her greatly. Then, looking toward the counter the voice was coming from, she saw Nikolai Sharmonov standing there, his fingers half-clenched rigidly. He was speaking in an angry demanding tone to the clerk behind the counter. Other people in the office were staring at him.

"Don't you understand?" he was asking, the tone of his words more like a curse than a question. "This is my child we're talking about! I have every right to inquire about my child. My flesh and blood, do you hear me? My very own son!"

The clerk was a silver-haired, middle-aged woman who looked shaken but stubborn and confident in the bureaucratic correctness of her position. She spoke quietly, hoping to make Nikolai lower his own voice by example. "I'm sorry, sir, but that's the law. Since you are not the person who put the child into the foster home, who formally signed the papers, then you must show me some proof that you are the child's father. Otherwise I can't—"

"For the love of God, woman, what sort of proof *is* there of such a thing?"

Tiffany was paralyzed, standing by the door. She did not know what to do. Her first thought was to leave quickly before Nikolai could turn and see her. Some instinct made her remain, though.

"If I bring in the child's mother," Nikolai railed at the woman, "she would tell you I am the father! But she won't come! She tells me she wishes to work through a lawyer, instead of coming here with me!"

"Sir, would you kindly lower your voice," the woman said nervously.

Nikolai was about to respond with a barrage of invective, Tiffany was sure, seeing the way his back and the back of his neck tensed at the request. The woman's supervisor came over, however, and said brusquely, "If you can't keep a civil tone in this office, I'll have to have the security guard remove you. You've been coming here almost every day for the past week now, and though I can't stop you from coming, I can stop you from abusing my clerks." He glared at Nikolai to show he meant business.

Tiffany could see the back of Nikolai's neck turning red. She knew what torment he must be going through, and she also knew that if he continued in this way, he would never obtain the information he wanted. She quickly moved forward and put her hand on his arm. He jerked his head to look at her. She said nothing to him, just kept her hand on his arm in what she hoped he would take as a reassuring way, while she addressed the supervisor.

"I'm a member of the media. I realize you don't recognize this man, but I want to tell you that he's an internationally known celebrity. Our government has gone to great efforts to make him comfortable here. I apologize to you for his losing his temper—" she glanced at Nikolai and saw him tense angrily at having her apologize for him "—but I'm sure you can understand his emotional state. We'll be quieter now, but we would appreciate it if you'd help with this matter. It's very important to him." She didn't really even know what it was.

The glares leveled at Tiffany were of very different natures. Nikolai was looking at her with anger for apologizing for him when he thought he was entirely in the right, though at the same time he seemed to realize that her stepping in for him this way was something he needed. He would probably fail in his purpose if left to his anger and his own devices, whereas Tiffany might save the day for him.

The clerk and her supervisor were glaring at Tiffany with resentment but also curiosity as to whether she really was someone they should take seriously as representing this angry domineering man, who also might be someone they should take seriously.

"If you have any doubts about our government's desire to treat Mr. Sharmonov with the utmost courtesy," Tiffany said, "I suggest you call Mr. Aronson at the State Department." She paused, seeing the two officials look impressed but still suspicious. "You may have a hard time getting through his secretary—he's quite a highly placed officer—but if you tell them it's concerning Nikolai Sharmonov, I'm sure he'll talk to you."

She glanced at Nikolai to see how he was taking her interference now. He was still hostile and chafing under the collar but was perceptive enough to remain quiet. Despite his harsh feelings about her he seemed to realize that if he wanted to succeed in his purpose, Tiffany's approach was more likely to win favor than his own.

The supervisor said to Nikolai and Tiffany, "Stay here, please." Though he said please, his voice was anything but courteous. Then he disappeared into a back office.

The clerk stood there looking uncertain. Tiffany led Nikolai away from the counter over to the side wall, where they would be less conspicuously the point of attention for the entire room. Gradually the people in the office returned to their own business.

Nikolai was breathing through flared nostrils, angry, but keeping himself in check. "I suppose you expect me to thank you."

"I expect nothing from you, nothing at all."

"Why are you attempting to help me?"

"I'd do the same for anyone who was too pigheaded to behave in a civilized way that would get them the information they wanted."

He didn't fly into a temper tantrum at this, as she had expected. His reaction was subdued. "Pigheaded, am I? You tell me *I* am pigheaded? From you that is a compliment."

"What is it you came here to find out?" she risked asking, seeing that his hostility toward her seemed a bit diminished. He might still be angry with her, but, for the moment at least, a truce seemed to be in effect.

"About my son. I came to find out about Dmitri."

"What do you need to know that Larisa can't tell you?"

His eyes narrowed. "Do not speak to me of that woman." He looked disgusted. He ran his hand frustratedly through his thick mane of golden hair. His disgust seemed to overcome him now, and he seemed on the verge of walking away from Tiffany.

"Nikolai, I know you and I aren't on the best of terms. But if you let me, I may be able to help you get the information you want."

"I know how you help people. You help them by promising one thing and doing another."

She looked him in the eye. "I'm sorry I included that film footage of you dancing Zhukov's famous solo. It was wrong of me to do so."

"And you'll take it out then?"

"Yes. I'll take it out. It won't be in the final cut."

He looked surprised, but then he grunted in acknowledgment, seemingly appeased.

"And if you'll let me, I may be able to help you get the information you came here for. You don't seem to be getting on too famously with the clerks in this office."

"I am not good at dealing with people like these," he admitted grudgingly. "I lose my temper." His face took on a pained look. He clearly did not want to show his vulnerability to Tiffany, but his feelings were bursting inside him and had to get out. "Don't they realize," he declared in an emotional voice, "they're speaking of my *son*? My *child*? I only wish to have him, to love him, to be near him, to save him from the bad foster home Larisa tells me he is in. That's why I came all the way from Russia, why I risked my life defecting."

Tiffany's eyes showed her sympathy.

Seeing her supportive gentle look, Nikolai continued despite himself. "I love children," he said quietly. "All my life I've loved children and wanted to be a good father. Larisa is not the woman I would have chosen as my wife, but when she told me she was pregnant, I asked her to marry me." His expression became bitter. "She said no. She defected to the United States. For two years I hardly heard from her. Then out of the blue she sends a letter saying Dimi is in a foster home being treated badly and that he needs me. So I come.

"And what happens *now*?" he nearly shouted, his

helpless rage bursting through to the surface. "She tells me I cannot see Dimi! She tells me to wait! She says that a lawyer is working on the problem, that it will take months and that if I act on my own I'll only make the situation worse." He dismissed her words with a sharp swipe of his hand. "I am fed up waiting! Dimi is my child! If he needs me, I must help him!"

Tiffany was touched. This was a loving caring side of him that she had seen only briefly—only that one night on the riverbank, before...before the horror had started.

"Nikolai," she said gently, "I'll be honest with you. I don't know whether there's any way you can have your son back if Larisa prefers to work through an attorney and won't come down to attest that you're the father. The law may be against you. But I can help you find out what the situation is with your son and whether there's any chance of your getting custody of him."

"Can you help me see if he's all right, if he's in a good home?"

"I think so. This is the first step—inquiring here to see what happened to him after Larisa put him up for placement. The next step is for you to get yourself a good lawyer who specializes in this field. Rolf knows lawyers; he can tell you who's the very best man to help you."

"Thank you," he said formally, with dignity. "I'm grateful for your help."

"I...I want to help you," she said.

"And I want to do something for you, too."

"That's not necessary."

"Here is what I want to do for you. I want to make you confront your mother and return to ballet."

"*What?*"

"I can see how it pains you to be away from ballet. From that night I saw you dancing alone, I could tell how greatly you love dance. And you have such talent, such rare skill. It is sacrilege that you should waste it by—"

"We won't talk of this," she said, a chill emanating from her like a gust of cold wind. "I told you that when you brought it up the first time."

"You're doing something for me. I want to do something for you. I want to make you see how greatly you need dance and make you confront your mother so that—"

"I said we won't talk of this!" She glared at him. There was no topic closer to her heart. She could not be rational about it. She reverted to a defensive animal each time she came up against the issue.

Seeing how upset Tiffany had become, Nikolai sighed and shrugged. He leaned back against the wall, signaling that he would keep his silence.

Tiffany was still so upset it took her a long time to calm down. They stood against the wall, neither of them speaking. Their fragile truce seemed to have been shattered.

Finally the supervisor returned to the counter from

a rear private office and indicated for them to come forward.

"I'm sorry if I was a bit abrupt with you, Mr. Sharmonov," he said. "I didn't realize you were—"

"Just tell me about my child," Nikolai cut in.

"Well, the fact of the matter is, I'm still not officially authorized to divulge information relating to the placement of a foster child. But I can tell you unofficially, of course... and I do hope you'll appreciate that I'm doing you a favor by revealing this...."

"Get on with it!" Nikolai roared. "Tell me!"

The man looked flustered. "The fact is, our records do not show any child put into a foster home by the woman whose name you gave me."

Nikolai looked startled.

"Your records—" asked Tiffany, "they're for Manhattan only, aren't they?"

"No, they're for the five boroughs. There is no record of any child put up for placement by a Larisa Zamyatin at any agency in New York City."

Tiffany and Nikolai both seemed to be thinking the same thought. Nikolai's eyes narrowed dangerously, and Tiffany put a restraining hand on his arm. "This doesn't mean she lied to you. She could have put the baby into a foster home outside of New York City. That's possible."

He said nothing; his expression was seething. He knew Larisa far better than Tiffany. He seemed to realize now, for the first time, what depths of deceit she was truly capable of.

"Don't jump to any conclusions," Tiffany warned. "We should look into this further before you—"

He jerked his arm free and glared at her, but he did not seem even to recognize her. He looked at her as if she were a stranger, then through her as if she did not exist at all. His face turned red and his jaw began trembling.

Tiffany frowned with helplessness. She had never seen him this way before; he seemed capable of almost anything. She watched him swivel sharply on his heel and storm out of the office.

For the first time since she had known him, Tiffany was truly frightened. The look on his face had been murderous. She knew where he was going—to find Larisa.

Tiffany was in a terrible dilemma. She knew she should call Larisa at the theater to warn her so she could avoid Nikolai until his temper cooled down. This was not only for Larisa's sake, but for Nikolai's, as well. But Tiffany also knew that if she meddled in this affair at the moment, Nikolai might never forgive her. He might hate her to his dying day. Now that his relationship with Larisa was clearly about to end, there was the possibility that Nikolai might in time come to think of Tiffany in a more tender light. She didn't want to do anything to make him hate her—not at present, when she was on the verge of having a second chance.

What could she do? She clenched her fists in

anguish and grimaced tightly. *I won't do it,* she told herself. *I have no business meddling in his affairs. Besides, maybe I'm being overly dramatic. I'm probably blowing his anger way out of proportion.*

"Well, can you beat that," muttered the silver-haired clerk in astonishment, staring at the empty doorway where Nikolai had passed. "I sure wouldn't get in *his* way right now."

"That fellow is going to kill someone," said the supervisor grimly, shaking his head.

Tiffany frowned in helpless dismay. She turned to the supervisor. "Where's the nearest telephone?" she demanded.

LARISA WAS AT THE THEATER rehearsing. It took several minutes for her to come on the line. Tiffany drummed her fingers on the side of the telephone booth, sick with anticipation. Finally the woman came to the phone.

"Larisa, this is Tiffany Farrow. I have something important to tell you. You have to get out of there. Nikolai is on his way over, and he's...he's not in control of himself."

"Whatever do you mean?" Larisa said blithely, infuriating Tiffany with her studied nonchalance.

"He's crazy with hurt, Larisa. And...and he *knows.*"

Larisa's voice lost some of its self-assurance. It seemed to waver for an instant. "I'm sure I don't know what you're talking about," she said. "He knows what?"

Though Tiffany was reeling with tension, she had her wits about her. She decided to try a gambit. She needed to find out the truth, so she pretended to know it already. "He knows you never had a child," Tiffany said. "He knows it was all a ruse, a scheme!" She said it as if she knew these things were so, which she really did not. She waited for Larisa's reaction.

There was a long pause. Then, in an almost hysterical voice, Larisa blurted out, "How can he know? How did he find out?"

Tiffany shut her eyes. So it was true after all. "Never mind that. Just get out of there. He knows, and he's coming after you."

Larisa seemed to realize she had betrayed too much. Tiffany had caught her by surprise, and Larisa had reacted out of hysteria, not thinking. Now it was too late to retract her admission. All she could do was say in a nasty voice, "I'm sure you had a hand in this. I'll make you pay, you bitch!" Then she hung up.

CHAPTER NINETEEN

BY THE TIME Tiffany had reached the ballet theater, the fireworks were over. She could tell from the stunned, almost traumatized looks of the people who had witnessed the scene that it had been explosive indeed. It had ended only minutes ago, just before Tiffany had arrived.

"Well, what *happened*?" she asked Steve Dunhill, who had been there filming the rehearsal and had witnessed the scene.

Steve took her outside into the hall, where he could get a needed cup of coffee from the vending machine while he talked. He seemed shaken up. "It was awful," he said. "That Larisa—what a she-demon."

"She was here when Nikolai came in?"

"I know you called to warn her, but your warning didn't do any good. It only made her realize she had no chance of salvaging the situation. So she made up her mind to cause as much damage as she could. She knew it was her. . . well, her last stand, so to speak."

He took a swallow of the black coffee. "Sharmonov stormed in like a madman and demanded to know the truth about his child. This was a revelation to all of us in the theater. No one even knew he had a child—or thought he had one, to be more accurate, since as it turns out he doesn't.''

"Larisa told him that?"

" 'Told' is not the word. She practically branded him alive with the information. She glared at him with sadistic glee and told him he was a fool. She said she thought she really was pregnant in Russia. But then, after defecting, she learned the pregnancy had been a false alarm. She saw no reason to tell him this, though. She's clearly resentful of his talent and of the fact that he's getting one hundred times the recognition she is. She told him that when he received the promotion to *danseur noble*, she realized she could use him to get the roles and acclaim she says she deserves. And if he was naively trusting enough to believe her story about the child in the foster home, then he deserved everything he got.''

Tiffany could understand why the dancers she had just seen appeared to be in a state of shock. She herself felt traumatized just hearing about what had happened. "My God," she whispered, "I knew she was a horrid person, but how could she be so cruel?"

"Insane jealousy, which evidently she's harbored for years. Cruel is not the word. She deliberately taunted him, enjoying watching how her words hurt him.''

"What did he do?" Tiffany asked in a whisper, almost afraid to find out.

"He almost murdered her—that's what he did. He

stood there seething and fuming, and then his hands went for her throat. All of us were so flabbergasted we couldn't even move to stop him. It all happened too fast. Larisa didn't even try to stop him; she just stood there laughing at him, intentionally provoking him."

"*Provoking* him?" Tiffany said in amazement.

"She had nothing to lose at that point. She knew her career was over. The NBT wouldn't have had anything to do with her in the first place if not for Sharmonov's insistence. And they were about to drop her anyway. She's not good enough to be in a first-rate company. So she figured that as long as she was going down, she'd take him with her." He winced at the recollection. "Finally Sharmonov came to his senses. It was her laughing at him that did it. He realized what she was trying to do. He stood there trembling for a moment, looking like a wounded animal. Then he released her and ran out of the theater."

NIKOLAI DISAPPEARED. For five days no one saw or heard from him. It was as if he had vanished off the face of the earth.

Tiffany was deeply concerned. After trying to locate him through the usual channels, she decided to ask Steve if he knew anything about his whereabouts. She suspected he might. Though the two men were not close, they had been on friendly speaking terms and had gone out for drinks once or twice.

"I do know where he is," Steve admitted, "but I'm not sure I should tell you. The fact is, he's in no condition to be dealing with people. He even told me as much. That's why he went into hiding—so he wouldn't have to deal with anyone while he's in such a state."

"I understand what you're saying, Steve, but what I'm thinking is this: even though he doesn't want to see anyone right now, maybe he *needs* to." What she was really thinking was that maybe he needed her right now. How he must be suffering.

Steve was a perceptive man. He sensed that Tiffany had been close to Nikolai once, though he was not certain of the nature of their closeness. He frowned for a long moment, then said with grave reservations, "If it were anyone else, I wouldn't tell them, but I will tell you. He's on the sailboat I keep out at pier eighty-three on the Hudson." He told her how to recognize it and where it was located.

Tiffany thanked him and left. Even then she did not know if she should go to Nikolai. After all, he clearly wanted to be alone. What right did she have to impose herself on him when he obviously did not want her? She debated the situation in her mind. The deciding factor turned out to be her realization that if he had been a possible danger to Larisa earlier, he could well be a danger to himself now, he could well have turned his violence and sorrow and rage inward.

She had to go see him. She would just check up on him, and if he didn't want her, she would leave. But at least she had to try to see him, in case he needed her. She left for the sailboat just after sundown.

When she arrived, there was no sign of life aboard. The boat was quite large and was tied up to the dock, which was deserted. Tiffany stood at the edge of the boardwalk, a bag of groceries in her arms.

"Nikolai?" she called out. There was no answer, no movement aboard the boat. "Nikolai? It's me, Tiffany."

Still no answer. The water rocked the boat gently. Tiffany pursed her lips and stood silently for a moment. Then she stepped up onto the deck and walked along to the cabin. The door was open; she stood outside it and looked in.

Nikolai was seated at the butcher-block table, leaning on his elbows, running his fingers through his disheveled hair. A growth of stubble beard five-days old adorned his face. His eyes looked bloodshot. He was bare-chested and barefoot, wearing only bell-bottomed white nautical pants. On the table before him was a ceramic mug and a half-empty bottle of Stolichnaya vodka. Nikolai looked at her in the doorway, made no expression or sign of interest, turned back to the ceramic mug. He raised it to his lips and took several swallows.

Tiffany came in. She looked for the kitchen part of the cabin. One corner of the room had a sink and small refrigerator and a propane-gas stove. She put her grocery bag on the countertop. "I brought you some things," she said, taking them out of the bag.

She put the fresh fruits and vegetables in the refrigerator, along with the two top-sirloin steaks she had brought. The refrigerator was practically empty, except for a torn remnant of a loaf of bread and some crusty cheese. She threw these out.

She had brought a jar of instant coffee. She put some in two mugs and boiled water in a pan on the stove—there was no pot. Then she carried the two mugs of steaming coffee to the table and set them down. She took a seat opposite him. He glanced at her and turned halfway silently.

"Oh, Nikolai," she said. "I'm so sorry."

"Are you? About what?"

She did not answer. There could be no doubt about what she was speaking of.

He laughed an unhappy laugh and rubbed the back of his neck with his hand. His neck was thickly corded with tension. "We say in Russia, *Ti ni emeech nichego, potomu chio nichego ni hochech.* 'You can't have something, therefore you don't want it.' It was meant to apply to the shortage of consumer goods, but it applies equally well to life in general."

He laughed that tortured laugh again. Tiffany's heart went out to him. "You know," he said, not looking at her, "I've always wanted children. I love children. I fell in love with my child, a child I never saw. I looked forward to being a good father to my child. But now...no child. The child is a figment of a scheming female imagination."

Tiffany did not know what to say. She reached out

and touched his hand, which lay lifelessly on the table. When he did not withdraw it, she squeezed it supportively.

For a moment he did not move, just continued staring off at the wall. Then he came alive. He stood up and began pacing about the cabin, gesturing animatedly. "Well, why should I care, eh? Why should Nikolai Sharmonov be unhappy?" He tried to grin but failed. "I'm a happy bachelor once more—carefree, living the good life in New York City. Yes? Is it not so?"

She did not answer. She held out the cup of coffee to him. "Would you like—"

He slapped it out of her hand, sending it hurtling across the room, smashing into pieces against the wall. "I do not want any damn coffee! I do not want any damn sympathy! You think I need sympathy? You think I'm not strong enough to bear this thing that happened to me? You think I'm weak and sensitive?"

"I don't think you're weak. You don't have to be weak to be sensitive. It's one of your strong points that you're a... a sensitive man, who—"

"I'm not sensitive!" he declared, his eyes fiery. "I don't care about children, about tenderness, about anything! I'll show you what I care about—all I care about!" He came around the table in a flash of movement and raised Tiffany to her feet. He embraced her and tried to kiss her. Vodka was on his breath.

She turned her head to the side, grimacing.

"What's the matter? You don't like being kissed by Nikolai Sharmonov?"

"Not like this I don't. Not when you're only trying to prove something to yourself."

"You don't like this? Don't lie to me. You like it. . . you want it." He grasped her chin and forcibly turned her face back to his. His lips descended on hers crushingly as he embraced her. She struggled against him. Her effort was in vain; he was far too strong for her. So she did the only thing she could do. She bit his lip.

"Ow!" He grimaced and jerked his head back. Then he glared at her.

"Let me go," she said.

"You think I need you? You think I love you, maybe? You think Nikolai Sharmonov needs anyone? Loves anyone? Never! I do not need! I do not love! This is not the world for love. Love becomes pain."

She tried to push away from him, but he held her tightly. "It doesn't have to be that way, Nikolai. It just seems that way now, while you're hurting so badly. But you said you. . . loved once before. It can be—"

"Ha!" he exclaimed, the drink and the pain pushing him over the brink, turning him into a different person—a person so deeply hurt that all he could think of doing was hurting back. "You're speaking of the time I told you I loved you? You believed me? I don't love you! All I want from you is this!" He grasped her breast.

"No!" she cried, shaking her head. "No, it's not true!"

"I don't need you. I don't love you." He spoke slowly, as if trying to convince himself. "Nikolai Sharmonov does not...need...or love...anyone." Then, to convince himself further, he declared drunkenly, "*This* is all I ever wanted from you!" And he tore at her blouse, ripping it open.

Tiffany went wild. She slapped him with all her might and scratched at him. She tried to shove herself away. "It's not true. It's not true!" she cried. He released her, and she staggered backward, tears in her eyes. She was breathing in ragged gasps.

It was the tears that seemed to bring him to his senses. He stared at them, and a look of tenderness slowly came over him. It was as if he had just now come out of a trance and was himself again, the person he had been before Larisa's horrible admission had turned him into a tortured animal. Tiffany was crying, shaking her head from side to side in desperate denial of what he had said. His words had pierced her to her very heart. Nikolai looked tormented seeing her pain, realizing he had caused it. He came forward and put his fingertips to her cheek.

Tiffany slapped his hand away and rushed past him out of the cabin. She ran down the deck, then over the plank onto the pier. Behind her Nikolai lurched out of the cabin onto the deck. "Tiffany!" he called after her desperately. *"Tiffany!"*

She ran without thinking, blinded with pain. She did not know where she was going. She found herself in a taxi. Moments later she found herself at Rolf Grayson's penthouse apartment, banging on the quilted leather door.

When Grayson opened the door and saw her emotional state, he frowned in shocked bewilderment. He stood straight and tall in his embroidered, silken, Oriental smoking jacket. "What is it?" he demanded. "What's happened?"

"Oh, Rolf," she cried, rushing to him, throwing her arms around him. "You care about me? You care about me, don't you?"

His arms closed around her protectively as she cried against his chest. "You know I do. You know I've always cared about you."

"You don't think I'm someone who could...who could never be loved?"

He put his hands to her small shoulders and pushed her away from him slightly, so that he could look at her. He saw the way the front of her blouse was torn and the way the tears were streaming down her face. Strands of her disheveled hair were wet and plastered to her face. "Who did this to you?" he asked. "Tell me who did this and I'll kill him."

"Rolf," she cried, reeling, "I need someone to care about me, to love me. I need someone strong who will...will...."

"Hush," he said, putting his finger to her lips. "We'll talk of this later. Meantime, you have to lie down and rest. I want to make sure you're all right." He put his arm beneath the back of her knees and lifted her up. He carried her inside, kicking the door closed with his foot, across the living room toward the bedroom. Tiffany noticed his butler looking concerned and agitated. "Lee," Rolf said, "get some brandy. Warm it and bring it in."

"Yes, Mr. Grayson."

Rolf carried her into his spacious bedroom and laid her on the enormous bed. He took a blanket from the closet and snapped it open in the air, letting it settle over her. Then he sat down on the side of the bed and took her hands in his. "You'll be all right, Tiffany; you're safe here."

"Oh, Rolf." She moved his hands to her cheek and let his fingers brush against her skin. "Rolf, you asked me to marry you once. Does that offer still stand?"

"You're not yourself now. We'll speak of it in the morning."

"Now! I want to know now!"

He seemed wary and, for the first time in as long as she had known him, vulnerable. "Tiffany, you're not teasing me?"

"I'd never do that to you."

His aristocratic face was not very good at showing emotion. But now, though his face was set and strong, there was a glimmer of feeling in his gray eyes. "My darling," he said, "I love you. You must know that. I love you now. I'll love you tomorrow. I can't imagine ever not loving you. Yes, I still want to marry you. I want it more than I've ever wanted anything."

She put her hand to the back of his neck and pulled his head down. She kissed him on the lips.

When Rolf's butler came in a moment later, carrying the warm brandy in a cup on a tray, Tiffany was lying with her cheek on the pillow, her eyes closed, pretending to be asleep. Grayson stood up from the bed and said in a low voice, "Never mind, Lee. We'll let her sleep for a while."

Tiffany heard footsteps on the carpet, then the door was softly closing. She opened her eyes and looked around the luxurious bedroom. *My bedroom*, she thought, testing out the notion. It was not what she had ever thought she wanted. But . . . .

How do I know what I want? she asked herself. Maybe this was what she had wanted secretly. Maybe this was what she needed. She didn't know. All she was sure of was that she had taken an irrevocable step and there could be no turning back.

She shut her eyes and prayed sleep would come quickly.

CHAPTER TWENTY

ROLF WANTED to make a surprise announcement of their engagement at an elaborate society ball he would give in Tiffany's honor. Tiffany was not keen on the idea. She preferred to play down their engagement as much as possible. Seeing how proud Rolf was of their impending marriage, however, she consented to let him announce it in any way he chose.

As it turned out, word of the purpose for the ball somehow leaked out in advance of the ball itself, dismaying Rolf. He couldn't understand how word had got out. He had told no one about the engagement except his social secretary, who was absolutely discreet. And Tiffany had told no one but her mother.

"Never mind, darling," Rolf said to her as they met for dinner the evening the news broke. "I don't suppose it was possible to keep news like this secret for very long."

"I don't know how the reporters found out," Tiffany said. "All at once, this afternoon, they appeared like a plague, falling all over themselves to interview me, to snap pictures, to ask if the rumor was true. I refused to talk to any of them until I talked to you first.''

"You did the right thing. They'd have been descending on me, too, if I hadn't been thirty thousand feet in the air at the time, flying back from that meeting on the West Coast." He smiled at her. "It doesn't matter that much whether we formally announce the engagement at the party or a little bit earlier. I'll have my secretary confirm it to the reporters first thing in the morning."

"Whatever you wish, Rolf."

He took her hand. "If you think you were deluged by reporters today, when they didn't even know if the rumor was true, you just wait until they get the confirmation. I have a feeling you won't be able to walk ten paces without stumbling over a reporter or two."

Tiffany thought he was exaggerating. She was totally unprepared for the tumultuous nonstop attention she received following Rolf's corroboration of their engagement. The news was not only carried on the society pages but also prominently featured on the news pages of the *New York Times,* the *Washington Post* and other major journals. Rolf Grayson was one of the nation's most powerful media giants, and when he decided to marry, it was news.

Reporters, gossip columnists, even film crews from the TV networks descended on Tiffany in droves. Paparazzi—celebrity-seeking photographers— dogged her every footstep. Though Tiffany took pains to avoid them, it got so that she could not even leave her apartment building for work without having to run a gauntlet on the way to her taxi. Rolf solved this problem by sending around a limousine to pick her up in the morning and take her home again at night. Later he put the limousine and driver at her complete disposal.

To the paparazzi and society-page journalists, Tiffany was a godsend. It would have been fine enough for them if Rolf Grayson's fiancée had turned out to be merely pretty and just a step above dull, but having her beautiful, intelligent and already newsworthy, as well, was like a dream come true. They had a field day with Tiffany, exploiting their readers' interest in her to the fullest extent possible. She found herself on the cover of two of the national celebrity magazines and even in the People section of *Time* magazine. Her telephone never stopped ringing. Finally she had it disconnected and installed a new line for her friends and business associates.

Rolf wanted her to give up her apartment and move into a suite of rooms he would secure for her in the building where he lived. Tiffany thanked him for his thoughtfulness, but told him she would rather not. "The wedding is only three months off," she said. "I'll move into your penthouse then, or we'll move out to your home on Long Island. But in the meantime, I think I'd like to stay where I am."

Rolf saw no purpose in her being so far from him, especially since they were getting together for dinner almost every other evening, but he didn't press the matter. The announcement ball was only a few days off, and after that it would be just a short time before they were married.

When the day of the ball arrived, Tiffany was nervous. She was not a stranger to society functions. Over the years she had dated a variety of celebrated and powerful men who had escorted her to almost every sort of social function imaginable. Never, though, had she herself been the star attraction.

She dressed very carefully in a de la Renta gown of emerald chiffon. It fit her figure and had an only moderately daring neckline. The simplicity of the gown set off the strikingness of her flowing hair. Her vivid green eyes gleamed brightly, accented by the color of the dress.

Her mother had wanted her to wear a gown more flamboyant and revealing, but Tiffany felt that a conservative approach would suit her better tonight. She had an important role to play now. She was no longer responsible only to herself. Now she was Rolf Grayson's fiancée, the woman he would present to the world as his wife. Besides, thought Tiffany, as she viewed herself in the full-length mirror of her bedroom, though the gown was not in itself very revealing, the slinky material did little to hide her firm rounded bustline and slender but curvaceous figure. No male at the ball would look at her without being envious of Rolf, she knew.

Rolf was wearing a trimly tailored tuxedo when he arrived to pick her up, and he looked extremely dashing. During the ride to the St. Regis-Sheraton, where the ball was to be held, Rolf produced a blue velvet-covered case the size of a long billfold and handed it to her.

"I know it's traditional to give you a ring on an occasion like this," Rolf said, "but if I gave you a ring that really expressed my feelings for you, there wouldn't be anything I could do for an encore. There's only one ring worthy enough of being offered to you. Now I can give it to you at our wedding. Meantime, I hope you won't object to a minor trinket like this for an engagement gift."

Tiffany opened the royal-blue case. For a moment she was speechless. Inside, sparkling with reflected light, was the most gorgeous necklace she had ever seen. It consisted of four rows of shimmering diamonds laid closely together, bordered on the top and bottom by a row of lilac kunzite gemstones. The mountings were invisible, making the necklace appear to be a wide strip of brilliant rainbow-colored light.

Rolf removed it from its velvet case and put it around Tiffany's neck. He undid the opal necklace she had been wearing and put it into the case.

"Oh, Rolf," she said, looking at him with affection and kissing him tenderly.

"I love you, Tiffany," he said, his expression overpowering.

"I...I...." She could not say the words back to him. She kissed him again instead. Then they rode in silence to the ball.

When they arrived, they were besieged by well-wishers as they moved across the marble floor. A small orchestra was playing, and couples were dancing. The St. Regis's ballroom was one of the most extravagant in New York, a bastion of Old World wealth and rococo elegance. Several hundred persons were in attendance now, having come to pay tribute to Rolf.

Tiffany recognized some of them. Since Rolf owned companies prominent in the communications industry, it was natural that many of their guests were well-known media figures. There were also several congressmen present, along with major industrialists and business leaders. A sprinkling of top military men had come, too, in formal dress uniforms far more flamboyant than the uniforms one saw them wear normally. The women at the party wore lovely gowns aglitter with jewels. Tiffany's mother was present, looking regal and aristocratic in an Edwardian-style gown.

The atmosphere was so heady Tiffany could not help but be buoyed by it. People were coming up to her and congratulating her, smiling at her, openly admiring her. It was a rarefied world of the rich and powerful she was entering now, and for the first time she was being treated by these people as an equal. She could see from the way Rolf gazed at her that she was presenting herself very well indeed, doing justice to her role as his fiancée.

Rolf was clearly dominating the gathering; Tiffany

was on his arm. Bright conversation swirled all about them, mixing with gay laughter and the clinking of champagne glasses raised in toast to them. Rolf's self-assured smile was a beacon that gave Tiffany strength during moments when she felt weakened by doubts over whether she should even be there. Of all the people at the ball, none was more dynamic and attractive than he. Looking at him, Tiffany told herself she should be happy to be marrying him. She refused to let herself dwell on the fact that she was not.

At one point a senator came up to Tiffany and Rolf and, after a few minutes of light banter, took on a serious look. He asked Rolf if he might have a few moments alone with him. Rolf excused himself to Tiffany, kissed her and walked away with the senator. It was then that Tiffany realized for the first time that not everyone present was pleased at their engagement.

"So you're the one who managed to snare him," said a very pretty girl about Tiffany's age, who had come up to her in a belligerent saunter. The girl wore a low-cut silver gown and an overabundance of jewelry. "Well, good for you, I say. I'm certainly not envious. If an outrageous mane of hair is what it takes to turn the trick, then more power to you."

After Tiffany walked away from her, another girl came up to her on the arm of a famous movie actor. She made no secret of the fact that she was interested in Rolf. Many women were interested in Rolf, for he was the sort of man who could not walk into a room without causing heads to turn because of his commanding presence. With this girl now, though, it was different. Her expression was not simply one of wistful interest but predatory envy. "Someone had to get him," she said, looking Tiffany over with a critical eye. "If I'd known that the 'career-girl act' would tickle his fancy, I might have tried it myself."

Rolf laughed when Tiffany told him about these incidents upon his return. "Don't let them bother you, darling. None of them is in your league, and they know it."

"It's the way they think of you that bothers me. They talk as if you're not even a human being, just some sort of carnival prize that goes to whoever is the lucky winner."

"Let them think what they want. I've got you. That's all I care about."

Dinner was six courses, featuring a roast pheasant with truffles that was wonderful. The chef had prepared it especially in Rolf's honor. Afterward Rolf led Tiffany onto the floor to dance. As they moved gracefully to the music, Tiffany allowed herself to feel the pleasantness of being held in his arms. She looked up and saw him smiling down at her. *If only I could let myself enjoy this,* she thought. *It can be a good marriage. If only I didn't keep thinking about how it would be if instead of marrying Rolf, it was....*

She forced the thought from her mind.

Minutes later, though, she could not force the thought from her mind, for she was confronted with a reality that made it impossible: Nikolai Sharmonov entered the ballroom. He was without a date. He stood inside the entrance, looking around purposefully, his expression somber. He was striking in an unconventional black leather dinner jacket, his golden hair swirling across his forehead. Tiffany's heart skipped a beat. He was not supposed to be here; he had not been invited—Tiffany had seen to that.

She had not seen or heard from him since that incident on the sailboat. He must have known she would hang up on him if he called or avoid him if he tried to see her, for he had attempted to do neither. But now he was here, and from the way his eyes fixed on hers with steely firmness, she knew he had planned it this way deliberately.

He started forward across the ballroom. Tiffany looked desperately for someplace to escape. There was an exit toward the rear wall. "Rolf," she said urgently, "I have to go. I'm sorry."

"Go? How can you possibly have to go anywhere? This party is in your honor."

"I know," she said, glancing nervously at Nikolai, who was quickly approaching. "I'm sorry, but I have to."

Rolf saw where her eyes were directed; he looked thoughtful. "Just what is he to you?" he asked. Tiffany had never told him it was Nikolai she had visited that night she had appeared at Rolf's door in such distress. As far as Rolf knew, Nikolai was no more than a brooding temperamental artist she had helped escape from Hungary. If he suspected there was more to it, he kept his suspicions to himself. In fact, he had even arranged for Nikolai to be guest of honor at his Foundation for the Arts benefit, to be held in two weeks.

"He's nothing to me," Tiffany said urgently. She turned away to rush to the exit, but Rolf took her arm and stopped her.

"Please, Rolf."

"You wait here; this is your party, and you're not going to leave it. If you don't want to see that man for some reason, he's the one who's going to leave."

"Rolf, I don't want a scene. Just let me—"

"No." His voice was firm, his eyes uncompromising. He turned and walked off toward Nikolai.

He came directly up to him, blocking his path. He said something Tiffany could not hear. Nikolai did not look angry, merely intense. He seemed to be considering Rolf's words. He glanced past his shoulder at Tiffany. She had an urge to turn her eyes away, but then a surge of defiant spirit took hold of her, and she raised her chin challengingly and held his stare. She would not let herself be cowed by this man. She had put up with more than enough from him already.

Rolf said something else to Nikolai. Nikolai looked at him. For a moment they stood facing each other, two tall commanding presences among the partygoers, who seemed only now to be noticing that something was going on in their midst. Nikolai looked at Tiffany once more, then he turned and left, cutting a path through the crowd. Rolf returned to Tiffany.

"What did you say to him?" she asked.

"I told him in the friendliest way possible that he wasn't welcome here. I told him I didn't know *why* he wasn't welcome," he added with a pointed look, making it clear he was aware that Tiffany was keeping something from him, "but that the fact remained that he wasn't welcome. And I asked him to leave."

"That's all?"

"What else was necessary? Whatever reason he had for wanting to talk to you wouldn't have been served by getting into a brawl with me."

"Thank you, Rolf."

He didn't answer. His eyes made it clear that he desired an explanation from her but that he would not press her for it.

Later in the evening Rolf made a short speech. He formally announced the engagement, which had already ceased being news, and he gave the date of the wedding. There was applause, which Rolf had Tiffany stand for at his side, and he put his arm around her.

Afterward, when he went off to speak to a few close friends, Victoria Farrow came over to Tiffany. She hugged her daughter. "Congratulations, dear."

"Thank you, mother."

"There's only one thing that bothers me," Victoria Farrow said, a look of concern darkening her features. "Why must the date of the wedding be so far off? November—why that's almost three months away."

"It's convenient for both of us. Why, mother? Is there anything wrong with having it then?"

"No. It's just that—well, so many things can happen between now and then. Wouldn't it be nice if you were to be married sooner, so you wouldn't have to be concerned about anything interfering?"

"I'm not concerned about that. Why are you?" Tiffany could see her mother was truly perturbed about the distant date. "Mother, why are you so anxious to have me married off to Rolf?"

"Why, I'm not anything of the sort."

"Yes, you are. You're so anxious you don't want me to wait even the three months of our engagement. You want the marriage to take place right away, so there's no chance of my changing my mind."

Her mother held her eyes. She did not deny Tiffany's accusation. "Dear," she said, "sometimes you are a bit... flighty. On something as important as this marriage, I see no reason why you should risk having anything happen to forestall it. There's no reason not to wed right away. I'm sure Mr. Grayson would be more than happy to."

"Mother, I won't change my mind and back out of the engagement. You don't have to worry about that." Tiffany was becoming irritated. "But I don't like you trying to push me into this marriage any quicker than I'm planning to go into it on my own."

Her mother responded with a bold look. "I must say, you have a peculiar way of phrasing things. Push you into it? Tiffany, I'm not the sort of mother who pushes her daughter into anything. If I volunteer my opinion on what I think is best for you, it's only for your own good, and I have only your best interest at heart. You do realize that?"

Tiffany knew her mother loved her and that she did what she thought was in Tiffany's best interest. But this didn't make Tiffany any less bothered by the feeling that her mother was pressuring her—just as she had been pressuring her all her life into doing whatever she thought best, despite Tiffany's own views on the subject.

Tiffany wanted to ask a question but hesitated because it could be considered insulting. Then she realized she was being silly. Victoria Farrow was the Rock of Gibraltar, and could certainly bear up under any offense from Tiffany.

"Mother," Tiffany asked, "did you let word out that Rolf and I were engaged? We didn't plan to announce it until tonight at this ball, but somehow the papers got wind of it."

"It was not 'somehow,' " Victoria Farrow said with unflinching confidence in the rightness of any move she might make. "It was my calling Dorothea, who is a dear friend, and telling her the happy news."

"But you know Dorothea is the biggest gossip in New York! She couldn't keep a secret like that if her mouth were stitched shut."

"And why should she? I'm very proud of you, Tiffany and I take pride in the fact that you're about to marry."

"You mean that I'm about to marry Rolf Grayson," she said hotly. "Mother, you can be so exasperating at times."

They looked at each other with clear understanding. Both of them knew Victoria had let word of the engagement leak out because she didn't want to take any chance that Tiffany would back out before tonight's event. Once one's intentions were made public, it was far more difficult to change one's mind.

Victoria now spoke in a voice that took the tone of a wise elder patiently instructing a child. "Tiffany, this marriage is good for you. You need to be married, and you need to be married to a strong man. You're too independent for your own good. Rolf Grayson is just the kind of man you need as a husband. And I have no apologies to make about the fact that I'll do anything I can to see this marriage come to happy fruition."

"Mother," Tiffany said helplessly, "you didn't even ask me if I love him!"

"You're a big girl now. You should realize there are more important qualities two people can bring to a marriage than love. He loves you—that's plain enough. And he'll be good for you, too. Whether you love him is not a very important question." She glanced at Tiffany in a warning way. "But don't let him know there's any lack of love, if there is. Men are much greater romantics than we are, dear, despite the popular notion."

"Oh, mother!" Tiffany said in exasperation. She wanted to pursue the point, but Rolf was coming across the floor to her, smiling, in the company of two other men. Tiffany recognized them both. One was the president of Rolf's syndicated television network and the other was the governor of California.

"Darling," Rolf was saying, "I want you to say hello to two good friends of mine."

TOWARD THE END of the evening Tiffany's mother asked if Tiffany would come home with her that night, instead of staying in her own apartment. Her mother's tone was subdued, and Tiffany could see that her agreeing seemed to mean a lot to Victoria. She had something she wanted to talk over with Tiffany.

"All right, mother," Tiffany said. The timing was good because she did not want to be at home alone this evening. She suspected Nikolai might try to see her, and she didn't want to have to deal with that. She didn't know why Nikolai had come to the ball— what did he want of her now, she wondered—but she really didn't want to find out. Tiffany suspected that her mother also sensed that Nikolai might try to see her tonight. Victoria didn't want this to happen; she was strongly opposed to any contact between Tiffany and Nikolai.

Late that night, as Tiffany lay in bed in the guest room, her mother came in. She sat down on the edge of the bed. Her mood seemed to be warm and gentle—and a bit disturbed. Tiffany sensed that her mother felt a need to explain herself.

"Dear," she said, "I know it's hard for you sometimes to understand why I want the things I want for you, but you see, it's only because I love you."

"I know that, mother, and I love you, too."

Victoria smiled in a subdued way. "You see, Tiffany, I know more about what the world is like than you do, and I want to spare you from having some unpleasant times. Marrying a man like Rolf Grayson will give you the security you need. When your father and I married, it was because we were good for each other, not because we had any particularly great love for one another. And it worked out satisfactorily. It was a practical sensible marriage, as I'm sure you'll agree."

"Yes," said Tiffany, though she did not really have a very good memory of her father. She had been so young when he had died on that African safari. The memories she did have of him were fond, but her memories of the relationship between him and her mother were not quite so fond. There had been no love between them. And though they got along without quarrels or unpleasantness, they had not seemed to take much joy from their life together.

"Don't you want a good marriage like your father and I had?" Victoria asked.

No, thought Tiffany, *I don't want a marriage in which I can't love my husband with all my heart.* But she didn't say this. To say it would be to admit that she was condemning herself to unhappiness in the years to come. She didn't want to even think this, much less say it. So she just squeezed her mother's shoulder and answered, "I won't back out of the marriage, mother; you don't have to worry. It wouldn't be fair to Rolf."

"Or to yourself," Victoria persisted.

But Tiffany would not say that. She lay back in the bed and pulled the blanket snugly up to her chin. "Good night, mother," she said, yawning.

Her mother bent forward and kissed her on the forehead. She stood looking at her with obvious affection, then she shut off the light and left the room.

CHAPTER TWENTY-ONE

THE NEXT MORNING Tiffany decided against phoning in to have the limousine pick her up at her mother's apartment building instead of her own. Though she did have a change of clothing at her mother's, she preferred to go back to her own apartment and change for work there. Her apartment was not far, and an early morning walk would do her good. She dressed in a simple cotton blouse and a tailored skirt and left.

It was a bit cool outside, and the traffic was already beginning to thicken. The sounds of the wakening city were like a background hum all around her.

She had not walked more than halfway down the block when Nikolai suddenly popped out from the alcove of a building, where he had obviously been waiting for her. He must have followed her to her mother's last night. He had not changed; he still had on the black leather jacket he had worn to the ball, though his necktie hung down and his shirt was unbuttoned at the neck.

He fell into step beside her and began walking with

her down the crowded street. Tiffany glanced at him, then quickened her pace. Nikolai quickened his pace, too.

"I don't wish to see you," she said.

"I have to speak to you."

"Leave me alone. *Please.*"

She crossed the busy street. He crossed with her. His chiseled face was stern and resolute. "Tiffany, that evening on the sailboat—I could kill myself with anger over what I said to you. You must believe me; my words that night—they were the words of a madman."

"I don't care to discuss it."

"I was crazy with grief, with anger. I had vodka poisoning my blood, too, which is unusual for me. I have never before got drunk. I was not myself. I'd give anything for that night never to have happened."

"It did happen," she said icily. She continued walking briskly down the crowded avenue, trying to lose him. He refused to be lost.

"Do you wish me to stop walking with you?"

"How perceptive you are! And here I thought I was being too subtle."

"I'll obey your wish, but only after I know you accept my apology. No, that's wrong. There can be no acceptance, no excuse or forgiveness for what I said. All I want is that you *believe* me when I tell you that those words I said were lies...lies torn from the darkest depths of my soul in a moment of grief."

She refused to answer. She tried to flag a taxi, but none was near. She began weaving and cutting through the crowd, trying to shake him off.

"I was crazed with hurt, and I lashed out at whoever was around. You were there. I did all I could to avoid having that happen. That was why I disappeared, why I went to stay on Steve's sailboat—to isolate myself so I could *not* lash out at those I cared for. I tried to avoid having that happen."

"Well, pardon me for wanting to help you," she said frostily. "If I'd known you preferred that bottle of vodka as your only company, I'd have gladly obliged you and stayed away."

"I don't mind your being angry with me; I understand your anger. All I want is that you tell me you understand what I'm saying to you now. Those words on the boat—they were lies; they meant nothing. They were false. . .completely false."

"I really don't care to discuss it. It doesn't matter to me one way or the other. If you mistakenly thought I cared about how you felt toward me, I can assure you—"

He grasped her and whirled her around to face him, holding her shoulders in a viselike grip. His face was rock hard, his eyes aflame. "Listen to me! Hear what I'm saying! The words were lies. Lies! I want you to believe that. I will leave you alone when I know you believe that."

"You're hurting my shoulders."

"The words were lies. Tell me you believe me."

"Will you let me go, please?"

"Say you believe me!"

"I'll scream if you don't let me go."

"Say you believe me!"

"I'll call for the police. I'm not kidding!"

"Say you believe me! Say it!"

"I believe you, damn you! Oh, damn you!" Suddenly she felt her eyes becoming moist. "What does it matter?" she asked helplessly. "That's past now. You're past now. You're part of my past. None of it has any meaning now."

He tried to comfort her, but she pushed him away. He made no further effort. He looked stoic, as if he accepted that he had no right now to try to comfort her in any way. When Tiffany tore free of his grip and began running down the street, he made no attempt to follow.

He did not give up, however. That evening, he called her at home. She hung up on him the instant she heard his voice and then took the receiver off the hook. The next day he appeared at the Grayson Building reception room and asked to see her. She ordered the security guard to have him thrown out if he refused to leave.

She sent word she did not want to speak to him or see him ever again. She said that if he tried to accost her once more as she left her apartment building, she would move and leave no forwarding address. Though Nikolai sent word back that he only wanted to talk to her, Tiffany knew the truth. He wanted to court her, to try to make her change her mind about marrying Rolf. Now that Larisa no longer had any hold over him, Nikolai evidently thought he could just pick up with her where he had left off that night on the riverbank. How wrong he was!

"I don't understand why you don't see him just once—which is all he's asking," Mary Blakely said a week later when she and Tiffany were in the sound-dubbing room. Tiffany was there to oversee a new take on the narrative that was to accompany her film. Mary was there as her assistant but was speaking to her now as her friend.

"How do you know he wants to see me only once?" Tiffany asked in an overly disinterested voice.

"He told Steve, and Steve told me."

"Steve talks too much."

"Still...."

"Still nothing!" said Tiffany, wishing she could sound unemotional. "Look," she said, making a deliberate effort to calm herself, "what would be the point? Why should I see him? Nothing will come of it."

"You used to be close to him once," Mary said gently.

"That's over with. A lot has happened since then, not the least of which is that I'm going to be married very soon."

Mary said nothing; she merely looked displeased. She was opposed to Tiffany's marriage to Rolf Grayson. As far as Mary was concerned, she knew what Tiffany needed, and Rolf Grayson was most definitely not it. Tiffany needed someone who was romantic and creative, strong and sensitive. Strength alone, such as Grayson possessed, was not enough.

Tiffany refused to discuss it further. She went into the glass-enclosed sound room and began going over the narration text with the announcer she had hired. She didn't return to the audio control booth until Mark Pernell entered to join Mary. In addition to being a first-rate film editor, Mark was also one of Grayson's top audio engineers. He was the man responsible for recording the session.

Mark was laughing as he took his seat at the audio console, a folded newspaper in his hand. "Hey, get this," he said jovially. "Tiff, looks like your boyfriend Sharmonov is having lady trouble. Seems that the poor fellow is just too homely and unexciting to get any dates."

"He's not my boyfriend," Tiffany said, knowing the young engineer was calling him that only to tease her.

"Well, whatever you call him, looks like he's just another poor slob who stays home on Saturday nights because no one'll go out with him."

"What are you talking about, boy wonder?" asked Mary, grabbing the newspaper out of his hands and scanning the article he was reading. Mark continued laughing, shaking his head in amusement. Mary glanced up at Tiffany, who was looking at her

with curiosity. "Listen to this," Mary said. She
began reading the article.

The internationally renowned dancer Nikolai
Sharmonov, who recently defected to the United
States, has canceled his previous acceptance of
an invitation to appear at next week's Arts
Foundation benefit. Mr. Sharmonov was scheduled to be guest of honor at the affair. The concert is being staged at Lincoln Center to raise
funds for various civic arts organizations. Mr.
Sharmonov expressed his regrets but stated that
he could not attend due to his inability to find a
suitable partner to accompany him to the event.

"Boy, is Grayson going to be ticked off at that!"
laughed Mark. "He's the chairman of the board of
that foundation. It's *his* benefit. And now this Sharmonov, the main draw the benefit was built around,
changes his mind and says he won't come."

"Oh, hush up," said Mary, continuing to scan the
article.

"But it's funny! I mean, look at it. Nikolai Sharmonov, the most sought-after celebrity in New
York...one of the most handsome, talented, dynamic guys around...not going to the benefit because he
can't get a date." Mark slapped his knee, breaking
up in laughter. "The poor guy probably has so many
beautiful dolls hanging around his knees in adora-
tion, he can't walk without dragging a few of them

after him. They surround him everywhere he goes. Maybe that's why he can't get a date—he can't see the trees for the forest."

Tiffany was pretending disinterest by jotting notations on her copy of the narration text in preparation for the session. "If you're through philosophizing about the state of celebrities' social lives," she said to Mark in a businesslike voice, "maybe we can get on to—"

"Hey, listen to this!" said Mary excitedly, reading further:

Mr. Sharmonov told the press that the only woman he would feel comfortable escorting to the benefit is Miss Tiffany Farrow, recently announced fiancée of media baron Rolf Grayson. It was Miss Farrow, readers will recall, who played an instrumental role in Sharmonov's defection. The dancer made it clear that no social relationship exists between him and Miss Farrow. He simply desires her to be his escort due to his stated shyness over appearing in public with women he does not know.

"Shyness!" declared Mark with hilarity. "Nikolai Sharmonov, shy about going out in public with members of the opposite sex?"

"Be quiet, Mark!" Mary ordered.

"Yes, ma'am. Your Highness."

Mary stopped reading the article aloud. She looked

up at Tiffany and summarized the rest of it. "He says that if he can't go to the benefit with you, he won't go at all, and you told him you're busy that night."

Tiffany looked at her. "Well, he's right. I am busy that night. And every other night, too. Now can we please get down to business? I've got an announcer in there to whom we're paying union overtime."

Mark glanced toward the glass-enclosed speaker's booth and winked at the announcer, who nodded at him in greeting. "Yeah, well, all right. If you want to be a killjoy about the whole thing."

They began working in earnest. Mark set his controls, put on his headphones and had the announcer speak a few lines so he could get the proper balance and pitch. Then he gave the cue, and started the quartz-movement clock above the speaker's booth, which the announcer would use to pace himself for the proper pauses during the film. Tiffany gave the announcer a few last-minute instructions through her intercom, then they began taping. Mary kept an eye on the visual scanner to make sure the narrative kept pace with the film. The announcer was not allowed to view the film as he spoke because his undivided attention had to be on the text he was reading.

They were halfway through the script when someone banged loudly on the control-booth door. This was so unusual that it made Tiffany and Mark jerk slightly and stare at the door. The double red light above the door was on to warn people that a taping was in session. A sign on the outside of the door beneath the light read: Taping in session. Do not enter or disturb.

Mark tried to keep his mind and eyes on his control panel, but when the knocking came once more, he gave up. Yelling "Cut!" into his intercom, he leaped to his feet and rushed to the door. He yanked it open as he declared, "Who the hell is the *idiot* who can't see a red light when it's right in front of his—" He broke off his harangue and stared, his mouth remaining open. When he spoke again, his voice was much more respectful. "Oh, hello, Mr. Grayson. What can I do for you, sir?"

"Is Tiffany Farrow in there? You're taping the ballet documentary, right?"

"Yes, sir. We were right in the middle of it, in fact, when you...uh.... Shall I get her for you, sir?"

Grayson stepped forward and looked into the room. He saw Tiffany, jerked his head for her to join him, then walked out again. Tiffany told the announcer in the soundproof booth to take a five-minute break. Then she left the control room to join Grayson in the hallway outside.

"Hello, Rolf," she said somewhat irritably. She did not appreciate being interrupted in the middle of a taping, no matter who was doing the interrupting.

"Tiffany, did you see today's *Times*?"

"No. But if you're talking about the article on Nikolai Sharmonov not coming to your benefit concert, Mary read it to me."

"That's exactly what I'm talking about. What in

God's name is the story with that son of a cossack? You know him better than I. This benefit is in his honor. He agreed to be the guest of honor before we ever started publicizing it. Doesn't he realize he's ruining the affair by canceling out at the last minute like this? People bought tickets specifically to see him there. He's going to make a laughingstock of me."

"I don't know what he realizes or doesn't realize, Rolf. I haven't seen him for a while. And I don't talk to him."

"Yes, well, that's one thing that's about to change."

"I beg your pardon?"

"I want you to reestablish contact with him—at least for one night. I want him at my benefit. Nobody is going to pull the rug out from under any benefit Rolf Grayson is chairman of. If he wants to be childish and insist on having someone he feels comfortable with as his escort, we're just going to have to humor him."

Tiffany chose her words carefully, her brow tense. "Rolf, don't you think it's my decision whether or not I want to accompany him?"

He patted her arm and made light of her concern. "Oh, come now, darling, this is certainly not worth getting excited about. I know you don't like the man, but—"

"I didn't say I don't like him," she said coolly. "I don't feel one way or another about him."

"Of course you don't! So why not humor the stubborn donkey? If he's going to be temperamental and brooding and stay away just because he can't have you as his escort, then by all means go as his escort! I'm sure you can put up with him for just a few hours.''

Tiffany thought about how Rolf had been willing to spare her from having to ''put up'' with Nikolai for even two minutes during the ball. But now that he had a personal stake in the matter, suddenly it was all right for Tiffany to put up with Nikolai for an entire evening.

''Besides,'' Rolf said, ''it's for a good cause. A number of this city's cultural activities depend on my foundation for support.''

Tiffany knew that Rolf's concern was not so much for the city's cultural needs as for preserving his own reputation as a dedicated fund raiser and patron of the arts. He had always been concerned with upholding his image in these areas. Tiffany did not mention this, though. She merely gazed at him for several seconds in silence, then nodded solemnly and said, ''As you wish, Rolf.''

''Fine.'' His expression turned harsh. ''This way I won't have to ruin that son of a bitch Sharmonov— which I was seriously thinking about doing. How dare he pull a stunt like this on me? I can make it so he never dances with a first-rate American company again.''

Tiffany knew it was not an empty threat. Rolf was a major supporter of the country's three leading ballet companies and was on the boards of two of them. He also wielded enormous power in the area of federal grants to the arts because of the influential people he knew. Backed up by his vast media empire, he was one of the three or four most powerful men in American cultural affairs.

"Thank you, darling," he said. "I'll have my secretary convey your acceptance." He smiled his usual smile, only now it seemed less appealing than it usually did. "You're a wonderful girl," he said. "Now go back to your taping. I'll see you tonight at dinner."

CHAPTER TWENTY-TWO

THE NIGHT of the benefit concert Nikolai appeared at Tiffany's door in a velvet tuxedo and ruffled silk shirt. He bowed. There was only the slightest hint of mockery in his voice as he said, "I'm honored you chose to accept my humble invitation."

"I was forced to do it, and you know it."

He took her hand and curled her white-gloved fingers around his arm as he led her to the car. Tiffany removed her hand and simply walked beside him—at a distance. She caught him glancing at her ice-blue gown and at the way her hair was combed back from her forehead and temples, giving a lion's mane effect. His gaze also took in the ornate diamond necklace Rolf had presented her with as an engagement gift. He made no mention of it, though.

Nikolai had engaged a chauffeured limousine for the evening. As they rode to Lincoln Center, his face lost its slightly taunting look and instead became open and honest—and intense. He half turned in his seat to look at her. Tiffany was staring straight ahead, not even acknowledging his presence.

"Why do you not wish to see me anymore?" he asked.

"I'm getting married soon. What could be a better reason than that?" She kept her tone businesslike, allowing no hint of emotion to creep in.

"Tiffany. Do you know that I love you?"

"I know that I believed it once, and I was terribly hurt when I found out it wasn't true, that you thought I was good for one thing only."

He grasped her chin and made her look at him. His face was alive with fury. "Don't lie to me! You know I love you! You know the words I said on the boat were false. So stop pretending you believe otherwise."

She tried to hold his stare but found her eyes lowering involuntarily. She did believe him; she knew how he felt about her. She wished she didn't, though. It only made things so much harder.

"I want you to tell me," he said. "Do you know that I love you? Do you know how deep, how great my love for you is?"

"I know, Mr. Sharmonov, that you got me into this car under false pretenses and that I'm going to leave it any minute now if you continue this line of discussion." She glared at him. "You never really cared about having me as your date for the concert tonight. All you wanted was to get me alone in this car so you could subject me to words you know I don't want to hear."

"They're words you're going to hear, whether you want to or not."

"Stop the car. I'm getting out."

"No, you're not. You're going to sit here and listen to me. This is the first chance I've had to talk to you in weeks, and I've no intention of letting it slip by."

Tiffany reached for the doorhandle, even though the limousine was in motion. He grasped her hands and held them, refusing to let go.

"Listen to me," he said. "I know Larisa filled your head with lies about me. She lied to me, too, deceived me with her evil scheming ways. But don't you see, Tiffany, that's all behind us now. The deceptions we fell for that drove us apart, the pain we suffered that made us lash out blindly at each other—they're all part of the past."

"Will you let go of me, please? I have no desire to listen to any of this."

"How can you act so coldly to me? There's no longer any reason! You know I love you. You know that throughout all the lies and deception my love for you never lessened—not in the slightest. And now, now that we both know the truth, there's nothing to keep us apart."

"Aren't you forgetting one tiny detail? I happen to be engaged to be married! Mr. Sharmonov—"

"Stop this Mr. Sharmonov nonsense!"

She hesitated; then seeing the honesty in his eyes, she relented. "Nikolai," she said softly. "I accepted Rolf's proposal. I can't go back on it."

"You can."

"I'm not the sort of woman who accepts a man's proposal, then changes her mind and runs off with someone else. There's such a thing as honor, you know."

"Honor be damned! Do you love me?"

"I...I did."

"And do you now?"

She raised her eyes toward the roof of the limousine helplessly. "What's the point in answering that? It accomplishes nothing."

"Do you love me? Tell me! Tell me the truth!"

"I won't tell you anything," she declared in response to his demanding tone. "You have no right to get me alone like this to ask me these questions. I owe you nothing, understand? Nothing!"

She reached for the doorhandle again with every intention of leaving the car the next time it stopped, of refusing to continue on to the concert hall with him. It was too late, though. They were now pulling up to Lincoln Center. A doorman opened her door; a red carpet extended across the entrance walkway directly up to their car.

Camera strobe lights were flashing, and news cameras were rolling. Reporters, jostling one another to shout questions, were kept at bay behind purple suede-covered chains that bordered the red carpet leading into the hall. Behind the reporters the crowd of eager fans and celebrity-seekers craned forward, anxious to see the stars disembarking from the limousines. When Nikolai exited from the car, a round of applause broke out and the crowd became animated.

Tiffany could not rush away now. Aside from the fact it would cause a sensation, there was also the matter of the sheer physical impossibility of doing so. There was absolutely nowhere to go. They were surrounded by paparazzi and a crowd of admirers. She could not rush through them.

Nikolai stood outside her open door and offered her his hand. After an instant's pause she allowed him to help her from the car. As they walked down the red carpet into the concert hall, a cheer arose from the crowd. "Nikolai! Nikolai! Nikolai!" someone shouted. Others called out his name, too, until soon it became a chant. In the scant few months he had been in the United States, Nikolai had become the darling of New York—not only of the members of ballet society, but of everyday citizens, too. They loved his quick wit and charming smile, which they saw often when he was featured on TV news broadcasts.

Nikolai waved in response to the avid greeting. He tried to smile, as well, but Tiffany could see the hardness at the corners of his mouth. He was in no mood to smile. They walked into Avery Fisher Hall, her hand on his arm. The box they were seated in was directly next to the one occupied by Rolf and the dowager society lady he was escorting. Rolf stood and nodded to Nikolai, politely but with reserve. Nikolai nodded back in the same fashion.

When Nikolai was introduced as the guest of honor at the beginning of the performance, he put his hand on Tiffany's elbow as he stood up, indicating he wanted her to rise with him. This was not strictly necessary according to protocol, and Tiffany refused to do it.

During the concert it was impossible for Tiffany to concentrate on the music. Her emotions were in turmoil, and her thoughts were focused on the words that had been said in the car and the fact that soon she and Nikolai would return to the limousine. Beside her Nikolai was staring straight ahead and to all appearances seemed intent upon the performance. But Tiffany knew better—a vein in his neck was throbbing, betraying his tension.

Finally the concert was over, and then—mercifully—they were outside in the cool brisk night air, hurrying to their waiting car. At last they were inside it, being driven away from the hall down brightly lighted Broadway.

Tiffany noticed something was wrong when, after several minutes, the limousine crossed a bridge and turned onto an expressway. She opened the glass partition and leaned forward in her seat. "Driver," she said, "you're going in the wrong direction. This is not the way to the reception...."

"Yes, ma'am," said the driver, but he made no move to leave the expressway.

When Tiffany tried to lean forward again to demand that he follow her instructions, Nikolai gently held her back. "It will do no good," he said. "He has his orders."

"Where are you taking me?" she demanded.

"Not far. A quiet place where we can talk."

"I demand that you take me home this very instant."

"Fine."

"What do you mean 'fine'?"

"I mean fine, demand whatever you like, but I'm not taking you back until I have a chance to talk to you."

She glared at him, then sat back stiffly in the seat, fuming. She folded her arms across her chest and looked straight ahead, determined not to say a word to him until he tired of his game and returned her to her apartment.

They drove for several minutes, leaving the city and entering an unfamiliar rural area that Tiffany did not know existed so close to Manhattan. They took several turns onto untraveled roads and finally stopped. Nikolai got out and offered her his hand. Tiffany remained in the seat, impassively. He took her wrist and pulled her out of the car, not roughly— but not gently, either.

"Take your hand off me!"

"I will, now that you've come out here to join me."

It was a cool night; the stars appeared very bright. There were trees near them, rustling under the gentle breeze. Moonlight illuminated the scene.

Nikolai led her away from the car, and they began walking slowly. He apparently had no destination in mind; he simply wanted a chance to talk to her away from the hustle and bustle of the city. It was a very pretty pleasant setting, and Tiffany was enjoying the cool night and fragrant air despite herself. The sounds of nature were appealing, too, after living with the noise of the city day after day.

He led her to a large boulder surrounded by grass, and he sat easily on it, one long leg extended to the ground, the other knee raised. "Tiffany," he said, "let's not play games. So many misunderstandings have come between us already. Let's be honest with each other now."

"Yes, let's. Here's what I honestly want: I want you to take me home and then get out of my life forever."

The silence that followed her statement made her aware of what she had said. She had said it because of her mood of helpless anger and frustration. Now she realized her words had been preceded by the statement that this was what she honestly wanted. But did she—did she want him out of her life forever?

"I'll tell you what I want," Nikolai said. "I want you to stop lying to yourself, to stop sacrificing yourself."

"Sacrificing? What are you talking about?"

"You love me, yet you intend to marry Grayson, who I don't believe you love."

"How presumptuous you are! You don't know who I love!"

"Then tell me—who do you love?"

She started to reply indignantly but closed her mouth instead and pressed her lips together tightly.

"Just as I thought," he said. "That's what I mean when I say 'sacrifice.' Why are you doing it? Why are you ruining your chance for happiness in this way?"

"Look, you. First of all I'm not saying that I'm ruining my chance for happiness, and second of all—well, some people believe in honoring their commitments. It would hurt Rolf terribly if I were to leave him after telling him I'd marry him."

"Would it? Or is that just an excuse you're giving yourself? Oh, it would hurt him all right—for a while. But the Rolf Grayson I met is made of steel and flint. His one true love is his business empire."

Tiffany refused to comment on this. She knew it was probably true. She couldn't admit this, though, because then Nikolai would demand to know the real reason she wouldn't leave Rolf to go to him. And that was something she could never tell him.

"Don't you see what you're doing?" Nikolai insisted. "You're sacrificing yourself. To avoid having to confront a painful situation, you sacrifice your happiness instead. Tiffany, darling, you have to realize what you're doing before it's too late."

"Don't call me 'darling.'"

"And it's the same with ballet. You sacrificed the

great love of your life because you didn't want to face the pain of confronting your mother."

"We won't talk of ballet. You have no right to talk to me about that."

"I have every right! I love you! I won't let you continue destroying your life, throwing away your chances for happiness."

"I won't listen." She put her hands to her ears and turned away from him, desperate not to hear what he was saying.

He pulled her hands away. He spoke directly to her face—harshly, as she shook her head, her eyes shut tight. "You gave up ballet! You sacrificed your happiness once. Now you wish to give up our life together. Can't you see how the two are related? Tiffany, realize what you're doing—before it's too late!"

"Who are you to tell me how to live? You're the man who fell for Larisa's lies and let your heart be torn with love for a child you never had!"

She saw that she had got to him. His eyes showed his pain.

"Nikolai," she said in a softer voice, "I...I'm sorry. I didn't mean to."

"What you say of me is true. I am maybe one of the world's biggest fools."

"Oh, no, Nikolai. That's not what I meant. I—"

He put his finger to her lips gently. "But at least, my darling, I'm willing to take risks for my love, to live my life unafraid. And because I love you, I'll teach you to do the same. I'll teach you that you must grasp for your happiness. You can't live your life in fear of confronting pain."

Tiffany didn't want to be taught anything. All she wanted was to be taken home and set free, allowed to return to the simple well-ordered life she had left only hours ago—hours that now seemed like an eternity.

"Nikolai, this is hurting us both—and for no reason. Please, take me home now. Let's just...leave things as they are. Nothing is going to change."

"One thing will change. You'll speak to your mother about why you gave up ballet. You will confront your feelings, not hide from them."

She shot him an icy murderous look, but he continued in spite of it. "You will do this one thing for me. And then I'll stay out of your life forever, as you request."

"It's none of your business, and I refuse." She moved away from him. She had no feelings of tenderness or affection for him now. There was nothing inside her but cold hostility. "I won't allow you to meddle in my affairs. The decision regarding my life in ballet was made long ago and is a closed matter. I won't reopen it."

His voice was cutting. "You will reopen it, or you won't go home tonight. You'll remain here until you agree to do this thing. This one last request I make of you."

Tiffany raised her chin defiantly. She started back to the car.

"The chauffeur is not a family man," Nikolai said. "He has no wife he must go home to; he can stay as long as I tell him to. I myself have no obligations calling me into town. And if you think you can walk back to the city, you're wrong. You'd never find your way along these unfamiliar roads."

She turned away from him, returned to the road and began striding down it, but she had no idea how long she must travel before she could find a familiar place or a passing car. It had been a long drive to this deserted area, and she had not been paying attention to directions.

Nikolai was walking alongside her, the limousine following behind him slowly. Tiffany removed her high heels and continued marching. When she reached a crossroad, she didn't know which way to turn. She chose the direction that seemed most reasonable but, after half a mile, realized she'd taken a wrong turn.

Losing her temper, she whirled on him, furious. "Why do you insist on meddling in my life?"

"Because I love you and won't see you destroy your chance for happiness."

"Well, I hate you! Do you hear me?"

"Yes."

She glared at him furiously. He glared back.

"All you have to do," he said slowly, "is agree to speak to your mother about why you gave up a career in ballet. You don't have to tell her you're returning to ballet. You don't have to change your decision about giving it up. All I ask is that you tell her it was she who made you give it up—and you sacrificed your own happiness to do it."

"I don't understand," she said flatly. "Why is this so important to you?"

"I won't tell you. Do it and you'll see."

She was getting tired of tramping down this rural lane in the moonlit darkness. "If I agree, you'll take me home and promise to stay out of my life forever?"

His expression was solemn, showing that he realized the weight of what he was agreeing to. "Yes," he said. "I promise."

"Then I'll do it. It'll be worth it to get you out of my life for good."

He bowed his head formally in the manner of a condemned man hearing a judge pronounce a death sentence upon him. Then he went to the limousine and held the door for her. Tiffany got in.

"Take her back," he said to the chauffeur. "Return for me later. I want to be alone awhile."

As the car sped away, Tiffany looked back at his tall solitary figure, illuminated by the moonlight. A pang of remorse gnawed at her, but she ruthlessly shut it out.

She had not been honest with Nikolai. She hadn't told him the main reason she wouldn't leave Rolf to go to him. She *couldn't* do it. That was the main reason. For Rolf was a vindictive man who would wreak a terrible vengeance on Nikolai. He'd destroy his career—which was all Nikolai lived for. He'd make his life one of misery and frustration by arranging that he never again dance with a company befitting his talents.

So really, thought Tiffany, there was no question of doing what Nikolai wanted. They could never share a life....

CHAPTER TWENTY-THREE

IT WAS NOT UNTIL two days later that Tiffany finally got up the courage to confront her mother about ballet, as she had promised Nikolai she would. Only then did she realize how Nikolai had tricked her.

She went into the confrontation already in an edgy mood due to an incident that had taken place with Rolf only a little while earlier. The matter had left Tiffany with a sour feeling.

Rolf had come into the company's research library on the twenty-first floor looking for her. It was six o'clock, and Tiffany was alone, boning up on Peru and the Incas for her upcoming assignment. The room was comfortable and quiet, and beyond the large windows spread the evening skyline of Manhattan. "I don't know what you're doing in here," Rolf said, smiling, "but I've come to rescue you. My six-o'clock appointment fell through, and I've got just enough time to take you to dinner."

"I can't do it tonight, Rolf," she replied. "I have to be at my mother's at eight. And meantime I have a lot of studying to do."

"Studying? For what?"

"For my Peru assignment, of course." She smiled at him. "Did you think I was already a walking encyclopedia of information on the Incas?"

He looked bewildered. "Darling, you're not serious? You don't expect to continue with that assignment?"

"Of course I do. Why wouldn't I?"

"Well," he said, laughing a bit uncertainly, "you're going to be my wife in a month or so. Then we're off to the Côte d'Azur for our honeymoon. And when we return, you certainly don't expect to continue working for a living."

Tiffany frowned and pushed the open books away from her so she could give her full attention to what he was saying. "Rolf, I like making films. It's one of the most fulfilling parts of my life. I don't intend to give it up just because we'll be married."

Rolf sat down on the edge of the table. He looked serious and a bit flustered. "Darling, there's no need for you to continue working. It's utterly unnecessary."

"We're not talking about need; we're talking about want."

He smiled paternalistically, as if Tiffany were a child unversed in the ways of the upper social strata. "As my wife, you'll have plenty of time to work—but not here and not for a living. You'll have your full share of social and charitable obligations to fulfill: organizing social affairs, fund raisers, tea parties for the wealthy women who form the backbone of this city's cultural life—that sort of thing. It's expected of the wives of men in my position, Tiffany. I thought you understood that.''

"I understood that many of the wives of prominent men do engage in such activities, but I never thought you'd ask me to do that if I didn't want to." She eyed him steadily, wondering how he would reply.

He understood the significance of her look; his tone became serious. "Darling, I won't ever ask you to do anything you don't wish to do. I love you too much to risk losing you that way. If you prefer not to assume certain social obligations, that's fine." He smiled a bit, trying to make light of it. "My social secretary wouldn't enjoy looking for a new job anyway. So we'll continue to let her handle those things."

"Good," she said. "Thank you."

"But I do wish you'd reconsider this idea of working for a living. I'd really rather not have my wife holding down a job. I'd like to be the full-time object of your attention and affection."

Tiffany put her hand on his. She forced a smile she did not really feel. She could easily imagine having a marriage in which she did not deem it necessary to continue as a filmmaker, in which the idea of devoting herself entirely to her husband would be, by itself, fully satisfying to her. But her marriage to Rolf would not be such a union. She could not conceive of making him the focal point of her existence, building her life around him. "Rolf," she said gently, "I really would like to keep my job. At least until we have children."

He looked at her very sharply. His look was so intense and immediate, it made Tiffany wonder what she had said to provoke it. "Well, you think about it," he replied, suddenly standing up. "I'll go along with whatever you decide, but you just think about it a little bit longer. Maybe you'll change your mind." He bent down and kissed her lightly, then he walked out.

Tiffany was still feeling uneasy from this encounter when she left for her mother's apartment. On the way she rehearsed in her mind what she would say to Victoria. She did not intend to go even an inch farther than she had promised Nikolai. She would tell her mother she had given up ballet for her sake alone, not her own.

Tiffany did not know why Nikolai wanted her to say this—what could it possibly accomplish—but she did know that she would say nothing more than that. They would discuss it for a moment or two, then Tiffany would quickly turn the conversation around to other matters. In return for her doing this, Nikolai would stay out of her life forever. She would no longer have to be provoked by him into questioning her decision to marry Rolf or her decision to give up ballet. She would be left alone to live her life in... well, maybe not in happiness, but at least in peace.

That was her plan, but the instant she entered Victoria Farrow's apartment, she realized that she had been tricked by Nikolai, that she had been set up.

"What do you *mean* you intend to return to ballet?" her mother demanded before Tiffany could even speak. Her face was flushed, and she was obviously ready for battle. "That matter was decided years ago, and I'll not have you going back on it."

"Going back on it?" Tiffany said, stunned by the unexpected offensive. "I'm not going back on it. I didn't say anything about returning to ballet."

"Don't try to fool me, Tiffany Farrow," said her mother, squinting her eyes and shaking a finger at her. "I know you never really resigned yourself to giving up ballet, even though we decided together that it was the best thing for you to do; I know you never fully accepted it. But I must say, I was surprised you didn't even have the decency to tell me yourself that you were going back on the decision. I had to hear it from the lips of a stranger...a man I'm not at all fond of—Mr. Sharmonov. He came to tell me yesterday you intended to return to ballet."

Tiffany understood. "So that's it," she said. Nikolai had this all planned. "Mother," Tiffany said, "don't you see, he's trying to—"

"I know very well what he's trying to do, young lady, and what you're trying to do. And I won't stand for it. I was very happy when you quit ballet five years ago because I knew you were making the decision that was best for you. Well, I intend to *stay* very happy. Your returning to professional ballet is simply out of the question." She nodded curtly, indicating that the matter was closed.

Tiffany had not intended to argue in favor of returning to dance—in fact, that was the very last thing she had intended to do. But now, seeing her mother so adamant in her refusal, she felt challenged. She had always been willful and strong-minded, even as a child, and nothing provoked her into taking a defiant stand more than having someone tell her she could not.

"Mother, even if I did plan to return to ballet, it wouldn't be a decision I'd change my mind about just because you insisted on it."

"Tiffany," said her mother forbiddingly, "this is not up for discussion."

Tiffany felt her blood beginning to boil. "How can you say that? It's my life, after all."

"It's your life, but if you don't have the sense to make proper intelligent decisions, I have to step in and make them for you. Returning to ballet now is out of the question."

"Why? Why is it out of the question?"

"You know very well why. We went through this before—five years ago. It's a life full of nothing but heartache and shattered dreams. It's not a life for an intelligent young lady like you."

"But what if I'm willing to put up with the heartache in order to have the joys? And what if I don't have any falsely romantic dreams that can be shattered?"

"You can love ballet, study it, eat and sleep it, live it as your life," her mother said, looking away, remembering what it had been like for her. "You can give yourself to it completely. And then one day you find out it was all for nothing...you sacrificed for nothing. Your future can be blighted in a single terrible moment." She was speaking bitterly, barely even looking at Tiffany.

"Mother," Tiffany said sympathetically, "I understand what you're saying. I know the heartache you went through. But it's different with me. I'm willing to endure the heartache to have the joy. To me the joy of dancing is worth it. Don't you see? I've tried to stay away from it. I haven't danced with a company or taken classes for years. And yet...I find myself returning to it every chance I get, practicing in dingy old studios wherever I happen to be...alone, in secret. If I couldn't dance, why life wouldn't be worth living."

She had never thought of it this way, but listening to herself speak, she realized that her words were true and straight from her heart. She had avoided thinking of it this way, avoided realizing the truth all these years, because she had feared having to confront her mother.

"We went through all this five years ago. I see no reason to go through it again."

"A lot has happened in five years. For one thing I've realized how much I truly love ballet. I couldn't have known that five years ago. Think of this, mother—think how greatly I must love it to keep doing it month after month, year after year, with no recognition, no applause, no teacher to give me a gentle criticism or an encouraging smile.''

"That doesn't matter," her mother said sharply, dismissing Tiffany's words as if they were totally beside the point. "You're about to marry a very wealthy, very sought-after man. You'll have to devote yourself to making him a good home, to upholding the image of Mrs. Rolf Grayson that he'll want you to project to the world. You certainly don't want to give up all that just to enter professional ballet, now do you?''

Tiffany reflected on the question quietly, realizing for the first time how serious it really was.

"Do you?" insisted her mother, refusing to relent. "You certainly don't want to give up that just to return to ballet?''

Tiffany shut her eyes. "Mother," she said quietly, "do you know what you're doing? You're trying to live your life through me.''

Victoria Farrow was offended at the idea. "How dare you suggest such a thing?''

"It's true. I'm sorry, mother, but if you'll look at it, you'll see that it is. You're telling me what *you* want, what's best for *you*, not what's best for me, and certainly not what I want. Because the truth is, what I want is to return to ballet, to dance professionally.''

Had she really said that? She felt amazed and stunned—and, for the first time in years, calm and at peace with herself.

"I knew you wanted that!" raged her mother. "I knew it!"

"Did you, mother?" Tiffany said quietly. "Then why didn't you let me have it? And why did you try to prevent *me* from knowing I wanted it?"

That made her mother stop short. For an instant she appeared uncertain about how to answer, then she raised her chin defiantly and thrust her shoulders back. She was, after all, Victoria Farrow, former world-famous star of ballet. "I wanted only what was best for you."

"Or," said Tiffany slowly, hesitating, feeling fierce resistance against pulling the words out, "what was least threatening to you."

Her mother looked shocked. "That's not true."

Tiffany sank down onto the sofa. So she had said it at last. She had known it secretly for so long but had never had the courage to face her mother and state it openly. Now that she had breached the once-inviolate wall, she knew she had to continue on, to force herself to say the whole truth. There might never be a moment like this again. "Mother, you were always afraid I might surpass you. You knew how good I was. You couldn't *not* know it; you were too great a dancer not to see the greatness in me. And I don't believe you could have lived with the possibility of my surpassing the skill and renown you'd achieved. So you did everything you could to stop me from becoming what I could be."

Her mother's eyes turned stony. "That's the most

despicable thing I've ever heard, and you should be ashamed of yourself for even thinking it."

Surprisingly, Tiffany laughed a short self-contemptuous laugh. She looked down into her lap. "If there's anything I should be ashamed of, it's being too much of a coward to face reality. I was so afraid of hurting you by saying this that I hurt myself instead." She stood up, went to her mother and took her hands. "Mother, I don't blame you for what you made me do. Truly I don't. I don't think you even knew the real reason you wanted me to give up ballet. It was too deep inside you."

Victoria Farrow pulled her hands away and glared at her. Tiffany felt great love and affection for her mother just then—and great sadness. Because she was sure Victoria could see that what she had said was true. It was a terrible truth to have to realize. It was so terrible, in fact, that Tiffany had been willing to give up ballet to spare her mother from having to confront it. It was exactly as Nikolai had said—she had been willing to sacrifice her own happiness for the sake of her mother's.

"Mother," Tiffany said, "I love you." Tears were streaming down Tiffany's cheeks. She felt terrible about hurting her mother, but she also still felt that strange sensation of being at peace with herself, of being courageous after a very long time of being cowardly.

She let her mother see her tears, unashamed at showing how deeply she loved her. "I wouldn't say these things to hurt you. Believe me, mother, it pains me horribly to have to hurt you. But I think I've reached the point now where finally I've become a woman. I'm no longer a scared little girl, afraid to face reality. I'm willing to take responsibility for my own life, and I'm willing to admit to myself that the way to live my life is *not* by giving up the only thing that makes it worthwhile."

Her mother was staring at her stonily.

"Do you understand, mother? Please say you understand and that you accept."

Victoria Farrow asked just one question, her voice sharp. "Do you intend to return to ballet against my wishes, regardless of all I've said to you?"

Tiffany drew in a deep breath. She knew she was being challenged. She sensed that this was one of the decisive moments of her life. She knew that somehow, in a way she could not yet fully understand, another important matter in her life was also hanging in the balance. She stood up straight and looked her mother in the eye. "Yes, mother. I will return to ballet."

Victoria Farrow raised her arm stiffly and pointed at the door. "Leave my house," she said, "and don't return."

CHAPTER TWENTY-FOUR

THE NEXT MORNING when Tiffany told Rolf about her decision to return to ballet, he was quite surprised. "But I thought you were so negative about ballet? I mean, you were always oversensitive to any mention of it, and I practically had to twist your arm to get you to cover the Volgaya story."

"I was never negative about ballet, Rolf; it was just a very sensitive subject with me. Now I've decided to go back to it—and professionally, this time."

"Are you still that good? It's been five years since you turned down that offer from the NBT."

"I've kept in constant practice ever since then."

"That's surprising, too. This whole morning is full of surprises. How come I never knew about it if you were practicing that often?"

"Oh, well, I . . . never made a very big deal of it."

"That you certainly didn't." He narrowed an eye at her warily. "You're not going to join NBT, are you?" he asked.

Tiffany understood the cause of his wariness. He suspected there might be some feeling between her and Nikolai, though he had never said so openly. He had been suspicious of this for some time.

"No," Tiffany said reassuringly, "I don't want to join NBT. I was thinking of auditioning for Paramount instead."

"Why Paramount?"

"For one thing it's an occasional company, and it doesn't tour. I'm not sure I want to live and breathe ballet twenty-four hours a day, as I wanted to when I was eighteen. I don't know if I want to devote my entire life to it now, as I did then."

"I certainly hope not. I want you to build your life around me—not ballet, not documentaries, not anything but me."

Tiffany squeezed his hand to reassure him. The fact was, she was not sure she wanted to give up film-making completely. If she joined Paramount, she could arrange it, after a while, so that she was an occasional dancer, rather than a full-time member of the company. This would let her continue doing films part-time, if she later found that she wanted to.

There was a more important reason, though, why Tiffany wanted to join Paramount instead of NBT: she could not bear the thought of seeing Nikolai day after day, dancing with him, feeling the touch of his hands on her body, while knowing there could be nothing between them ever. She could not endure having him refer to her in a harsh impersonal tone as "Mrs. Grayson."

She hadn't seen Nikolai since that night on the rural road. True to his word, he had not tried to contact her. He had promised to stay out of her life forever, and he was keeping that promise. Tiffany felt such powerful mixed feelings about him! At first she'd hated him for tricking her into confronting her mother, for setting up the situation so that she had been forced to confront her, even though she hadn't intended to. But it was hard to keep hating him when she knew that he'd done this only because he loved her; he had realized how miserable she was away from ballet. The end result was that Nikolai had given Tiffany a new life that would hold joy and passion—the life she had always wanted as a ballerina—while he himself was condemned by his own promise to a life of misery away from the woman he loved.

Tiffany moved to the window abruptly and looked out. She had to stop thinking of this. It only made matters worse. She was going to marry Rolf soon, and nothing could change that. The invitations had been sent out. The arrangements had all been made. Rolf loved her very much, she knew, and would be terribly hurt if she left him for Nikolai. Worst of all, he would be vengeful and furious. He would arrange it so Nikolai could never dance with a first-line company again, just as he had once threatened. Tiffany knew what ballet meant to Nikolai. For him to be condemned to dance in second-rate companies for the rest of his life would be utter torture. She wouldn't subject him to that. So preparations for the wedding went on unimpeded.

"Well," said Rolf, "I can't say I'm overjoyed at this sudden new direction in your life, but at least you're not joining a full-time company where you'd have to rehearse constantly and tour.''

"Yes," she said, "with Paramount I won't have to do that. Another reason Paramount is good for me is that when we have children, I won't want to dance often at all, or make movies or anything else. With Paramount I can—"

"Wait a minute," he said. He stood up from his desk and came over to her. His expression was serious—and familiar. Tiffany remembered seeing this same expression previously, the last time she had mentioned children to him.

He shook his head slowly. "I don't want children, Tiffany. The last thing I want in my life at this point is a bunch of brats running around the house." His look was forceful. He tried to soften it by smiling slightly. "Tiffany, I want it to be just you and me, with no one else to make claims on your affections. I want your love all for myself."

Tiffany looked at him steadily, seeing his strength and his vulnerability, his tenderness and his callousness all at once. "Rolf," she said, "I love children, and I've always wanted to raise a family."

"I'm sorry, but I feel strongly about this. I believe children should be raised in a home where they have a father and mother who are both actively involved in bringing them up. I don't want to be actively involved. I just plain don't want to be a father. I've got an empire to run here, and I'll have a wife to love. That's enough for me. I don't want to take time away from either to spend it on raising any kids." He looked at her hopefully. "You do understand?"

"Yes, and I hope you understand, too. I love children, and I want to raise a family."

Rolf frowned hard, concentrating, trying to brainstorm a way around this problem. He turned away from her and began pacing in front of his shelf of Oriental sculptures. He had a fondness for the Orient, and the knickknacks scattered about his home and office reflected this. Finally he sighed in resignation and took Tiffany's hands. "Darling, I love you. If I have to become a father in order to have you, then I'll do it." He kissed her hands with surprising tenderness.

Tiffany was touched by the tenderness and decided not to say anything further, but she was disturbed. She was thinking that this was not the way to have a harmonious marriage or to raise healthy happy children—having one parent agree to do it under duress. She felt that children should be raised in an atmosphere of warmth and affection by parents who loved them and rejoiced in bringing them up. But what could she say? Rolf seemed willing to do anything to keep her, to make any sacrifices, no matter how great.

"I have to go now," she said. "I have an appointment with Gladstone of Paramount. I'm auditioning for him this morning."

He nodded and kissed her, and Tiffany left.

Two weeks later, on the day before Nikolai's debut performance with the NBT, Tiffany was in her office when Jaynie announced that she had a phone call. At first Tiffany thought, hopefully, that it was her mother calling to say she would go to the performance after all. But then she realized with disappointment that she was being unrealistic. Her mother had not called her since the evening Tiffany had said she was returning to ballet, and each time Tiffany called, her mother was cold and abrupt—and barely civil.

It was foolish to think her mother would phone her now to tell her she had changed her mind about going to the NBT debut. When Rolf had graciously sent Victoria the tickets, she had sent a brief unfriendly note to Tiffany, saying she would not have anything to do with any performance by Nikolai Sharmonov.

Tiffany was deeply hurt by her mother's coldness to her, but there seemed to be nothing she could do—except recant her decision, which she would not do. She prayed that somehow, someday, there would be a reconciliation, but the signs did not look good.

"It's Julian Temple," Jaynie said, "from the NBT."

Tiffany picked up the telephone and said hello.

"Tiffany, how are you!" Temple began boisterously. "Gladstone over at Paramount told me the good news—you've returned to ballet and you've been rehearsing with his company for the past two weeks. He says your audition was the best he's seen in years."

"I'm sure he was exaggerating," said Tiffany modestly.

"I'm sure he was not. Gladstone is almost as much

of a curmudgeon about compliments as I am. If he says you're good, you're good. But tell me, Tiffany, did I do anything to offend you?''

"Offend me? Of course not, Mr. Temple. Why would you think that?''

"Because you're dancing with Paramount, that's why. I told you years ago that if you ever changed your mind about leaving ballet, there'd always be a place for you at NBT.''

"That's very kind of you, Mr. Temple, but—''

"Kindness be damned! It's purely selfish. I run a tight ship here and when I see quality, I want it. So why did you go with Gladstone?''

Tiffany gave him the same explanation she had given Rolf, telling him how she preferred a company that didn't tour and that demanded less than a full-time commitment.

Temple seemed only moderately appeased. "Well, I do understand," he said grudgingly, "but I can't say I like it. I hate seeing talent like yours stuck away in a company like Paramount. Not that it isn't a fine company, mind you. It just isn't NBT.''

"I'm happy, Mr. Temple, happier than I've been in years.''

"Well, if you do change your mind...." He let the words hang, then he changed the subject. "Listen, here's what I really called you about. This afternoon is our last chance to rehearse before tomorrow evening's performance, and Natasha Panova got invited to appear on a TV talk show at the last minute. Naturally I let her go. Lord knows, we can use the publicity.''

Tiffany was familiar with the tenuous economics of ballet. Even in New York City income from performances was never high enough to pay all the costs of sets, salaries, costumes, et cetera. That was why contributions were so avidly sought and any chance to get free publicity was jumped at.

''Can you come down and fill in for her during the rehearsal? Just for this afternoon. It's a piece I know you're familiar with—Gladstone told me it's in your repertoire—the third act of *Le Corsaire*.''

Tiffany's heart raced. She would love to dance *Le Corsaire* with members of the NBT, and this would be a perfect opportunity, too, because she knew Nikolai would not be present. She had read in the television log that he would be appearing on the Dax Newton Show this afternoon. That was probably why Temple had let Natasha Panova miss such a crucial rehearsal—because Nikolai would be missing the rehearsal to appear on one talk show and Natasha's prima-donna ego demanded equal treatment.

''You know how important this rehearsal is,'' Temple said. ''To tell the truth, I'd never even have let Natasha go on that talk show, except that... well, she's a real spitfire, if you know what I mean.''

''I understand, Mr. Temple. Yes, I'll be happy to stand in for her.''

''Wonderful. Be at the Fortieth Street studio at

four o'clock sharp. And thanks again, Tiffany. Goodbye.''

He hung up quickly before Tiffany could ask him why he had said the Fortieth Street studio. She put down the receiver slowly. That seemed strange, she mused. The Fortieth Street studio was the NBT's auxiliary studio, not its main one.

When she arrived at the old studio, she had an even stronger intuition that something strange was going on. The studio seemed deserted. The white-haired manager behind the desk told her to go on up to the small practice room on the second floor, where she was expected.

The instant Tiffany opened the door to the upstairs practice room, she saw a sight that jolted her. The room was empty except for one solitary figure: Nikolai Sharmonov, who stood at the *barre* doing *pliés*. He wore a black, strap T-shirt that showed his bulging sinewy shoulder muscles and powerful chest and arms. The warm-up pants he also had on were stretched over his lower body.

He continued doing his *pliés*, one hand on the *barre*, the other over his head. "Hurry up," he said, his face powerful and commanding. "I'm already warmed up. Now you warm up quickly, then we'll begin."

CHAPTER TWENTY-FIVE

TIFFANY COULD DO NOTHING but stare at him disbelievingly. "You can't be here," she said in a weak voice. "You're supposed to be on the Dax Newton Show."

"I am on the Dax Newton Show, and if I had the time, I'd go home and watch it. I gave a wonderful interview. I complimented myself on it right after yesterday's taping." He narrowed an eye impatiently. "But since tomorrow evening is my premiere performance, I don't have time to go watch. My *pas de deux* still needs work. So come, let us begin. This rehearsal is very important to me."

Tiffany stood in the doorway facing the mirrored wall, not entering the room. She was having a hard time accepting that he was really here, that she was really here, that they were alone together. She had not seen him in such a long time. "Nikolai," she said, "I don't want to dance with you." She made a move to back away.

"You're going to desert me during my last rehearsal before my performance?"

"You can get somebody else."

"At four o'clock on a Thursday afternoon? Someone who is good enough to partner me in the LaSalle version of the *Corsaire pas de deux*?"

Tiffany did not know what to do. She felt keenly distressed. To leave him now at such a crucial moment would be a serious blow. But to stay, to dance with him in one of the loveliest *pas de deux* in classical ballet, to feel his strong hands upon her body lifting her, to see his chiseled face so near to hers—she did not know if she could bear it.

"Nikolai," she blurted out helplessly, "you planned it this way!"

He did not deny it. He came forward across the room and stopped only when she began edging back out the doorway. "Of course I planned it. I told Temple you were the one I wanted to have partner me for this rehearsal. But don't seem shocked. I told you months ago: you dance *Corsaire* better than I have ever seen it danced. I want you to dance it with me now."

Tiffany wanted to leave. The thought of being close to him now, knowing it would be the last time, was torture. She would be Mrs. Rolf Grayson in weeks. To have Nikolai's body brushing against hers as they danced would be unbearable.

"I'm sorry," she said. She turned to leave.

"Tiffany!" His voice was commanding and not at all friendly.

She turned back to face him.

"You owe this to me," he said. "The fact that you have returned to ballet—that is my doing."

"That's right, it is!" she declared accusingly. "You tricked me! You manipulated me!"

"Yes. And because of it, your life will now be more fulfilling and satisfying than ever before. Tell me, is it not true?"

She held his stare for a moment, then lowered her eyes. "All right," she said quietly. "I'll dance with you. I do owe it to you." She looked up sharply. "But after this, we'll be even. I'll owe you nothing else ever again."

"Fine. That's just how I desire it." He came forward and took her wrist, pulling her into the room, then he slammed the door and turned the lock. Turning to her, he looked down at the open waist-tied cotton shirt and long corduroy skirt she wore over her leotard. Almost savagely, without warning, he pulled open the shirt and ripped it off her. Then, while she was still too dumbfounded to move, he unhooked her skirt and pulled that off, too. He tossed the clothes into the corner, near the costume rack.

Tiffany's hands went up to cover herself instinctively, and she looked shocked and horrified. "What are you doing?"

"Did you intend to dance in those? Come. We are behind schedule already."

Her leotard and tights were perfectly proper dance attire. Yet under his piercing unabashed gaze, she felt as if she were stark naked. She had never felt this way before when dancing. *These clothes are proper*, she had to keep reminding herself; *they are the accept-*

able working clothes of my profession. Despite this she could not help feeling as if she were somehow wickedly exposed.

To take her mind off her unaccustomed feeling of near nakedness, she went to the *barre* and started her limbering-up exercises. Nikolai went across the room and ran through a series of lightning swift turns and leaps. His Russian style of ballet was somewhat more acrobatic than the subtler American style, and this showed clearly as he worked off his excess energy. When Tiffany was ready, he put on the record and took up his position behind her, his strong hands on her waist. Then they began.

The *pas de deux* from *Le Corsaire* was Tiffany's favorite piece, and she knew she danced it wonderfully, so she was shocked when Nikolai yelled "Stop! Stop!" after only a few minutes. He stalked over to the record player and jerked the needle off the record.

"This is terrible!" he declared, turning to her. "You call this dancing? How dare you defile such a beautiful ballet!"

Her mouth opened wide in indignation. "How dare you accuse me of defiling anything?" she shot back. "This is my best piece! I know how well I do it."

"Yes?" he countered angrily. "And do you know how well you do it when you are so tense, when you are cold and stiff like an icicle?" He shook her by the shoulders, back and forth, to show just how rigid she was. "You have no looseness, no flowing. You are going through the motions, yes, but certainly this is not what you call dancing."

She glared at him, hurt and angry. Fire coursed all through her. He glared back, refusing to give an inch. The horrible thing was, she knew he was right. She had only been going through the motions. Her dancing had been technically correct but totally uninspired. There had been no passion in it—none of the giving herself over to the essence of it that changed dancing from mere body work into a transcendent experience of beauty and grace.

"I need you to dance with me now," Nikolai said angrily. "I need it very badly. But if you insist on being a robot, then go! Leave me! I do not need robots as my partners."

She shut her eyes tightly. She knew what the problem was. She was *afraid* to give herself over to this dance. She was keeping herself distant and unemotional. Ballet was so sensual and emotional to her that it made her terribly vulnerable, and she feared being vulnerable now, because. . . .

Tiffany knew the real reason: because her true feelings might come out, because the message her heart was sending her was one she didn't feel able to cope with. She had to keep her guard up. And yet she couldn't dance this *pas de deux* with her guard up, being distant and unfeeling. It would not work that way, and it would not be fair to Nikolai, for this rehearsal would then be useless to him.

She turned to face him. "All right," she said quietly. "I'm ready. I-I'll try to do better."

He looked at her appraisingly, as if deciding whether to continue. Then he nodded curtly and started the record again.

The rousing strains of the Riccardo Drigo score surged through the air; Nikolai took up his position behind her, and their dance began. Tiffany started out coldly again—she couldn't help it. But gradually, as the dance progressed, she let down her guard, let her resistance fade. And then the magic of ballet took over, and she was soaring, flowing, more intensely alive than she had ever been.

"Yes," said Nikolai, "now you are dancing." He lifted her, moved with her, turned with her. The longer they danced, the more his eyes filled with admiration. "Now you are *dancing*," he declared. Coming from him, it was a compliment that coursed all through her, inspiring her on to even greater feats, even more dazzling achievement.

They moved as one, with a harmony and beauty that was almost spiritual. Tiffany had always been in love with this *pas de deux* but had never thought she'd find a partner who was her equal in it. It required such precision, balance and speed that no male dancer she had ever seen had seemed able to master it completely. Now as Nikolai partnered her, it all came together with flawless perfection. What a wildly liberating exultant feeling! Dance had never been like this! Tiffany was intoxicated with the throbbing of the music, the swirling of the room. The male musky scent of Nikolai was in her nostrils, the sight of him filling her vision—his arrogant profile, his glowering blue eyes. Then, as she bent backward over his arm, his lips descended on hers. Time seemed to stand still. Before she could protest, he twirled her out as the choreography demanded.

They danced apart. He twirled her back in. "I love you," he said as he held her. "I love you, my darling." Before she could respond, he was turning her out again. They danced apart now, never missing a beat, their movements in perfect harmony. The grandeur of the ballet and of the swelling music surged through Tiffany. They came together, and Nikolai lifted her in a soaring arc, then set her down, his face bent over hers.

"Marry me," he said, his eyes passionate and intense. "Be my wife. Be my love. Be mine always."

"Nikolai, don't."

"Yes!"

"Please don't."

Their dancing continued as the music surged on, and they performed brilliantly, beautifully. Each time they came close, Nikolai would speak.

"Do you love me?" he asked.

"Don't ask me that." Her voice was tremulous.

"Do you? *Do you?*"

"Yes!" she blurted out, the answer bursting from her heart.

"Marry me."

"Nikolai, I...I can't! Rolf would destroy you; your career would be ruined!"

She had not meant to tell him this. Their dancing continued, and she was pirouetting away from him. She glided back toward him, and they danced together, she up on point. She could see his expression now. He was smiling at the knowledge that she did love him, and there was a glint in his eyes, too, which was very strange. *Why is he looking that way,* Tiffany wondered. *It's as if he has some plan, some secret knowledge of how to get what he wants. But what could it be?*

She learned soon enough. As Nikolai's movements progressed from the classical into the personal, he let his hands sweep slowly across her breasts, rather than in an arc above her head, as the choreography called for.

"You stop that!" Tiffany said in an intense whisper, her eyes going wide.

His hands went around her waist as the dance demanded, but instead of remaining behind her, he pivoted her to face him and pulled her against him. Her breasts crushed against his chest; she could feel the heat of his body through the fabric of her leotard.

"Stop it, Nikolai!" she hissed as they began sidestepping in unison. She tried to break away, but he held her. "I know why you're doing this," she said, struggling to fight down the wicked flames of feeling that made it almost impossible for her to speak. "You—you think that if you can excite me...if you can seduce me, I won't marry Rolf. You know I'd never let myself marry him if I made love to you now, so you're trying to seduce me to put an end to the wedding."

He didn't answer. Instead he lowered his head and began kissing her throat.

"Stop it," she cried as his hand moved down her back and over her derriere. Neither of them was dancing any longer. They stood in the center of the room as Tiffany endured the ravaging flames that preyed upon her body. "It won't work, Nikolai," she whispered through gritted teeth, her nostrils flaring as she struggled against him. "I won't let you... excite me. You hear? I won't let you... seduce me."

"Of course not," he said, a sudden grin flashing across his features.

"I won't let you stop me from marrying Rolf," she breathed. "I won't let you ruin your career over me. I—" She gasped suddenly as she felt an electric shock of pure pleasure. His mouth was at her breast, capturing her nipple even through her leotard. "Oh, Nikolai, stop that!"

She couldn't bear it any longer; her will was crumbling. Already her body was betraying her with its flashes of passion that ignited each place his hand touched. Even his words were weakening her will to resist. "I love you," he kept saying. "*Moia dorogaia*. I love you, my darling."

With an intense effort of will Tiffany gathered her strength and pulled free of him. She stumbled back a few paces and waited there, half crouched, struggling for breath, her eyes like those of a frightened animal.

Nikolai stood straight and looked at her. He made no move to go after her.

She remained like this for a moment, breathing in gasps. Then she said in a trembling voice, "Nikolai, I have to. . .to leave now. I can't stay here with you." She knew that if she stayed her resistance would crumble in the face of his overpowering love. It was his love that was affecting her so deeply, and both of them knew it. The sensuality was part of it, but his love was the hardest thing to resist. She stared at him a moment in anguish and helplessness, then turned to leave.

"Stop." His word was a command.

When she slowly turned back to face him, she saw that his face was hard, his eyes smoldering.

"Come to me," he said.

She shook her head vigorously.

"Tiffany," he said, his voice dropping ominously low, "I love you. I love you more than life itself. But if you walk out that door, I never want to see you again."

"Nikolai," she pleaded, "he'll destroy your career!"

"I make my own decisions about what I want from life. I love ballet, but I love you more. My life without you is nothing. With you it is everything. I've made my decision. Now you must make yours."

She stood helplessly, unable to speak.

"If you leave me now, don't ever come back. I won't want you. It'll mean you haven't yet learned my lesson. You can't sacrifice your happiness for the sake of others. As much as I love you, I don't want the kind of woman who lacks the courage to learn that lesson." His eyes were commanding. "Don't think of how Grayson may be hurt! Don't think of how my career may be ruined! Think only of this: what do *you* want?"

Her eyes pleaded with him. She was in torment. For a long moment she stood motionless by the closed locked door. Then Nikolai spoke one last time, and this time his eyes showed racking doubt, and his words were painfully drawn out. "Maybe... you really... don't love me at all."

"Oh, Nikolai," she cried, "I do!" A sob broke from her throat. She saw him open his arms to her, and she rushed into them. His arms closed around her. He kissed her searingly. Then, one arm beneath her knee, he raised her up and carried her over to the costume rack in the corner. A variety of colorful costumes from the troupe's dress rehearsal hung on the rack. Nikolai yanked down a thickly brocaded gold-and-scarlet cape. He spread it on the floor and gently lowered Tiffany onto it.

He knelt beside her, a look of love in his eyes. His fingertips stroked her cheek tenderly, stroked down to her shoulders, then caressed her breasts. Tiffany drew in a gasp of air at the sensation. She shut her eyes.

"Open your eyes," he said tenderly. She did so, knowing he wanted to see the look of love there. This, too, was a challenge to her. "Do you have the courage to face my love openly?" he was asking silently.

Her eyes were half-lidded now, and she could not stifle a slow moan as Nikolai's hands cupped her breasts and gently caressed them. His mouth came down to the side of her face, and his tongue began doing enticing things to her ear.

When his hands went to the top of her leotard and began pulling the garment down past her shoulders, Tiffany could not help but tense her body. She did not resist, though, as he slithered the material down over her breasts, baring them to his eyes, then lower still until it was completely off. His hands went to the hem of her tights. She reached out and grasped his wrist at the last moment, involuntarily, to prevent him from skinning these, too, down her legs. He looked into her eyes, though, saying nothing. Tremulously she removed her hand from his wrist.

Then she was naked before him in her creamy fair-skinned loveliness. His gaze traveling along the length of her body was like a physical caress, and Tiffany felt it almost physically; her skin began tingling with a sensuousness that nearly drove her mad. She felt an ache of loving desire...desire for Nikolai.

He lay down beside her, and his hands traveled over the hills and valleys of her body, almost seeming to melt her skin everywhere they touched. His mouth moved down her shoulders and across her breasts. The sensation was tormenting. Tiffany's hands were in his golden hair, touching, tousling. She felt his tongue trace a path down from her tingling nipples to her stomach and move in a slow torturous circle. Her breath was shallow and rapid.

Nikolai looked at her and smiled. "You are as lovely as a Venus," he said. "You are the most lovely woman on earth." He stood up. She knew what he was going to do now. He was going to undress. She turned her head away.

"Look at me," he said gently. And when she did so, he pulled off his cutaway top, baring his muscular chest with its forest of softly curling hairs. Then his hand went to the drawstring of his pants.

Tiffany bit her lip. She was not used to any of this, her sense of modesty was shrieking at her to turn her head away, to cover her nakedness. But she did not do so because Nikolai did not want it. And so she watched as he undressed completely, pushing his clothes down past his strongly muscled legs.

Again Tiffany gasped. Nikolai stood before her completely naked, his broad shoulders thrust back, his hips arched slightly forward. Tiffany recalled the one time she had seen his body—in the moonlit darkness of the Danube riverbank. She had ruthlessly forced that image from her mind over the past months. Now she was confronted with it again, and now it was all right. He stood before her in all his iron-hard glory, even more tormentingly erotic than she had remembered.

Tiffany became excruciatingly aware of her own nakedness as he came down beside her, his hands and lips and tongue roaming at will over the roundness and softness of her body, touching her at her most sacred secret places. She looked in the wall of mirrors for a moment and saw both Nikolai and herself as he did loving wonderful things to her. Her own hands slowly began answering his, touching him, feeling his muscles and the heat of his body.

Her skin was on fire. Her heart was overflowing with love. And then, as the music crashed and soared around them, they danced the most beautiful dance in the world...the dance of love.

CHAPTER TWENTY-SIX

TIFFANY SAT before her dressing mirror the next evening, vigorously brushing out her hair. She was nervous with anticipation. Rolf was scheduled to pick her up at any moment for their date to see Nikolai's premiere. She had made up her mind she would tell him the news sometime tonight—the news that their engagement was over.

She got up from the dressing mirror and began walking about fretfully. Oh, if only life were simpler! She hated to have to hurt Rolf like this, but she knew there was no other way. She had learned the lesson Nikolai sought to teach her—that she must grab at happiness, not shrink from it for fear of causing pain. She knew her life would be meaningless if she were married to anyone but Nikolai, and she would say so to Rolf, but she dreaded having to do it.

As she finished dressing, the wall buzzer sounded. It was the doorman downstairs, announcing Rolf's arrival. "Send him up, please," Tiffany said.

During the tense minutes she waited for him to arrive, she thought of how Nikolai had offered to be with her now when she broke the news to Rolf. As much as Tiffany had wanted to have his support, she knew it would be wrong to accept his offer. Rolf deserved to hear the words from her own lips in private. And if he wished to respond with anger or pain, which he had every right to do, Tiffany would not shrink from facing his emotions.

The doorbell rang. Tiffany looked at the door for an instant, then she took a deep breath and went to answer it. She was doing the right thing; she knew that in her heart. Realizing this, though, gave her little consolation.

She opened the door. "Hello, Rolf," she said.

Rolf breezed past her into the room. He seemed in a highly agitated state. When she shut the door and turned to face him, he came directly up to her. His brow was furrowed. "Darling," he said in a grave voice, "I have something to tell you."

"What is it?" she asked quickly, concerned. "Is anything wrong?"

"Yes."

For an instant Tiffany felt a twinge of horror. Had he somehow found out about Nikolai and her? Had he learned of it before she even had the chance to tell him? She was in terrible suspense and started to ask him how he had found out.

Before she could do so, though, Rolf blurted out, "Darling, it's wrong! It's wrong; it's wrong! Forgive me, but—" He took hold of her shoulders and said, "It won't work between us. I'm sorry, Tiffany."

"It. . .it won't?" she said.

He shook his head sadly. "You must think I'm a terrible cad, calling the wedding off at the last moment like this, but it's the only thing to do. I've given it a lot of thought, ever since that morning we spoke about having children. I told you I was willing to let you have your way despite my not wanting children. Do you remember?"

"Of course I do," she said softly.

He began pacing the room. He seemed deeply distraught. "Well, the fact is, darling, as much as I love you, this is one concession I just can't allow myself to make. Letting you continue working for a living is one thing. That I was willing to put up with. But this subject of children...." He came to her again. She could see how troubled he was and how important it was for him to explain his feelings. "The fact is, darling, I'm not the kind of man who appreciates children—particularly not when they're infants. If we had children, don't you see, I'd only be putting up with them to satisfy you. But I don't think that's the proper way to raise children."

"I agree, Rolf. I don't think it's the proper way, either."

He seemed hopeful. "You do see my point then?"

She took his hand. "I do, and I think you're a very good kind man for thinking of the welfare of our... of children first, even though it means sacrificing something you want dearly."

He hugged her tightly, grateful for her understanding. "You're such a wonderful girl—how I love you.

But you do see that there's nothing we can do about this but call off the wedding, don't you?" He looked suddenly hopeful at a passing thought. "Unless you've changed your mind about children being so important to you."

She shook her head sadly. "They're very important to me, Rolf. I've always wanted to be a mother, and I know I'll be a good one. I want to raise a family. The man I marry will have to want that, too."

He looked at her longingly for a moment, then sighed in resignation. "I knew that. All the way over here I was hoping it might not be true, but I knew it was."

Tiffany lowered her head.

He put his finger beneath her chin and raised it so she would look at him. "Do you forgive me?"

"There's nothing to forgive. You're doing the right thing. And...I'm doing the right thing, too." She thought of telling him that even aside from the issue of children she would not have gone through with the marriage. She thought of telling him that she loved Nikolai and that she would marry him. But looking at Rolf, she could see that that would be a very cruel thing to do. Why should she trample on his feelings, just so she could have the satisfaction of knowing she was being completely honest with him? If she told him now, she knew, it would be for her sake, not his. Looking at his expression, she could see that the very last thing he wanted to hear from her was that she was forsaking him for the love of anoth-

er man. Tiffany closed her lips and made up her
mind. She would not say anything.

He embraced her and gently rocked her back and
forth. "You're a wonderful girl," he said. "A truly
wonderful girl."

She hugged him back, feeling very warm toward
him, warmer than she ever had before. He was a
good man, and at the moment he needed something
from her. She moved her head forward and kissed
him lightly. The act was not wasted on him. She
could see in his eyes how grateful he was for her sympathy and understanding. He hugged her even more
tightly.

They spoke very little on the ride over to Lincoln
Center, where the premiere was being staged. The
silence, though, was not tense. It was a comfortable
silence, like that between two comrades who did not
have to speak to reassure themselves that they were
still in each other's good graces.

When they arrived, Rolf led her to his private box.
It was then that Tiffany received her second surprise
of the evening. As she and Rolf were taking their
seats, Tiffany looked over to the box Rolf had reserved for Victoria Farrow and saw that her mother
was actually seated there. The last word Tiffany had
heard from her mother was that she refused to attend
any performance by the man who, Victoria was convinced, had persuaded Tiffany to return to ballet.

Tiffany's face lighted up upon seeing her mother.
She was delighted she was here. Could it really mean

what it seemed to—that her mother was taking the first tiny steps toward a reconciliation? Did Victoria's attendance here mean that she did not still scorn Nikolai for his role in Tiffany's return to ballet—and, by extension, Tiffany herself for returning to it?

Victoria Farrow turned her head and looked at Tiffany. She had the same regal bearing and great dignity she always displayed. There was no smile on her lips, but Tiffany had not expected one. Such was not her mother's nature. She had been hurt; her advice had been rejected, and to smile now would be out of character. But as Tiffany watched with bated breath, she saw her mother nod to her, shutting her eyelids for an instant. Then she turned back to watch the rising of the curtain.

Tiffany felt so happy she could burst. It was not a full reconciliation, but it was a start. There would still be a bit of coolness between them, but at least it was a beginning—a sign that the breach would be healed. As Rolf took her hand and squeezed it, she turned her eyes to the front and watched the curtain rise on the first act of *Le Corsaire*. This was the crucial moment. Nikolai had to prove himself to a skeptical, demanding, highly critical American audience.

THE BALLET ENDED. The curtain dropped. For an instant there was absolute silence. The tension was electric. Tiffany glanced apprehensively to the left and right. There was light scattered applause. Then suddenly came a thunderous explosion of clapping. The audience had been stunned by the magnitude of the performance they had witnessed. Now, in delayed reaction, they rose to their feet almost as one, and the ovation went on and on.

The dancers marched back onto the stage for their bows as the curtain rose. The applause was generous for the supporting dancers and quite loud for Natasha Panova, but it was absolutely deafening for Nikolai. He was forced to return for curtain calls again and again—eight in all. Each time he took Natasha with him by the hand, graciously sharing the applause. Tiffany felt a bright spot of happiness in her heart to see her mother on her feet, also, joining in the standing ovation.

The applause was still resounding ceaselessly as one of Julian Temple's assistants made his way through the throng to Grayson's box and approached Tiffany. "Mr. Sharmonov asked if you would join him backstage."

Rolf had heard. He looked at Tiffany, who looked back at him, desperately wondering how he would react.

Rolf nodded to her and managed a smile. "He'd *better* ask you backstage, so he can express his gratitude," Rolf said. "None of this would be happening if it hadn't been for your helping him to defect."

There was a strange glint in his steely eyes, and Tiffany wondered if he knew more than he was saying. After all, this was no ordinary man—this was Rolf Grayson. Rolf gave no further signs, though. He turned his eyes back to the stage and continued clapping, joining the rest of the audience, whose applause rang through the majestic hall, filling it to the highest balcony.

Tiffany kissed Rolf on the cheek. Then she followed the stage worker back down the aisle and into the wings. From the wings she watched as the traditional bouquet of red roses was delivered to Nikolai on the stage, and he in turn presented them grandly to Natasha. But then she noticed something that was most definitely not traditional and that perhaps the others in the hall had missed. Nikolai withheld one scarlet rose from the bouquet, secreting it in the hand he held behind him. Then, when the curtain fell for the final time, he raised the rose to his lips and kissed it and walked back into the wings to Tiffany. He bowed from the waist and presented one scarlet rose to her, his eyes bright, his lips grinning that proud, charming, fiercely individualistic grin that was his alone.

"My love," he said to her.

A new round of applause broke out now, smaller, more intimate. It was from the members of Nikolai's newfound family—his new ballet troupe. They were applauding joyfully as Nikolai took Tiffany in his arms and kissed her.

For a truly SUPER read, don't miss...

SUPERROMANCE

EVERYTHING YOU'VE ALWAYS WANTED A LOVE STORY TO BE!

Contemporary!
A modern romance for the modern woman — set in the world of today.

Sensual!
A warmly passionate love story that reveals the beautiful feelings between a man and a woman in love.

Dramatic!
An exciting and dramatic plot that will keep you enthralled till the last page is turned.

Exotic!
The thrill of armchair travel — anywhere from the majestic plains of Spain to the towering peaks of the Andes.

Satisfying!
Almost 400 pages of romance reading — a long satisfying journey you'll wish would never end.

SUPERROMANCE

Available wherever paperback books are sold or through
Worldwide Reader Service

In the U.S.A.
1440 South Priest Drive
Tempe, AZ 85281

In Canada
649 Ontario Street
Stratford, Ontario N5A 6W2

What readers say about SUPERROMANCE

"Bravo! Your SUPERROMANCE [is]... super!"
R.V.,* Montgomery, Illinois

"I am impatiently awaiting
the next SUPERROMANCE."
J.D., Sandusky, Ohio

"Delightful... great."
C.B., Fort Wayne, Indiana

"Terrific love stories. Just
keep them coming!"
M.G., Toronto, Ontario

"I couldn't put it down!"

M.M., North Baltimore, Ohio

"The new SUPERROMANCE...
[is] just that – 'Super.' "

J.F.B., Grand Prairie, Texas

"Just great – I can't wait
until the next one."

R.M., Melbourne, Florida

"I am anxiously awaiting
the next SUPERROMANCE."

A.C., Parlin, New Jersey

*Names available on request.

SUPERROMANCE

Longer, exciting, sensuous and dramatic!

Fascinating love stories that will hold
you in their magical spell till the last page
is turned!

Now's your chance to discover the earlier
books in this exciting series. Choose from
the great selection on the following page!

Choose from this list of great
SUPERROMANCES!

#1 END OF INNOCENCE Abra Taylor

#2 LOVE'S EMERALD FLAME Willa Lambert

#3 THE MUSIC OF PASSION Lynda Ward

#4 LOVE BEYOND DESIRE Rachel Palmer

#5 CLOUD OVER PARADISE Abra Taylor

#6 SWEET SEDUCTION Maura Mackenzie

#7 THE HEART REMEMBERS Emma Church

#8 BELOVED INTRUDER Jocelyn Griffin

#9 SWEET DAWN OF DESIRE Meg Hudson

#10 HEART'S FURY Lucy Lee

#11 LOVE WILD AND FREE Jocelyn Haley

#12 A TASTE OF EDEN Abra Taylor

#13 CAPTIVE OF DESIRE Alexandra Sellers

#14 TREASURE OF THE HEART Pat Louis

#15 CHERISHED DESTINY Jo Manning

SUPERROMANCE

Complete and mail this coupon today!

- -

Worldwide Reader Service

In the U.S.A.
1440 South Priest Drive
Tempe, AZ 85281

In Canada
649 Ontario Street
Stratford, Ontario N5A 6W2

Please send me the following SUPERROMANCES. I am enclosing my check or money order for $2.50 for each copy ordered, plus 75¢ to cover postage and handling.

☐ #1	☐ #6	☐ #11
☐ #2	☐ #7	☐ #12
☐ #3	☐ #8	☐ #13
☐ #4	☐ #9	☐ #14
☐ #5	☐ #10	☐ #15

Number of copies checked @ $2.50 each = $_____
N.Y. and Ariz. residents add appropriate sales tax $_____
Postage and handling $_____ .75

               TOTAL $_____

I enclose_____.
(Please send check or money order. We cannot be responsible for cash sent through the mail.)
Prices subject to change without notice.

NAME_____
                   (Please Print)

ADDRESS_____

CITY_____

STATE/PROV._____

ZIP/POSTAL CODE_____

Offer expires November 30, 1982   20556000000